THE SECRET KEEPER

RENITA D'SILVA

Boldwood

First published in Great Britain in 2024 by Boldwood Books Ltd.

Copyright © Renita D'Silva, 2024

Cover Design by Becky Glibbery

Cover Photography: Shutterstock, Dreamstime, [Miguel Sobreira] / Arcangel

The moral right of Renita D'Silva to be identified as the author of this work has been asserted in accordance with the Copyright, Designs and Patents Act 1988.

A CIP catalogue record for this book is available from the British Library.

Paperback ISBN 978-1-83617-256-7

Large Print ISBN 978-1-83617-255-0

Hardback ISBN 978-1-83617-254-3

Ebook ISBN 978-1-83617-257-4

Kindle ISBN 978-1-83617-258-1

Audio CD ISBN 978-1-83617-249-9

MP3 CD ISBN 978-1-83617-250-5

Digital audio download ISBN 978-1-83617-252-9

Boldwood Books Ltd
23 Bowerdean Street
London SW6 3TN
www.boldwoodbooks.com

For my nieces Bhavna Rachel Pais and Eila Maria D'Silva
and my nephew Jaisal Simon D'Silva.
Beloved, glorious stars who bring such joy into our lives.
May you shine bright and share your luminescence far and wide.
SO very blessed in you.

"*And now here is my secret, a very simple secret: it is only with the heart that one can see rightly; what is essential is invisible to the eye.*"

— *ANTOINE DE SAINT-EXUPÉRY*, THE LITTLE PRINCE

PART I

1

RANI

India, 1938

Rani scurries down the winding corridors of the palace, pulling the veil of her maid's sari further down, the better to cover her face, her anklets chiming in time with her heartbeat, especially loud when she passes sentries or courtiers, afraid of being caught out. But the maid's sari is the perfect disguise; she does not merit a second glance, just another of the plentiful anonymous serving the king and his entourage, keeping the palace and its extravagant furnishings polished and blemish free.

The first few times she navigated her way out of this maze of a palace, she'd got hopelessly lost.

But now she is surefooted.

Any minute now...

There. She spies one of the exits into the fort that surrounds the palace. It is a bejewelled archway framing a sliver of bright gold sky scudded with pillowy clouds, pierced by the uncompromising grey rectangle top of this section of the embattlements.

Silhouettes of guards, swords glinting, cast shadowy aspersions upon the golden spill of light as they march back and forth.

Head down, she hurries through the gateway, her veiled gaze fixed on the tantalising slice of sky.

She's almost out of the exit, bowing acknowledgment to the guards when...

'Wait.'

The deadly ceremonial sheathed sword, concealed under her sari, which she has stolen from her father, bumps against her thigh, sharp as a tiger's tooth and just as dangerous.

2

ESME

England, 1990

'Feel free to sit where you'd like; use the couch if you prefer.' Dr Coates smiles.

Her voice is mellow, like sinking into a lavender-scented pillow at the end of an arduous day.

Esme had found her in the directory under 'Counsellors' – Dr Sally Coates had a whole host of degrees and publications after her name. But what clinched it for Esme were the testimonials:

I was floundering, no clue what was wrong with me, unable to face the day. A few sessions with Dr Coates and I feel good as new.

Sally Coates is a miracle worker.

Esme could do with a miracle or two, which is why she is here.

A large room. No adornments. Just plain, white walls like blank pages.

A couch also upholstered white, piled high with marshmallow-pink cushions, the effect that of a summer sky at dawn kissed by dreamy cloud puffs.

A walnut desk, polished and gleaming, behind which sits Dr

Coates, a notebook open in front of her, a box of tissues beside it, twirling a pen in her hands, unvarnished nails, long, elegant fingers, like the rest of her. A tall, dignified woman, wearing a plain black dress and very little makeup, if any, brown hair pulled back in a bun, bright, intelligent eyes behind square, no-nonsense kind of frames. A pleasing face, one Esme instantly trusts. At least judging from looks alone, she's made the right choice.

Esme eschews the couch – tempting though it is – for the high-backed chair opposite Dr Coates. Time enough for it, if she chooses to continue the sessions depending on how this one goes.

The chair is surprisingly comfortable and she sinks gladly into it, surreptitiously kicking off, with great relief, the new shoes she'd bought in the sales – 75 per cent off. Too good to be true, of course, as they've started to bite.

'So, what brings you here today, Ms—'

'Please call me Esme.'

Dr Coates smiles warmly, 'Very well, Esme. And I'm Sally. So, what prompted you to seek me out?'

Esme scrunches her toes, takes a deep breath. 'My dad passed away recently.'

The phone had rung just as Esme was getting into her bath.

It was something she looked forward to after a long day at work, her little treat to herself before facing the no doubt sleepless night ahead – she suffered terribly from insomnia since her breakup – when all the thoughts she'd managed to evade during the day ambushed and tormented.

She considered letting it ring, inhaling the bergamot-infused steam, feeling her body, more unwieldy every day, relax in anticipation, the weariness which seemed to have settled into her very bones, making itself comfortable, very much at home, ease a little.

But... it could be Robbie, calling from uni. She could go days without hearing from her son and then he'd call twice in one week, at the oddest of times, expecting her to answer with that careless entitlement of youth, piqued when she didn't, complaining the next time they talked, 'Ma where were you? I tried and tried to call you.'

It could be her brother, who also could go months without keeping in touch, and then ring out of the blue to say, 'I read this and thought of you,' and go on to recite, dissect and discuss whatever it was that he thought she'd enjoy.

Or... it could be Philip, reaching out.

Why would he, when you broke up with him?

But, as always, hope had trumped reason and she'd shrugged on her bathrobe, fraying, threadbare, once purple – her favourite colour – now grey, but deeply cherished.

Robbie had gifted it to her one Christmas years ago, bought from money he'd earned cleaning cars and doing odd jobs for the neighbours, and she's worn it every day since.

She'd picked up the phone mid-ring, the sudden silence in the wake of the interrupted shrillness seething, ominous.

'Hello?'

'It's Eve.'

A woman.

Her body slumped, all the oomph going out of it, and she realised, disappointment acrid in her throat, that she'd been expecting to hear Philip's rich voice that always brought to mind hot chocolate spiced with cinnamon.

Eve. She didn't know an Eve except for...

Of course.

Eve, the director of the hospice.

She didn't recognise the soft cadence in this woman's usually crisp voice.

And she knew then.

She'd collapsed onto her bed, tears brimming, salty, bitter, even before Eve spelled out the words, 'He's gone, I'm afraid. I'm so very sorry.'

Much later, when she stumbled into the bathroom, the bath-water was stone cold, like her father's body, she imagined, unable to stop shivering, the bathrobe no comfort...

3

RANI

Childhood

Rani was her father's pet.

Her earliest memory is of her father whispering, 'I might no longer be crown prince of Divanpur but I am the father of a queen.'

'Baba,' she'd giggle, 'I'm not a queen!'

'You are *our* queen, Rani, precious one. It's why we named you Rani. It means queen in Hindi.'

They spoke English at home – Baba insisted upon it, but he also made sure that Rani and her brother were fluent in the language of whichever country they happened to live in during their eclectic childhood spent travelling all over Europe.

'Why are you no longer crown prince?' Rani would ask.

It never failed to bring a smile to Baba's face. 'Ah, you want to hear your favourite story, then?'

'Yes.' Rani would beam. For although it sounded sad, it was really a happy tale of how Baba met Mama, her favourite story until her little brother's birth superseded it.

'During my holidays in my second year at Cambridge—' her father began.

'Where you met fellow Marxists,' Rani interrupted, for she had heard this story so many times, she knew it by heart.

'That's right. We were holidaying in Europe and while in Düsseldorf, one of my friends wanted to buy something for the girl he loved and we went to this jeweller the locals recommended. We were served by the most beautiful girl I had ever set eyes on.'

'Mama,' Rani breathed.

'Yes,' Baba would say, smiling at Mama, his gaze warm and soft in that special way it became when he looked at her. 'I knew then and there that we were destined to be together. My friends went on to the next country on our meticulously mapped itinerary. I stayed back in Germany. And, well you know my gift with languages. I pick them up so easily.'

'I do too.'

'So you do.' Baba smiling broadly at her. 'Our Rani, our queen.'

'What happened next, Baba?'

'Well, I visited the shop every day and wooed your Mama in German that got better and better. Her father kept sending me away...'

'Opa,' Rani giggled.

'He's indulgent with you but with me, then, he was very harsh.' Baba winced in remembrance.

Rani giggled some more. She knew how this story ended.

'But I kept going back. And my sheer persistence paid off.'

'You married her.'

'I did.'

'So you had to give up your throne for your father wanted you to marry an Indian princess but you wanted Mama.'

'I did but I don't regret it one bit. And,' her father leaning close, his spiced breath hot and ticklish in her ear, 'do you want to know the best bit?'

She already knew, and like always, her stomach tightened with anticipation, even as she breathed, 'What, Baba?'

'The best part is that you came along, soon after, making us a family.'

'Yes.' She snuggled closer to her father. 'You haven't been back to India. Do you miss it?'

'I do. But I carry it within me. And with you and your Mama, I've travelled the world. Seen so much. Have had such a rich life. You and Mama are *my* world, my life, my home.' Baba planted a kiss on his wife's lips, above their daughter's head.

'You married Mama...'

'She gave birth to a queen...'

'...and you lived happily ever after,' Rani cheered.

'I am living happily ever after.'

'The best story ever. Better than all the fairy tales in the world.'

'And do you know something, Rani love, you are the icing on our cake, the one who makes everything worthwhile. You are our lucky charm, our good fairy.'

She beamed. 'I am?'

'You surely are. And more beautiful, precious and intelligent than any fairy in this world and the next.'

* * *

Baba and Mama's meeting became Rani's second favourite story when Arjun was born, her first encounter with her new sibling taking precedence from then on.

'We were so worried, there being such a big age gap between

the two of you, that you might not take to him,' her father loved to say. 'But when he was born...'

'Yes?'

'You paused at the threshold to the room. Your Mama was holding him. I was worried that you might be jealous, feeling left out, usurped. But then I saw your expression. You were mesmerised. You entered the room on tiptoes. "I don't want to wake him, Baba," you whispered, already a caring big sister. And I knew then that we had fretted for nothing. We should have trusted our wonderful Rani, mature even at nine, to always do the right thing.' Baba smiling warmly at her. 'Your mother placed your newborn brother in your lap. And...'

Her father always had a faraway look at this point, a wistful smile playing on his face as he gazed into the past.

'And?' Rani prompted, even though she knew what came next.

'Your expression as you held him. I'll never forget it.'

'What was it?' she whispered.

'Awe and magic and wonder and most of all...'

'Most of all?' Rani prompted.

'Love.'

* * *

Rani was her father's shadow throughout her glorious nomadic childhood living all over Europe: England, Austria, Germany, France, Italy. She absorbed languages and knowledge like a sponge.

'That's my girl. Quick to learn, curious, eager for new experiences,' Baba would proudly declare while indulging her every whim.

He fed her love of knowledge. Taught her to think, question. Cheered when she argued. 'See her spirit. Chip off the old block.'

Rani also absorbed her father's philosophy and made it her own. Socialism. Equality for all. A society run by laymen, not autocrats.

She read her father's copies of Marx's manifestos from cover to cover. She would engage in heated discussions with Baba and his socialist friends, Baba smiling fondly at her, his eyes gleaming with regard when she came up with a particularly good argument and his friends praised her: 'Your daughter is quite something, old chap.'

'Isn't she just? Takes after her father.' Fond pride twinkling in her Baba's gaze. Rani warmed by it.

'One up on her father, I'd say.'

Baba's celebratory laughter like festive fireworks.

'But you are a prince.' Acquaintances shook their heads, perplexed when Rani's father declared himself a staunch socialist.

'Which is why I'm all the more against dictatorship,' Baba proclaimed.

Rani grew up believing in the right to a society where all were equal, fiercely against the oppression and injustices of an unequal world.

Her father was her mentor and her best friend.

'You two are inseparable,' her mother would laugh. 'Nothing can come between you.'

But India did.

4

ESME

A warm voice jolts Esme back into the present.

She's in the office of the counsellor she'd picked out of the phone book, whose number she'd dialled before she lost her nerve. She is curled up in the chair opposite this woman who, although a stranger, doesn't feel like it, her shoeless feet now tucked under her. The room smells sweet, of vanilla and understanding.

'I am sorry for your loss,' Sally says and Esme can see that she is, her brown eyes shining with empathy.

'Dad and I weren't particularly close, so I've been really stunned by the grief. It seems endless.'

'Coming to terms with the death of a parent is very hard, regardless of what your relationship with them was like.'

'I...' Esme sniffs. 'I meant to visit him more. I did. But...'

It had shocked her to see how he'd changed, shrunk more every time she visited, the clothes that had once fit him so beautifully hanging off his skinny frame. His bony shoulders slumping. His hands shaking. His tie askew, collar undone.

It hurt to see this old man in place of the intelligent, always smart and well-turned-out father she remembered.

And so her visits became longer and longer apart until they shrivelled into none at all.

Sally pushes the box of tissues towards her. Esme takes one, blows her nose noisily.

'My father, he...'

A magpie flies past the window behind Sally, which spills golden light into the room, illuminating the white walls, incandescent brightness.

The magpie is a blur of black and white. A fluster of wings. One for sorrow.

'He was very remote. Closed up. He kept himself at a remove, always.'

He'd always been quiet, reserved. And she'd learned, like her brother Andy had, to let him be, to retreat into herself, which is why her enduring memory of childhood was of them together but apart, Dad providing for them materially but emotionally and physically distant.

During her visits to the hospice, they couldn't break the habits formed during a lifetime together, their conversation paltry, stilted, forced. Esme trying to hide her shock, her sorrow, at his decline. She wanted to tell him she loved him, she resolved to, before every visit, but the words died somewhere on their journey between her head and her mouth. The silence would fester, pulsing with unsaid words, held back declarations, until she broke it with an abrupt goodbye and left, crying all the way home.

'And I...' Esme shreds the tissue in her hand. 'I...'

'Yes?' Sally prompts gently.

'I'm afraid I've turned out exactly like him.'

5

RANI

The sleek letter on intricate headed paper had arrived just as Rani, at sixteen, was thinking of her future. She wanted to read languages at Cambridge, following, inevitably, in her father's footsteps.

Her father was all for it.

They were making arrangements to move to England – they were currently in Austria where, like in the rest of Europe, tensions were building, the rumours that Hitler was going to invade Austria getting stronger with each passing day – so she could get settled in before beginning the process of applying.

'Always think ahead.' Another of her father's maxims.

Then the letter.

It reeked of self-importance. It exuded gravitas with its solemn, gilt-edged linings, its smell of exotic lands, the oceans it had travelled.

Never for a moment did Rani imagine that it had the power to so completely alter the direction of all of their lives.

* * *

Baba had glared at the letter as if it was a grenade.

'Let's light a fire. That's the best place for it,' he said.

Mama went to him. Laid a gentle palm upon his shoulder. He rested his cheek against it.

Rani looked at the two of them, her parents. Baba's face resting on his wife's hand. Her other hand stroking his hair. His eyes closed.

It was an image she would always carry within her. A treasure she would cherish.

'You should read it,' Mama said, softly, tenderly.

Afterwards, Rani would revisit that moment again and again; *he should have gone with his instincts. Burned it.*

But on that fateful day, Mama picked up the letter. Handed it to Baba.

He looked at it for a moment, shuddered, and then tore it open in one decisive swoop, like he did everything in life. Quickly and without hesitation, facing down whatever it was he needed to do, especially that which he found distasteful.

So many emotions flashing through Baba's face as he read the letter.

His face was a study in upset when he finally looked up at them.

'My father is dying. He wants to make peace. Meet his grand-children.' He smiled at Rani and at Arjun, who was in Rani's lap, playing with her hair, as he said this, his eyes haunted, shimmering with withheld emotion. 'He wants us back.'

And although he looked sad, angry, hurt, his voice thrumming with bitterness and angst, Rani noticed, for she knew her father very well, something else warring with this amalgam of feeling and winning. Hope. Happiness. Anticipation.

And she knew then that although her father had denied it, he had missed India. Perhaps even his father too.

And she knew also as she noticed her father link his fingers with Mama's, as he smiled up at her, mouthed, 'thank you', that they would go to India.

6

RANI

Things started to change even before they arrived in India.

As the ship sailed to warmer climes, as every day they came inexorably closer to the land of his birth, Baba's excitement was palpable.

Mama beamed as she stood by his side, his gaze fixed upon the horizon beyond which lay the country where he'd grown up. The land he left behind, denounced, when he, according to his father, committed the twin cardinal sins of not only falling in love, but with a white woman at that (and not even white nobility but, of all people, a Jew from merchant stock).

Mama linking hands with Baba as he stood on deck looking east. Arjun running up to throw his arms around their legs. The sea lapping the ship behind them. The three of them grinning, Arjun from between his parents' knees, silhouetted against sun and sea. Dreamy blue merging into white gold, beyond which lay India. A happy tableau. Another image Rani would always carry with her.

Branded behind her eyelids.

Watching them, she was aware of a curious lump in her throat. She blinked back sudden tears.

They were all smiles in anticipation of the happy occasion. Reason for celebration.

Baba reuniting with his family. Returning to his homeland.

Yet throughout this journey, Rani had been plagued by nightmares.

She had been beset by foreboding.

7

RANI

Their first evening at sea, they were invited to dine with the captain and other first-class guests, Indian nobility and British Raj officials.

Baba, for the first time, used his full name, the name he had used only a diminutive of in Europe. 'I am Prajanya Raj.'

The other guests looked up, the music of cutlery on plates on pause.

'Of the Divanpur Maharajas?'

'Yes.' Baba was matter-of-fact.

But Rani, who noticed how he was shredding his bread roll into crumbs, knew he was nervous about slipping back into the persona he had abandoned years ago.

Silence at their table while around them in the dining room aromatic with spices and grilled meat, rice and bread and caramelised sugar, the melodious chatter of guests, the clink of glasses, the respectful murmur of attending waiters, as they brought in platter after platter of freshly prepared delicacies.

The captain and the other guests scrutinising them. Baba. Mama. Rani. Arjun.

'You are the son who's been...'

Baba's mouth tightening, pulling down at the corners ever so slightly, only Mama and Rani, privy to Baba's every expression, taking note. Arjun was oblivious.

Baba's smile firmly in place. 'Yes.'

Mama's hand under the table seeking out her husband's.

Now the captain beaming, 'I say! A real pleasure and honour, Your Highness.'

'I'm not...' Baba protested. But the tightness in his jaw had eased. He was smiling and it was genuine. And seeing his pleasure, Mama smiled too.

'Well, they say the maharaja talks of nothing but you. He maintains the kingdom has not been the same since you left. I hear they've been planning celebrations in anticipation of your return for weeks, since you wrote to say you were coming, despite his majesty being ill.' The captain motioned to a waiter to top up the glasses of everyone at the table. 'A toast to the crown prince.'

'Hear hear.'

Rani watched her father being toasted. Arjun raising his cup of juice, Mama her wine, laughing happily. She felt sick. Her father would have eschewed this, even just a few days ago. The trappings of wealth, power and renown.

Her father was changing.

As if he knew what she was thinking and wanted to reassure her, Baba sought her gaze, raised his glass to her and winked.

She had felt comforted then, briefly.

But that night, in their luxurious cabin, her bed gently rocking to the rhythm of the sea, a rousing blur of royal blue as glimpsed through her porthole window, she couldn't sleep. And every night after, as she watched her father being sought out and feted, supremely comfortable in his new 'crown prince' persona. Dread sitting on her stomach, choking her chest.

'Baba is changing,' she said to Mama, laying her head in the crook of her mother's neck as they watched their beloved father and husband being admired.

'He's happy to be going home, *meine liebe*, my love,' she said, gently patting Rani's hair. 'It's been so long and I know that however much he's tried to hide it, a part of him has been hurting. Let him have this.'

Her mother couldn't understand. She couldn't see Baba shrug off the very principles that had made him the man he was, accepting everyone's adoration as his right instead of being embarrassed by it.

Before, 'Why are they fawning?' He'd have grumbled. 'Just because I was born into a king's family, by virtue of the simple accident of birth? It's wrong. They shouldn't be clustering around me, hanging on my every word. We are all equal.'

No longer.

8

RANI

'What about me?' Rani had asked when Baba said they'd go to India.

'You, my darling?' He looked puzzled. Taking a minute for his starry eyes to focus on his daughter.

'We were going to move to England so I could apply to Cambridge.'

'You can apply from India.' He waved her concerns aside as if they were nothing.

But when he said that, he hadn't met her eyes, his gaze wavering, and it worried her.

Whatever happens I will go to Cambridge, she told herself on board the ship, as she noted that she and Mama were the only women at the captain's table. The other nobles' wives, veiled like secrets, were relegated to their cabins.

That made the monster choking Rani's chest more vicious, the vague foreboding all the more pressing.

'Why are all the other women covering their faces? Why are they not at the table?' she queried.

'That's the custom,' her father said.

'It's wrong.'

Baba looked around, making sure no one had heard Rani. Something he'd never have done before. Worrying about what people thought.

'You've got a feisty one there.' One of the men fawning over him winked.

'Yes,' Baba smiled back but where before he'd have said it proudly, now it was pained, faltering, as if Rani *was* really embarrassing him.

Afterwards, he came to find her. She was sitting on deck, staring at the sea which whispered and ruffled, grumbled and sang, seagulls joining in the chorus. The wavelets twinkling silver gold.

She did not look up as he sat himself down beside her.

The water was calming. An oasis of blue green stretching away to infinity.

'Rani,' Baba said softly.

There was uncharacteristic hesitation in his voice.

She looked up at him then, this man she adored. This man she had looked up to unquestioningly, who was now proving himself lesser than she had thought.

'India. They do things differently there.'

'I thought that is why you went away, made a life for yourself in Europe.' Her voice sharp.

He sighed. His hands crossed behind his head. Looking at the sea. Avoiding looking at her.

She turned away too, watching the seagull hovering on the wide white awning of sky like a stray thought at the edge of consciousness.

We are just dots to them, she mused, and the thought was a comfort.

'I just... you'll have to think before you speak, Rani.'

And now she was incensed. 'You taught me to speak my mind!'

He sighed again, for longer. 'I did but...' He took a breath. 'It's gone on for so long, this feud. I just...'

'The feud is between your father and you. Why should I change who I am?' Now that she'd started, she couldn't stop. 'And why here? To please people you and I don't even know. To indulge their idea of how a woman should behave.'

Her father nodded then. 'Fair point.'

She was surprised. She hadn't expected this new, changed Baba to concede. She realised then that she was changing too, in how she felt about her beloved father, her expectations of him. He had always given weight to her opinions and taken them seriously. Before.

'I'd forgotten how the country changes me. Makes me wage a constant battle between who I am, the principles I hold dear, and what is expected of me, between what I want and what is perceived as my duty.'

'We aren't even there yet,' Rani said, softly.

'Exactly.' Baba rueful. 'It's why I left.'

That evening, he was her father of old. The man she loved and looked up to.

But the next morning, when the shout thrumming with excitement rippled across the ship that land would be sighted soon, India, and he stood on deck gripping the rail as if it was a lifeline, his eyes fixed on the horizon where the dot of mud brown was delineating into a strip of land, his gaze longing and hope and eagerness, she knew somehow that she'd never have him to herself again.

And so, she watched her beloved family standing against the ship's railing just before land came into view, the three people she loved most in the world smiling wide in anticipation of the future, with a feeling she would later understand was nostalgia and wistfulness.

Her mother held out a hand to Rani. 'Come and join us.'

'Come on, love,' Baba beckoned, even as her brother smiled cheekily, one hand tucked into each parent's palm.

Rani tasted salt that had nothing to do with the sea spray the wind whipped into her face, and everything to do with an urge to capture this moment, commit it to memory, her heart thick with a premonition that nothing was ever going to be the same again.

She had closed her eyes then, thrown her face up to the sun, bright hot and dazzling, until she felt arms around her and sank, gratefully, into her father's musk and ginger embrace.

9

ESME

'Why do you fear you've turned out like your father?' Sally asks, her voice soothing, like flowing water.

Their second session together. After the first, Esme had gone home and cried, but these were cathartic tears. And for the first time in what seemed like forever, she was able to sleep for a solid five hours, a marked improvement on the patchy, nightmare-tortured two to three hours she'd been getting.

'I... I'm afraid of commitment.' *Philip*, she thinks, *I'm so sorry. I'm here, I'm trying. I only hope it's not too late for us.*

'Your father was too?'

'Yes.'

'But he was married?'

'Mum died when I was a baby. Dad brought us up...'

'Us?'

'My brother and myself.' Esme takes a breath. 'I don't remember my mum.' Her voice small.

'What about your brother?'

'He doesn't either. And Dad never spoke about her. We knew not to mention her. He'd become even more closed up.'

'I see. He never remarried?'

'No.'

'No one significant?'

'No.'

'You might not have known ab—'

'He went to work, came home and worked some more. Or read. He was always either reading or working. There wasn't anything, anyone else.'

'Ah.'

'He did not share himself with anyone. Not even us.' Her mouth salty wet.

If she was to frame her childhood in a snapshot, it would be this: her father, back from work, sitting in the armchair by the fireplace, lost in words. Esme at the table, doing homework, Andy out somewhere on his bike. When she was stuck on a question, calling, 'Dad, I need help.' Embers crackling in the fireplace. Orange flames topped by dancing blue. The scent of roasting meat. Pots clanking in the kitchen. Her father looking up at her, after she'd called him twice, sometimes thrice, too absorbed in his book, blinking, that familiar, preoccupied, slightly abstract look on his face.

10

RANI

India, 1937

Her father's brother was waiting for them at the port. It was like watching Baba's clone, the resemblance uncanny.

He was wearing a bejewelled turban and robes that glittered and dazzled, and a wide smile that didn't.

He joined his palms and bowed respectfully as his older brother stepped off the ship, but Baba, who was glowing in a way Rani had not seen before, gathered his younger brother into a hug.

Uncle smiled when introduced to Arjun but upon seeing Mama and Rani, his face tightened, the grin freezing.

He took Baba aside and there was a heated discussion.

Rani could see, although they were talking in whispers, that it was urgent and intense. The glow leaving Baba's face, his back rigid.

Mama wringing her hands as she too picked up on the tension.

Uncle turned to the army of turbaned men clad in shimmering robes – not as intricately patterned or as brilliant and choked with jewels as Uncle's but eye-catching all the same – clustering behind him, who, Rani realised, were waiting to do his bidding. At a gesture from Uncle, a couple of them scurried away, only to return shortly carrying two pieces of glittery, sequinned silk.

All the while, the brothers talked but it was evident it wasn't a happy discussion. Her father's shoulders tense, the muscles in his neck straining.

Now he turned, walking up to Mama and Rani. His eyes tormented as he looked at his wife and his daughter in turn.

'My father, he's old-fashioned.' A pause while his jaw worked, even as he struggled to speak.

Come out with it, Rani thought, heart sinking.

Uncle watched, his face grim.

'You will be required to cover your faces with these veils.' Baba shamefaced and apologetic as he handed them the fluttering wisps of silk.

Now Rani understood their purpose.

'And you'll be staying in the zenana, the women's section of the palace.' The words strangled, even as they were delivered in a stumbling rush.

'What does that mean?' Rani challenged.

'The zenana is located in the interior of the palace, a whole, vast section set apart for royal women.'

Before Rani could interject further, Mama nodded gently. She said, softly, even as she wore the silk like a scarf, 'Don't you worry about us.'

Baba's gaze now capturing Rani's. Pleading with his eyes. 'He's an old man. Dying. He's my father. I must humour him.'

'*You* must. Why should I?'

Uncle's eyes flashed daggers at her.

Baba sighed. 'Please.'

Uncle turned away, his palms bunched into fists, angry, Rani could see, with his older brother remonstrating with a child instead of ordering her to do as she was told.

She thought of what Baba had said on deck that evening: 'I'd forgotten how the country changes me. Makes me wage a constant battle between who I am, the principles I hold dear, and what is expected of me, between what I want and what is perceived as my duty.'

She loved her father. And despite their differences, her father loved his own.

She fingered the silk, soft as a heart tender with love, slippery as a newly minted resolution.

It was just for a short while, to please a dying man, her grandfather. But it went against her principles, her every instinct.

Mama squeezed her hand, her eyes iridescent, framed by the veil the colour of sea spray gilded rose by evening's glow.

Do this, she was conveying, silently, *for your Baba.*

Rani nodded, inwardly sighing.

Her father smiled in relief.

11

RANI

India was like nothing Rani had imagined.

Heat and dust and obscene wealth lording over unimaginable poverty.

Not that she got more than the merest glimpse of life outside the palace – viewed through the barrier of veil her uncle had procured for her and her mother to wear – during their journey from the port to the palace.

And once at the palace, Rani and Mama were relegated to the zenana without a by your leave.

The zenana was a cloistered section within the palace which was guarded even more securely than the palace itself, and better fortified than any prison.

Mama and Rani were led through winding corridors until they came to a gate set into high walls that were topped by broken glass, the sharp, uneven edges pointing at the sky, glinting forbiddingly in the blinding sunlight, dazzling white.

Women clad in khaki saris and matching turbans stamped with the royal insignia, sporting belts adorned with spears, cudgels and knives and carrying *guns*, patrolled the wall.

The zenana, it dawned on Rani, as she and Mama were led inside, was a gaol of women, albeit luxurious, ensconced within high walls. Even the children she saw playing in the lawns and courtyards were girls.

'No boys over five,' the maid, wearing a sari the celebratory ruby of joy, chosen to accompany them because she was the only one who could speak English, explained haltingly, when Rani questioned this. 'Older boys stay at main palace and then go boarding school.'

The zenana was a town in itself – buildings interconnected by canopied walkways, surrounded by elaborate gardens where peacocks showed off their magnificent plumage, immaculate lawns ringing with the musical chatter of women, the tinkling of anklets, singing bangles, children's laughter, glorious as applause, palm trees, fruit orchards, rose arbours, twinkling pools. Monkeys regarded them curiously while hanging upside down from mango and jackfruit trees, clutching babies to their stomachs. Children played hide-and-seek while women flitted about in kaleidoscopic saris like exotic birds, no veils as there were no men so no need to cover their faces, their hair gleaming in ebony plaits and buns, their voices as gentle and soothing as the burbling waters of the various fountains dotted about the courtyards separating the regal and splendiferous, domed and turreted abodes.

'Each of these belongs to a maharani,' the maid pointed out.

Finally, after walking past several buildings, attracting attention from children and monkeys alike, maids stopping what they were doing to surreptitiously point at Rani and Mama and whisper among themselves, they arrived at a domed, pillared building more vast and spread out than all the others.

'The maharaja wanted you to have the biggest residence. His first wife, the maharani Usha had to move to that building over there – she's not happy about it.' The maid explained, pointing to a building to her left.

First wife? mused Rani. *We would have preferred not to stay here at all. Why can't we stay with our father and brother? Why do we have to be separated from them and wear veils in the presence of men?* she cried in her head. She had tried remonstrating with her father yet again when they arrived at the palace, but both he and her mother had pleaded with her to please go with it for the time being, respect the maharaja's wishes as he was so very ill.

The interior of Rani and Mama's residence in the zenana was sumptuous, brimming with antiques and treasures. There were endless rooms furnished with tapestries, chandeliers casting glinting rainbows on the exotic furniture, wall hangings, antiques studded with jewels, mirrored screens, kaleidoscopic and glittering, assaulting the eye with their dazzling brilliance. Maids dusting and polishing, mopping and cleaning, their anklets providing chiming accompaniment. The ceilings painted with nuanced scenes of battle, the stately carpets draping the marble floors gloriously soft and intricately patterned.

The maid gestured for them to sit and Rani sank into a chaise lounge, enveloped by its silky velvet caress. Mama reclined opposite on an elaborate divan and smiled at Rani as maids arrived, bearing food. Honeyed cashew nuts, spiced peanuts, caramelised almonds and salted pistachios, dates and papaya, mango and watermelon and jackfruit, Indian sweets shaped like flowers, decorated with silver foil, studded with nuts and shiny with syrup, spicy fried snacks, platter after platter. The zesty, sugar-soaked aroma making Rani's senses tingle and her stomach advertise how hungry she was with an embarrassing growl.

Mama reached for a samosa. 'Aren't you eating, *meine liebe?*'

Despite her valiant efforts at normalcy, Mama appeared lost and more than a little out of her depth.

No, Rani wouldn't eat. This wasn't home; it couldn't be, for, despite its opulent luxury, all she could see was what was missing: her brother, her father. Their family spliced in two, divided by walls and gender.

* * *

Just as Rani had feared, her father changed even more in India, became a domineering stranger.

If someone had told Rani that her father would become like *his* father, the man he professed to hate, whom he'd rejected and whose way of life he'd spurned, adopting socialist ideals, marrying a German Jew instead of taking over the throne and merging kingdoms by marrying the princess his father chose for him, she would have laughed, disbelieving.

If she hadn't watched him transform, conform, and what's more, force his family to conform to ideals he'd rebelled against, she wouldn't have believed it.

But he did. And it devastated her to see him turn his back on his principles, take on everything he'd rebelled against before her shocked and disbelieving eyes.

Her mistake was believing her father when he asserted it was temporary. A small concession to humour his dying father.

Rani and Mama were yet to meet Baba's father, the excuse being that he was not up to it. But Rani found out from Arjun that he had had an audience with his grandfather. 'He even smiled and patted my cheek,' Arjun told Rani. 'His hands were very cold.'

'Why can't Mama and I see your father, given the reason we are here is because he wanted to reconcile with you and meet your family?' Rani asked Baba.

'He's ill and not up to visitors, as I've told you already,' Baba said shortly.

'But Arjun is the exception as he's the heir to the crown prince?' Rani challenged.

And to this, Baba had no reply. Rani would not accept that her own father would transform so, even as she worried that when his father died, and Baba was crowned king, he would grow to enjoy the power he was invested with, forget his principles and worse, renege on his promises to his wife and daughter. Turn his back on his vow that his daughter would attend university.

Forget their happy life before. A tight, close-knit family unit.

Forget *everything*.

* * *

'But Baba,' Rani cried, when her father and Arjun visited them in the zenana, 'what about my education?'

This was when she still believed he'd listen to her, hoped whatever he was doing was just a phase. Before she became completely disillusioned and gave up on him.

'All in good time, my love. For now, you—'

She didn't let him finish. 'So Mama and I are stuck in here, having to wear veils and twiddling our thumbs...'

'Just for a while...'

'What about equality? For man and woman? For everyone?'

Her father looked around to make sure no one had heard, colour seeping into his face. 'Shhh, Rani.'

'Ashamed of your daughter or the principles you propounded so passionately?'

He was quiet, looking distinctly uncomfortable. Her father, who once, not too long ago, was so proud of her outspokenness, encouraging it, cheering her on with glowing regard, 'That's my girl.'

'How long do we have to stay here?'

Her father didn't answer.

12

RANI

The zenana was extravagantly spacious, yet beyond claustrophobic, her mother determinedly cheery but in unguarded moments when she thought no one was watching, Rani could see Mama drooping.

Rani felt for her. Displaced from home in a country so far away, in a closed-off section of the palace reserved only for women, living – except for Rani – with strangers, apart from her husband and her son for the first time. In luxurious surroundings, with all the trappings of royalty, yes, but no freedom. A prison with all the comforts bar the warmth of loved ones. This country with its alien customs and language she just could not muster – she didn't share her children's instinctive flair for languages.

Harsh, unrelenting sun heralding day after day of the same trapped boredom, for there was nothing for the royal women confined to the zenana to do except dress up and wait for and upon their men whenever they deemed fit to visit them. Their duty was to provide their men with male heirs: the more the better. But the tragedy was that they couldn't look after their own

children even if they wanted to – there were specially trained
ayahs for this. And in any case, the royal heirs were whisked away
to the main palace and onwards to boarding school when they
turned five, the girl children married off by the time they attained
puberty. It was not deemed queenly to care for your own child, to
cook or do any menial task when there was a maid for the very
purpose. In the absence of anything constructive to fill their time
with, the women thrived on gossip and one-upmanship, which
went against Mama's gentle, sweet nature.

Mama had come to India for love of her husband but her
husband had abandoned her in here with women who resented
her for being the soon-to-be-king's wife, given the biggest and best
residence, and worse, a *firangi* foreigner and the only white
woman, who'd barely been here two minutes. Rani did not let on
that she was picking up the language more with every passing day
– within a few weeks, she could understand what all the other
women cloistered in the zenana with them were gossiping about:
her grandfather's and uncle's many wives (another shock), some of
them younger than Rani! Her grandfather's wives were bitter
because they'd been stripped of their status as queen consorts,
her uncle's because they would have been queens if not for this
white usurper.

Rani's mother was pleasant and kind and genuinely friendly
to all the other women in the zenana, greeting them politely in
the broken words of Hindi she had mustered. It was more than
they deserved, these vipers with their venomous snake eyes who
grumbled viciously about poor, beloved Mama.

'Talk to Baba, please,' Rani had urged. She was not talking to
her father herself. Only very rarely on those occasions when she
couldn't get out of it and then very formally. 'Ask him to allow us a
holiday to Germany. To visit with Opa and Oma.'

'He's finding his way back into the fold of family. He needs us with him.' Mama sighed.

'*This* is needing us?' Rani laughed harshly, humourlessly, waving a hand around her. 'He doesn't see us. He's left us in here to rot,' she hissed viciously.

'Rani, love, not for long,' her mother whispered and Rani noted the hope and longing in her words.

'And in any case,' Mama added, 'things are not any better in Germany.'

Oma's letters recently were desperately bright and yet failed to mask the undercurrent of unease that pulsed through them.

Mama, instead of being cheered by the letters, which was clearly Oma's intention, was troubled. She'd hand each letter to Rani. 'Tell me if I'm wrong but from what Oma is not saying, it appears things are getting worse over there. I hope your Opa is not up to his usual tricks, propounding his socialist views, being involved in the resistance against Nazis and their divisive policies.'

Good on you, Opa, Rani thought.

Mama caught the smile she couldn't hide. 'I know what you're thinking. But I'm worried. Your Opa's been arrested once before but thankfully, due to his connections, he was able to get out unscathed. But with Hitler getting more openly anti-Semitic by the day, passing all these laws designed to exclude, tax, fine and punish Jews, making us aliens in our own country, I—'

'Mama,' Rani said. 'Opa and Oma will be fine. They own the biggest jewellery store in Dusseldorf and perhaps all of Germany...'

'But—'

'And not only that, Opa, as you said, has connections among the most influential—'

'That will no longer offer protection for Jews. Here, read your

Oma's latest letter – there's talk all Jewish passports will need to be stamped with an identifying J—'

'But surely that's...' Rani had thought herself inured to outrage more potent than the one she harboured against her father – but she felt it now. So incensed, she couldn't get the words out, about this abomination in Germany, the country so close to her heart, for it harboured her beloved grandparents.

'Reading between the lines of your Oma's letters, it is clear she wants to leave...'

'Leave?' Rani experienced a stab of panic and upset thrumming alongside the anger. Germany was her grandparents' home, where Rani had spent several wonderful summers. It was the repository of treasured memories.

But that aside, it was the *principle* of the thing. 'Germany is *their* country. Why should they leave?'

'That's exactly what your Opa says.' A soft smile played on her mother's face, briefly displacing the worry. 'You're so alike.'

Rani had thought she was like her father. She'd been proud of it. But after her father's betrayal, once they came to India, she was grateful to be told she was like her Opa.

Her mother cupped her face gently. 'It will get better, my heart, both here and in Germany.'

Rani wanted to believe her.

* * *

'Don't you see what you've done to Mama?' she'd asked back when she was still speaking to her father, on the rare occasions when he found time in his busy schedule to deign to visit them in the zenana.

Mama was fetching schnecken, a sticky, sweet, German cinnamon roll, loved by her husband and son, and which, after much to-and-froing of instructions translated via Rani, she'd managed to get the maids to prepare in anticipation of their visit. The maids would have served the schnecken but Mama wanted to do at least that, given she was not allowed in the kitchen to prepare it herself like she'd wanted to – the maids had been scandalised when she'd suggested it via Rani.

Arjun was playing in the vast grounds with the other children. Her brother had the run of the palace. He got to participate in the darbar, where the king and his nobles held court, received subjects, passed laws, settled disputes and discussed and deliberated the needs of the kingdom, making sure everything ran smoothly and well, while Rani was imprisoned in the zenana with bitter, gossipy women.

Another wound.

Rani had loved her brother absolutely from the first time she set eyes on newborn Arjun in her mother's arms. That love for her sibling had only intensified, despite their enforced separation, the male-centric society trying to drive a wedge between them. Yes, she was jealous of the liberties that Arjun, at eight, less than half her seventeen years, had that she was denied. But not *of* him. Never her brother, who was just as befuddled as she was when Rani and her mother were hidden away from the men, their most basic freedoms taken away.

'You want for nothing,' her father said tightly, waving a hand around at their luxurious surroundings, the gold-embossed tapestries, the jewel-encrusted mirrors, the upholstered, velvet couches, the shimmering, silk cushions, the many servants waiting to attend to their every need, one bringing rose water with pomegranate seeds, another bowls of nuts and a variety of syrupy, ghee-drenched, raisin and nut studded, silver and gold dusted, saffron-infused Indian sweets in all the colours of the rainbow.

'Mama doesn't know the language. She's stuck in here. Bored.

Lost.' Rani's voice sharp with the anger that flared knowing her
father had chosen to deliberately misunderstand her. This man
who used to boast that he'd turned his back on wealth and kingship because humanity was more important. 'She's supported you
through everything, unquestioningly. Have you spared even a
single thought for her?' At that moment, she hated her father,
donned in his kingly regalia, his army of courtiers standing defer-
entially to attention.

'I'm...' he began.

And as she watched him scramble to come up with a response,
she knew, if she hadn't already, that he hadn't thought of either
her mother or herself, only, selfishly of himself.

'Your majesty...' one of the courtiers interrupted with an
urgent message from the court.

Although he wiped it away almost immediately, Rani clocked
the brief expression of profound relief that graced her father's
face at having not had to answer his daughter's question.

When Mama returned with a plate of schnecken, it was to a
husband who was already leaving.

And again, Rani noted the hurt that Mama masked behind a
too-brilliant smile as she packed the delicacy from her childhood,
her way of showing love, for him to take with him, which he probably wouldn't even eat, Rani thought bitterly, turning away. They
had gone from a family who were open and honest with each
other to one hiding their feelings behind brittle smiles. Baba had
done this to them, taken an axe to their family, sawing them down
the middle, destroying their closeness, segregating them along
gender lines.

Arjun, their saving grace, blissfully unaware of the seething
tension, grabbed a few schnecken, even as he threw his arms
around Mama, 'My favourite, thanks, Mama', planting syrup and
sweat-laced kisses on Rani's cheeks, eating as he walked away,

waving with hands clutching more, Mama's smile as she watched her son go in his father's wake so heartbreaking that Rani closed her eyes even as they prickled and stung with briny heat.

* * *

Rani and Mama missed Arjun intensely.

When he visited the zenana, the boy was breathless with stories of his exploits, the friends he had made with whom he was exploring the palace's many nooks and crannies.

Her brother said, 'I miss you,' to them both but Rani could see that he was enjoying himself too much to actually do so.

Arjun was revelling in being fawned over, treated like a king-in-waiting and Rani didn't begrudge him that. What she did begrudge him was the freedom to roam, to *be*, unhampered by veils and rules.

It rankled and upset, this difference between men and women, the women cloistered away, treated like possessions, toys, pets, with no minds of their own, several wives for each man.

'Will you take more wives too?' she'd asked Baba out of her mother's hearing – she didn't want to hurt Mama any more than she was already.

Her father coloured. Turned red, bunching his palms into fists. He was working to rein in his anger. 'Rani. You're going too far.'

'And you're not? You've reneged on every so-called principle you lived your hypocritical life by. Why not this one too?'

'I love your mother.'

'You have a funny way of showing it, shutting her away like a prisoner, with people she doesn't know, in a country alien to—'

'Only until I've established myself, got my subjects here to trust and accept me. If I start breaking rules left and right, they might not—'

'It's not breaking rules to show them you're proud of your wife and to treat her as an equal. It is showing them what's right.'

'They will think I'm breaking with tradition and lose their trust in me. I can't barge in, take over and change too much too soon. I need to win their faith. As it is, I've married outside the community...'

'Oh, so you're ashamed of Mama, is that it?'

'Rani, I don't expect you to understand,' her father exploded and walked away, shaking his head.

'Have *you* tried to understand what it's like for us, living in here?' she'd shouted at his retreating back.

He did not give any indication of having heard.

'That's right, run away, why don't you,' she muttered to herself, biting back hot, salty tears. Although she was disillusioned by her father, a stubborn part of her always hoped he'd see sense, listen to her. She'd hoped they'd have a heart-to-heart like they'd had on board the ship. That he would include her in his confidence. Explain.

This is why his words hurt more than she could bear: *I don't expect you to understand.*

Before, he'd always patiently explained until she understood even the trickiest concept in whichever subject he was trying to teach her. He'd always maintained that she was bright beyond her years, that she grasped the point he was trying to make, that she understood *him*. She wanted him to tell her why he was doing what he was doing. Give her a good enough reason, not fob her off with excuses.

That is why she pushed. The Baba of before had always encouraged her to speak her mind. But now, when she did, he accused her of 'going too far' or didn't respond. So she eventually stopped talking to him. From hurt at being displaced, pushed away, and from the repeatedly thwarted desire to be his confidante again.

She wanted reassurance that although he had several courtiers and nobles to discuss state matters with, he still needed her.

Then she would have forgiven being stuck in the zenana, forgiven him anything.

13

RANI

'Mama how can you take it?' Rani railed, over and over. Her mantra.

Her mother sighed, 'Give him a chance.' Her mother's chant.

Rani wanted to shake her mother as she often had since they came to India, for being so accepting of the situation they found themselves in.

But as one hot, humid day followed another with weary sameness, Mama too had wilted. 'He needs time to find his way.' She said it with a weary acceptance instead of her usual bright optimism.

'How long?' Rani asked.

But her mother had no answer.

* * *

Then news arrived from Germany that Mama's parents, Rani and Arjun's beloved Opa and Oma, had passed away in a motorcar accident. It was a terrible blow and it couldn't have happened at a worse time, clashing as it did with Baba's coronation.

Baba's father had passed away in his sleep a few weeks after they arrived in India. The court was in mourning for weeks but Rani found it hard to grieve for a man she had never met, even if he was her grandfather.

When she heard that Opa and Oma died, on the other hand, Rani was devastated. She wanted to travel to Germany with Mama but...

'Your Baba needs me here beside him,' Mama said, her eyes dark and sunken with grief.

'He abandons you to the zenana but when you want to travel home to say goodbye to your parents, he suddenly wants you with him?'

'Your Opa and Oma are dead. They won't know either way. My duty is to my husband.'

What about his duty to you? Rani wanted to cry. *And Opa and Opa may not know about their only daughter and her children, whom they'd so adored, not being present to bid them farewell, but you and I do.*

But Mama was rent, devastated, undone by sorrow and so Rani put her arms around her mother and held her as together, they mourned the two people they'd so loved.

In the event, it would have made no difference if Mama had been present at Baba's coronation or not. She had to watch her husband ascend to the throne with pomp and ceremony, the new bearer of the ancestral sword of the Divanpur maharajas, from behind the curtained upper balcony of the court, where she was cloistered, alongside Rani and the other royal and noble women.

When Rani couldn't bear to watch her mother, reduced by grief for Opa and Oma to a mere shadow of her vibrant self, pine any longer, she requested an audience with her father.

'Say what you want to say here with us, his close family and courtiers present,' her uncle challenged.

She ignored him, turning to her father. 'I'd like a *private* meeting with you, Baba.'

'Give me fifteen minutes,' he said to his brother and courtiers.

His brother turned away with a huff, and from the way his stiff shoulders pierced the taut air, Rani knew he was angry.

As if she cared.

She was too.

Fifteen measly minutes was all her father was willing to spare her after asking permission from his brother first!

She came straight to the point. 'Mama is lost and grieving. She couldn't even travel back home for the funeral as she had to attend your coronation, where, again, like in the zenana, she was cloistered. You claim to love her. How could you be so selfish?'

'Things are very uncertain in Germany, Rani, with Hitler's oppression of the Jews. He's asking for their passports to be stamped with a red J. There was no guarantee she'd have been able to travel back to India,' Baba said, eyes flashing.

'Would that be such a bad thing? At least she would be in her home country with people speaking her language instead of stuck inside the zena—'

'Not that again! Rani, there's almost certainly going to be war in Europe. Mama is safer here. And in any case, how come she isn't complaining?'

'She's giving you a *chance*.'

'Why don't you do the same?'

'Because I see exactly where this is going. You used to be against totalitarian regimes. You are condemning Hitler. What about yours?'

She'd gone too far. She could see it in the way Baba clenched his fists to hold in his temper. 'My brother is right and I've let you get away with too much,' he said tightly, turning away from her.

And that, for Rani, was the last straw. Her father agreeing with Uncle with regards to her.

As that endless summer dragged on with Rani trapped within sweltering walls, as she felt her whole life, her future sweating away, melting with the heat, she understood that she couldn't rely on her father as she had all her life until now to sort the problem, come to a decision. And even if she could, she wouldn't go to this version of her father, Uncle's clone, for *anything*. She would have to do it herself, change the status quo, for Mama's sake as well as her own, as her father wouldn't.

14

RANI

First step, Rani decided, was to find a way out of the zenana and, if that worked, the palace. She wanted to experience the true India, outside these vulgarly opulent, yet stiflingly claustrophobic, walls, where a select few were waited on hand and foot, their every whim catered for by an army of obsequious servants.

She also wanted, if possible, to find her father's childhood friend, who, her father had told her back in the happy days before royalty destroyed their family unit, had lived in the village just outside the palace walls.

If successful, she'd then consider what to do next.

And so Rani meticulously planned her escape from the palace. It gave her something to aim for, took her mind off her worry about her mother, who, in her grief for her parents and her perpetual waiting for her husband to find his feet, was a shell of the happy, bright woman she'd once been. It stopped her agonising over whether she'd realise her dream of studying at Cambridge. For very soon, it would be too late...

One step at a time, she told herself.

She'd try and escape the palace first. Then once she'd

achieved that, she'd abscond to Cambridge. And she'd take her mother with her. Perhaps once they left, her father would come to his senses...

But first, leaving the zenana. How to get past the guards?

She sat on the bench just within the high walls and pondered the question, unmindful of the searing sun baking her uncovered head, crisping her body, and watched the maids leaving for the day exchange cheerful greetings with those arriving for the evening shift.

And that was when it came to her.

Over the next few days, she cultivated one of her maids, Priya, who was the same build as her, bribing her with money and the elaborate saris her father had bought for her but which she'd never worn, stubbornly wearing the same few dresses she'd carried with her from Europe (with a veil, grudgingly, when her father and uncle and Arjun visited). She studied the maid's dialect. The way she spoke, walked, her every mannerism. She fed her gossip she'd invented and kept an ear out to hear it repeated back with embellishments, as gossip was currency here in the festering confines of the zenana. When she didn't hear anything back and was satisfied of Priya's loyalty to her, Rani asked her for one of her saris, paying her handsomely for the privilege.

Priya was the only one in whom she confided her plan.

She had to, as she was to be involved in the subterfuge. Rani had decided against telling Mama, who was upset enough without having to fret about her daughter. And she didn't want to be dissuaded; she'd made up her mind.

'I'm going to feign a headache and tell everyone I'm not to be disturbed except by you as you will be tending to me. For the time I'm away, you'll have the run of my suite. Help yourself to anything you want, make yourself at home. I don't need to say this but I will anyway. Do not, at any cost, let anyone in.'

'But what if we're caught?' Priya's expressive eyes were liquid with fear. 'My job feeds my family, my younger brothers and invalid parents.'

'I will take the blame. You will be safe, I promise.'

'What if your mother knocks, wanting to check on you?'

'She knows I will be sleeping it off and I'm not to be interrupted.' Rani had already pretended that she was ailed by debilitating headaches a few times and her mother knew now to just let her be until she felt well again. And anyway, since Opa and Oma's deaths, her mother was not herself. Mama used to be ever the optimist, before. Always straight-backed and well turned out and elegant, now she drooped. Her lips, usually upturned in a smile, dragged down with lines of grief. Rani doubted she'd even notice her daughter was getting one too many headaches, 'resting' a tad too long.

'Don't worry,' Rani reassured Priya, smiling briskly, 'we will not be caught.'

15

RANI

And so, with everything in place, Priya ensconced in Rani's suite masquerading as Rani with a headache and not to be disturbed, Rani took the plunge.

She pulled her maid's sari closer around her, the veil covering her face as she slipped past the guards in the zenana, cheekily wishing them good day, taking care to mimic Priya's accent.

She kept her head down as she navigated the myriad walkways of the vast and winding palace with its many antechambers and interconnected mansions, forbidding turrets, countless courtyards, glinting pools, landscaped gardens. It took her a while to get used to them, her skill in directions not matching up to that of fluency with languages.

She got lost several times, ended up in all-male enclaves, but mostly managed to avoid getting caught by, among other things, hiding behind mirrored screens, intricate tapestries that swept the velvet carpeted tiles, and once, even pretending to be a statue in a room full of stuffed animals: tigers about to pounce, snarling cheetahs, majestic lions, leopards with teeth bared in manic grins, stately giraffes skirting the painted ceiling depicting gory scenes of Gods at war; an experience that she still had nightmares about. She was only stopped once but she pretended to be new and lost and the irate courtier sent her on her way with a warning, grumbling all the while under his breath about good-for-nothing maids.

But she persisted, and after a few such forays, she did finally find her way out.

Once outside the palace, its opulent claustrophobia and vulgarly luxurious trappings giving way to mud roads and huts and the desperate reek of poverty, the gut-wrenching, stomach-turning agonies of a hand-to-mouth existence, ironically, Rani could breathe again.

She took a freeing gulp of dust-sprinkled, spiced air, looking up at the wide, white sky, beneath which basked small huts with cracked, mud walls and holey, tarpaulin roofs.

She stumbled down narrow streets packed with carriages, neighing horses, bullock carts, the bullocks with curved horns lethal enough to gore tender flesh, pedestrians and businesses, hawkers and flea-plagued dogs, scrawny chickens, scrawnier cats, flies galore, small huts brimming with whole families nudging each other, naked urchins, also flea-tormented and mud-caked, sleeping in ditches beside animals in a similar near-starved state, caved stomachs, protruding ribs, open sores of wounds.

She had a vague plan – to find, if possible, her father's childhood friend, Murli the milkman's son.

'He would come to the palace to deliver milk with his father, riding on a bullock's back, and we formed a tentative friendship. I'd ask him questions about his life outside the palace walls and for me, his stories of never having enough food, of living in a one-roomed hut with not only his parents and siblings but grandparents too, with walls of earth that leaked in winter and baked in summer, seemed fantastic, romantic, more of a fairy tale than the ones I was made to read. I think it was then, trying to contemplate the difference between us, the food I wasted without thought, the multitude of empty rooms in the palace, choked with priceless antiques but soulless, that I started asking questions that would eventually lead me to embrace socialist and communist ideologies.' Sitting on her father's lap, snugly secure in the embrace of his solid arms, Rani would listen breathlessly.

'Did you see this hut where Murli lived?' she'd asked.

'Oh no! As crown prince, I was expected to behave a certain way, not mix with ordinary people. I was born with a silver spoon. And yet... I had everything except freedom.' His voice bitter, like when you bit into a fruit expecting sweetness but got a seed instead. 'I only managed to talk to Murli secretly while his father was delivering the milk. Perched on his bullock, he was just the right height to reach my window. We had a code – he'd tap three times so I knew it was him – but we didn't really need it. As soon as I heard the shuffling of the bullock's hooves, I dismissed all the maids. Then I'd wait beside the window, ready to throw it open when he knocked.' Her father's smile wistful, his gaze far away. 'I can still recall the heady feeling of secrecy, my friend's bobbing head between the branches of the jacaranda tree, his hot, sweet breath mingling with the perfume of the purple blooms. If you didn't look down, you would think he was conjured from the tree, a smiling, talking, human-face-shaped jacaranda bloom.'

Rani had laughed with delight, clapping her hands.

Her father had smiled, eyes shimmering. 'He told me he lived by the river. That he and his siblings played on the riverbed during the drought, shimmying across to the opposite bank and stealing mangoes from the orchard there as the whole river dried up!'

Rani tried and failed to imagine sun so potent that it would swallow a river whole, used as she was to very cold winters and mild, temperamental summer sun.

She'd fallen asleep that night and for weeks after picturing this India she had never seen, where breathtakingly opulent palaces perched within dazzlingly high walls, outside of which squatted mud huts housing three generations in one room, a river that evaporated in the summer and overflowed during the rainy season bearing silent witness beneath a sweltering, fireball sky.

When she escaped from the palace that first time, she wanted to see with her own eyes this river that had so captured her imagination as a child, and, if he still lived by the river, meet her father's childhood friend, whom he'd talked about with such affection and credited as the catalyst for his conversion to Marxism and socialism.

After half an hour wandering down the maze-like gullies spilling with humanity, lives lived in the streets, hot air scented with spices and sewers, reeking of desperation stroking her cheeks, she'd asked for directions to the river.

She'd been directed down alleyways, past mountains of disintegrating rubbish and debris taller than the mud huts housing the villagers, atop which children Arjun's age played, digging in it for treasure (rats there with the same purpose scurrying away), dancing with glee upon discovering a shiny scrap of metal, scrambling down it like a slide, bits of paper and pebbles and rotting veg flying everywhere, yellow teeth beaming from delighted, dust-streaked faces.

Rani's eyes stung, even as her stomach blistered with a fiery ball of rage as she contrasted it with the vastness and wasteful extravagance of the palace, the hundreds of unoccupied rooms chock-full of purposeless treasure, the huge table groaning with delicacies at every meal, the hundreds of servants tending to the bored whims of a select, overprivileged, undeserving few.

She walked on, past girls her age or younger tending to pots bubbling on open hearths, pregnant bellies protruding, bedraggled children with hungry gazes tugging at their mothers' legs, jogging crying babies on their young hips, looking at her as she passed, their eyes through their veils ringed by varying expressions of despair, indifference, pain, envy.

For the first time since she arrived in India, Rani felt shame push aside the hot indignation directed at her father. Here she was complaining of being hard done by, deprived of a Cambridge education, bored stuck in the zenana. She was *lucky*. So very, very lucky.

For the first time, she truly understood all those socialist maxims she had imbibed from her father and his books and blindly spouted, courting the admiration of Baba and his cronies.

Empty words, she saw now. Without meaning. Easy for her to say when she had everything, had never known trouble, hunger, lack.

Here, these children with less than nothing were finding joy in a rubbish heap while she complained, fretted, raged at being bored.

I will do something with my life, work to make a difference, bring about change, she vowed as she traversed the dusty strips of paths between huts and hawkers, under the unrelenting gaze of the sun.

16

RANI

A sharp turning and suddenly, open space, straggly, dust-choked crops, flecks of green visible through the ubiquitous orange. And there, a glint of silver, brightly shimmering in the haze, drawing the eye like the shiny metal held aloft the rubbish heap in that child's hand. A meandering trickle of an excuse for a river, muddy fields sinking down to it, red earth, giants of trees – gnarled branches, deciduous roots – bending down as if to drink from the water, which, perhaps to make up for its meagreness, gurgled and danced in warm welcome.

A holy man squatted on the riverbank, a necklace of black beads adorning his bare torso, a beard of matted, grey-speckled black hair trailing down his chin and onto his chest, bare head gleaming – with perspiration, but the effect was that of a glowing halo, as if he was truly blessed, eyes closed, praying to a shrine set into the hollow of a peepal tree, smothered by garlands, the tangy-sweet perfume of marigold.

Skinny goats and skeletal cows desultorily sniffed at the parched, yellowing grass dotted around the bank.

Women washed clothes in the water, their colourful saris glimmering in the golden sunlight, music of laughter and chatter as they gossiped like parakeets, the grey outcrop of rocks by the bank strung with kaleidoscopic flags of drying fabric. After they'd finished washing, the women perched on the rocks, sharing *paan* – betel leaf filled with chopped betel nut, slaked lime and tobacco, and woes, feeding babies while their older children splashed in the water, danced in the mud. All the while, the holy man prayed, eyes shut, lost to this world.

And then she spied it.

A hut perched on the bank at the bend in the river. A bullock tethered to a small excuse for a tree, looking placidly at Rani as she approached, the crows alighting on its back paying no heed to the periodic swishing of its tail.

'Hello?' she called at the entrance to the hut, a faded cotton sari, flapping in the occasional, humid, gritty breeze serving as a door.

It was pushed aside and a figure emerged, squatting low to exit from the small entrance of the mud hut.

She blinked as the figure, lithe as a leopard, stretched upright to full height, broad shoulders blocking the sun, a halo of ebony curls, face in shadow.

'Murli?' she asked, tentative, suddenly shy.

The purpose that had led her to bribe and cajole her maid into subterfuge, escape from the palace, come here, suddenly flimsy, evaporating in the glare of this shadowy gaze.

'Who's asking?' The voice flowing gold.

The man moved and, now she could see his face, was pinned by the scrutiny of his sunflower eyes.

'I...' She cleared her throat. 'I'm Rani.'

'What do you want with my father?'

Ah, so this was Murli's son. She was in the right place. Decisively, she pushed back her veil, threw her head up high. She would not be cowed.

She met his assessing gaze, this man whom she saw now was too young to be Murli, being a couple of years older than her, if that. Darkly handsome, a shadow of a beard, full lips pursed in a frown, thick eyebrows gathered in a glower over those bright eyes full of liquid light.

She found the Hindi words she wanted, digging for them in her memory, which was inexplicably uncooperative, suddenly, then said, carefully, 'He was my father's childhood friend.'

'My father had many childhood friends,' he growled.

'My father is called Prajanya Raj,' she said.

That scowl became more pronounced, a dark cloud casting aspersions on a dazzling white sky.

'The new king,' he spat.

'Do you judge everyone by their fathers or just me?' she asked boldly.

The man scowled at her for a few more seconds, each of which felt like hours.

Sweat beaded at the nape of her neck, travelled down the blouse of the borrowed sari.

Then, 'You call that Hindi?' And he smiled.

It was like a benediction she did not know she was yearning for. It transformed him, his golden eyes burning bright in that stubbly, rough-hewn face, that twinkling gaze reaching right into her heart, broken by what she thought of as her father's defection.

From that moment, she was lost.

17

RANI

After that first meeting, Rani escaped the palace nearly every afternoon.

Murli's son was called Prasad, she learned.

They sat among the branches of the peepal trees sweeping the parched, cracked riverbed, legs swinging pendulums, and they talked about everything under the sun, his bullock regarding them with drowsy, amber eyes.

He was a labourer, he said, but work was scarce in the village. 'Baba has found work in town. It involves long hours of back-breaking slog. He is allowed home for visits only when a project is finished. He hasn't been back for months now.'

'He is no longer a milkman?' Rani asked.

'There was a severe drought a few summers ago. The animals did not have food, so could not produce enough milk. The maharaja sacked him.'

He tried to keep his voice even but Rani sensed the bleak, bitter undertone. She wanted to take his hand, squeeze it, offer comfort. But she didn't dare. She was the granddaughter of the man who had, without a second thought, deprived Prasad's father of his livelihood.

'I'm so sorry,' she said. It was all she had. It was nothing.

'There is work in town, but I can't go.'

'Oh, why not?'

'Ma... she's not well. I have to be here for her.' His voice tight, clipped but carrying a thrumming current of pain.

She hurt with him, for him. This man touched her heart, ignited her emotions in a way nobody had ever done before.

Then, his voice bright, 'Hey, don't look so sad. It's good I'm here. I get to spend time with you.' He smiled at her then.

And it was as if a beam of sunlight was focused only, exclusively upon her, a radiant, glorious gift.

They talked about their childhoods and he was so avidly interested when she told of her cosmopolitan upbringing, visiting grandparents in Germany, living all over Europe.

'We've had such different childhoods,' he marvelled. 'You've travelled the world. I've not set foot outside of this village. And yet, here we are, talking, sharing. Friends.'

Friends. She felt a jolt of incandescent, intense happiness reverberate through her body.

'I might not be well travelled, but I am an expert at climbing trees. I'm only sitting down here on the lowest branch in deference to you.' Flashing that cheeky grin that she found irresistible even as she rolled her eyes to show him she wasn't impressed. 'That skill was very useful to us as children as we were always hungry and would supplement our meagre boiled rice meals with stolen fruit.' Then, nudging gently at her arm, his touch sending thrilling shivers up her spine, a smile glittering jewel bright in his voice, 'Ah don't be upset, there was always plenty of fruit to steal. Hell to pay the few times we were caught of course, but worth it for a full stomach. And it wasn't all bad. Swimming in the river during the rains, skimming stones, helping with chores, milking and wood cutting and hoisting, squelchy mud fights and fashioning intricate mud palaces with my siblings.'

'How many of you in the hut?'

'Ah let's see. Myself and my three sisters, Ma, Baba, Baba's parents...'

'Your grandparents too?'

'And the goat when there was the tiger scare – we couldn't risk it getting eaten, your grandfather preferred goat's milk to the cows'...'

'*Tiger* scare?' She looked around, at the children playing in the strip of muddy water that was all the river was now – the monsoons were late – at their mothers chatting as they washed clothes and set them to dry, at the sadhu who was being visited by the villagers bearing gifts of milk and sweet rice that they could ill afford so he would liaise with the Gods for rain.

He laughed. 'Don't look so scared; he's probably terrorising another village right now.'

'He's still *alive*?'

'Of course, who'd be brave enough to kill him? The villagers did set traps, but no luck.'

He shrugged. She shuddered. He laughed, bringing to mind shooting stars, shimmering constellations.

To take her mind off the fizzing electricity his laughter excited within her, she asked, 'How did you all fit in the hut with the goat as well?'

He shrugged. 'We made do. We all slept together in the one room anyway...'

'It's one room?'

'Yes, come, I'll show you.'

Nimbly, he jumped off the branch, held out his hand to help her down.

His touch sent sparks all down her arm and into her body, setting it aglow.

As they walked to the hut, he said, 'It was tough when the goat was in with us. For one, it kept farting and burping, so it was incredibly smelly, not to mention noisy...'

She giggled, although she was horrified for him, for all of them. He'd endured so much and yet still, he was so happy, positive, full of life.

'...and of course, the bullocks and cows felt left out and kept wanting to come in too, mooing and lowing mournfully all night.'

'Oh my.'

'Thankfully, the tiger moved on after a week, and the goat went back outside. Sadly, though, she was bitten by a cobra and died.'

'Oh no...'

'But by then, your grandfather no longer wanted our milk anyway.' His voice acrid, the smile thrumming through it quite gone.

'I'm sorr—'

'Well, here we are.'

They'd arrived at the hut.

'You have to bend down to enter. Mind your head. There's more room now my sisters are married and our grandparents have sadly passed on.'

More room? It was smaller than the closet reserved for her underclothes at the zenana, the walls fashioned from mud, the floor...

He read the question in her eyes. 'Cow dung. Ma used to sweep a fresh coat on every morning. I do it now.'

The hut was dark after the blinding sunshine outside. But when her eyes adjusted, she saw that despite it being tiny and cramped, it was neat. One small section, partitioned by a billowing sari curtain, was the kitchen and storage area, housing a couple of earthen pots, clothes and sundries all meticulously arranged for maximum space and efficiency.

'We cook outside,' he said. 'Wash in the river.'

Suddenly, what had looked like a bundle of clothes in the corner moved, spoke in a tremulous voice. 'Is that you, son?'

A small army of cockroaches scuttled from beneath the bedclothes and scurried past Rani, nearly brushing her leg.

Rani took a step backward, bumping against the mud wall, releasing a shower of dust. Prasad put a hand in hers and once again, that spark. Her whole body buzzing with it. He gently angled her towards what she now saw was a woman, shrunk so much she was but a skeleton, papery skin creased over a measly collection of bones.

'Ma,' Prasad's voice so tender, it hurt Rani's very core. 'I've brought a friend.'

The woman's eyes, milky with cataracts, Rani assumed, blinked a couple of times. Her mouth, small as a baby bird's, widened into what Rani guessed was a smile. 'Good. That's...' The rest of her words were swallowed up by a bout of prolonged coughing.

Prasad squatted beside his mother, rubbing her fragile back, every bone in her spine visibly jutting through her tissue-thin skin and sari, until the coughing fit passed. He pressed a gentle kiss on her insubstantial cheek. Again, it ignited pain deep within Rani.

'You rest now, Ma.' His voice soothing as a lullaby.

Rani ached for Prasad, for his mother. Her eyes stung but she held her tears in check. She couldn't cry when he was being so matter-of-fact, taking it all in his stride.

Afterwards, out in the sun, blinking to adjust to the blinding light, the vast, open space a luxury after the confines of his home, he said, 'The hut leaks during the monsoons and is powdery during the summer...'

Rani recalled the dust she'd dislodged when she bumped against the wall.

'It triggers Ma's asthma. She doesn't have long.' He sighed deeply.

She wanted to hold him, offer comfort, but she was too shy. This man wowed her, he made her strangely nervous, set her whole being aflutter. She was in awe of him, how he owned his life, troubles and all, how he seemed content despite scarce work opportunities and having to look after an invalid parent.

After a bit, 'How old is she?' Rani asked softly.

'Forty-five.'

'*Forty-five?*' Rani was horrified. That was younger than her father! The woman she'd seen looked nearly eighty.

As if he knew what she was thinking, Prasad said, voice threaded with bitterness and sorrow, 'It's the same with everyone in the village; life expectancy is very low. As it is, Ma never recovered from the death of my sister.'

She looked up at him. 'You said your sisters are married?'

'Two of them are. The other, well, she didn't get to grow up.' Shadows stealing the light from his eyes. 'She was the youngest. Always smiling. Happy. A real trouper. Black fever took her. We all got it. She didn't recover...'

'But... the doctor...'

He smiled and it was so very, very sad. 'We barely had enough to eat. How could we afford the doctor? We didn't even have rice to offer to the wise man for one of his potions...'

'I'm sorry,' she said, laying a tentative hand on his.

He looked at her, eyes shimmering. 'I know.'

And once again, she was lost in the depths of those soulful eyes.

Then, his voice changing, becoming steely, shot through with fiery determination, 'I dream of a world where everyone can afford basic necessities. Food, water, medicine. It's not too much to ask, is it?'

'Not at all.'

His hand was still in hers and she squeezed it. He squeezed back. Her heart felt full.

18

RANI

Prasad was passionate, lively, fun.

'How old are you?' she asked. He seemed so very grown up and yet, he could be just as silly as her eight-year-old brother sometimes.

'Eighteen.'

'Only a year older than me.'

He pulled himself to his full height, looked down at her, hands on hips, eyebrows raised. 'That makes all the difference, child.'

She laughed.

She told him about getting lost in the multitudes of alleyways the first time she came to find his father.

'What!' he scoffed. 'They're all so distinct. There's the Muslim area with the mosque, the Hindu side with its many shrines to various gods and goddesses everywhere you look, but just in case you miss them, the rotting flowers and cloying incense are a dead giveaway.' A cheeky smile. 'Then there's the vegetable market, the alley with the fabric and carpet vendors, the...'

'Really? Show me,' she challenged.

And he did, leading her patiently through each section, stopping to talk to all the vendors, passing the time of day at every hut. He seemed to know *everyone* and they him. And because she was with him, she was hailed with the same happy bonhomie. They insisted on sharing their watery gruel, cooked on outdoor hearths and spiced with the tart and smoky flavour of the mango and tamarind twigs used for kindling, with her. She knew they were going without to include her. It was humbling to be eating with all of them together, a handful of rice each, rather than she and her Mama in a huge room, the table creaking under the weight of food. Those few grains somehow tasted better than all the palace delicacies.

'Everyone likes you. You're charming. You have that effect on people,' she told him.

'But *you* charm *me*,' he said, grinning at her warmly.

Her entire body glowed.

He was curious about her life.

'Why are you here with me when you could be enjoying the luxury at the palace?'

She was hesitant to complain, moan, when she had so much, everything.

He seemed to understand without her having to put it into words. 'You are not your father or your grandfather. You are here with me, enjoying my company. At least I hope so.' Flashing that irresistible grin, even as he dug in his pocket, pulled out a raw mango, and from the other, some sea salt. He sprinkled the salt onto the mango, held it out to her.

'Yes, I definitely am.'

Her heart bloomed in the radiance of his gaze.

She took a bite of the mango, tart brine explosion in her mouth.

He laughed. 'You come here for this. Better than all the gourmet offerings at the palace, eh?'

She pictured the table at the palace, vast as three of Prasad's huts put together, packed with food, most of it uneaten. What happened to it, all those dishes, more at every course, untouched?

She swallowed the mango, and smiled as the sweet, sour, salty aftertaste lingered on her tongue. 'Much better.'

He threw back his head to the gilded heavens and laughed, a cascade of glorious celebration.

After a bit, 'Tell me about you,' he said.

Despite the disparity of their lifestyles, he seemed genuinely interested, invested in her answer.

She told him of how she grew up a socialist, beliefs picked up on her father's lap, and how angry she was that her father had turned his back on his ideals when they came to India. 'What hurts and angers me more than anything else is that he is swayed by the trappings of kingship, all these people bowing allegiance to him, dancing to his every whim, the very things he scorned. How could he change like that, in a blink?'

'Power does that to you, I'm afraid,' Prasad said, his eyes shining with empathy for her upset.

He *listened* to her, no derision or boredom in evidence.

'Don't you hate me for what my grandfather did, deciding to cut off your livelihood on a whim?' she couldn't help asking.

'What?' He was shocked. 'Why would I hate *you* for what your *grandfather* did?'

She was touched and impressed by how he cared for her and about her, felt for her despite her circumstances being so very different from his own, caused in part by her family.

'You must think me spoiled to complain when I have so much,' she said, finally able, because of his understanding, to voice what she was thinking.

His eyes when he looked at her were soft. 'Rani, you are hurt by your father not keeping his word, not sticking to his values, the values you learned from him. That's a big deal. I would be hurt too, upset, betrayed.'

If she wasn't already in his thrall, she would have been then. In any case, it was at that moment that her allegiance shifted, from her father to this man who understood, who cared, who saw her. It didn't matter that her father did not listen to her any more. Prasad did.

'How can my father be so blind to the plight of his subjects?' she said, getting it all, her anger, her upset off her chest. 'How can he shut himself away in the palace, a very exclusive, unreal place, and believe all is well? How can he not know that his brother and his courtiers are telling him only what he wants to hear? It was the very thing that riled him about *his* father and yet he can't see that he's doing the exact same. It's so frustrating.' She took a breath. 'When I wear Priya's sari and walk out of the palace, no one gives me a second glance, not the guards, not the sentry manning the moat, except to tell me to hurry away as the king's motorcar is on its way. Dressed in Priya's attire, I am invisible. It is incredibly freeing but also very sobering. Then coming here, seeing how you all live, I... I've understood the true extent of the disconnect between rich and poor and also how blind everyone is to the poor while the rich get more than their fair share of attention. There must be something we can do to change things, instead of just accepting the status quo.'

His eyes lit up, then, 'This is the beginning, Rani.'

She was momentarily distracted by the sound of her name on his lips – it was sheer poetry.

He was saying, earnestly, 'I believe strongly that if more of us feel this way, act upon it, one day, we will live in a world where everyone is equal, no matter where they come from, mixing freely, like you and I are now, with no thought to our different status and position in life.'

'A world where everyone has enough to eat, a place to live, access to medical help when ill,' she added.

He looked at her, eyes shining. 'Yes.'

Once again, she glowed from the pride in his voice, the passion in his gaze, her body fizzing.

'I would like to do something constructive,' she said, as much to distract herself from what his gaze was doing to her body, which wanted to angle towards him, touch him. 'I'm so bored in the zenana. So jealous of my little brother's freedom. It's a luxurious prison.'

As soon as she said it, she wondered if she had gone too far, given he lived in the one-roomed hut he'd shared with his extended family and a goat, his sister losing her life because they couldn't afford a doctor or even the potions of a wise man.

But...

'I understand,' he said. 'We are bound too, by poverty, by the shackles of an imperialist society.'

He understood. He sought her opinion, respected it, welcomed and gave weight to her ideas, took them into account.

With him, she felt validated.

It was a gift, after weeks of being treated as nothing more than a mannequin in the zenana.

19

RANI

The next afternoon, as Prasad and Rani swung on the trees lining the riverbank, hot breeze flinging baked dust in their faces, she said, 'I can't come tomorrow as Baba and Arjun are visiting us.'

She couldn't keep the joy out of her voice at the prospect of seeing her little brother. She missed him so. Not for the first time, she thought of how much Arjun would enjoy this, her clandestine afternoon adventures with Prasad. She'd considered bringing him along but no matter how carefully she planned it, he would be missed and they'd be caught. She couldn't risk it.

'Oh.' Prasad sounded so very disappointed.

It thrilled her heart. She was saddened too that the visits clashed – she must miss seeing one of the people she cared for if she wanted to see the other. And again, the hot fire of rage at her father, that it had come to this. Visits with him and her brother once a week, if that. Their family fractured.

'I'll miss you.' Prasad sounded... *vulnerable* and it was then that Rani dared to hope that perhaps he too experienced that electric thrum she did in the other's presence: that *need* to be with them.

He always seemed so grown up and assured; she'd felt privileged that he wanted to spend time with her. Now she considered the possibility that perhaps he felt the same way about *her*.

It made her bold. 'I'll see if I can get away earlier.'

'Don't get too cocky.' He laughed but she sensed that beneath the guise of levity, he was serious. 'I don't want you to be caught.'

'I won't be.' She was confident. Elated. Flying high on the vibrant wings of joy.

As if reinforcing what she was thinking, he said softly, 'Don't you feel like our friendship was meant to be?' His eyes bright as he looked warmly at her. 'Our fathers were friends and now we are.'

'Ah, but we're better friends than our fathers were,' she said.

He beamed. Then, 'Wouldn't it be nice if we really did manage to bring about change, a world where everyone was equal?'

'We'll try,' she said and meant it.

'Then...' he said and now his gaze, directed at her, was smouldering. It made her yearn. It made her want. 'We could be more than friends.'

Her body fizzed at his words; her heart thrilled. There was again that hint of tentativeness, a hesitation, a frisson of vulnerability to his voice, the last bit raised as if in question.

She met his gaze unflinchingly, even as her body moved closer to his, as if of its own accord, a magnetic pull she couldn't, didn't want to resist.

'We could be more than friends *now*,' she said.

And there, among the branches of the peepal tree, starburst rays angling through the woody canopy enveloping them in a gilded haze, she kissed him.

20

RANI

Rani had been abandoned by her father. In Prasad, she found a soulmate.

She had been flailing since coming to India but with Prasad, she was energised. She had purpose.

He looked up to her. He loved her.

They concocted plans of how to be together.

'I'll run away,' she said. 'I just won't go back to the zenana. I'll stay here with you.'

But her voice trembled at the thought of leaving Mama all alone, at the mercy of venomous women who only wanted her sweet mother's downfall, of not seeing Arjun, her lovely, mischievous brother whom she loved with all her heart.

And Baba...

'Give me time,' her father had pleaded on his last visit, when she refused to talk to him. 'I will bring about change, Rani. I just need time.'

She had not looked at him, acknowledged him, but his voice, his words had rent her heart. She wanted to believe him.

She loved him.

And there was Priya, who was helping her with her deception, scared every time Rani left the zenana in her guise, no matter how much Rani reassured her that they wouldn't be caught.

'My family depend on me. This job is our livelihood,' Priya cried every time.

'No,' Prasad said. 'Running away is not the answer.' He was possessed with an uncanny ability to divine Rani's thoughts. 'Your father will find out and there will be hell to pay. We need to put him in a position where he can't refuse.'

'How do we do that?'

'You know him best. Can you think of something?'

'I *used* to know him best,' she said, unable to keep her voice from shaking.

He took her in his arms, kissed her. 'It's all right, you have me now.'

She did. It was.

21

RANI

Eventually, Rani came up with a plan that Prasad tentatively agreed with.

It was daring, fantastic, involving huge risk on Rani's part.

But... if they carried it off, it would not hurt anyone.

Except, perhaps her father.

But he had hurt her, hadn't he?

'*You* could be hurt, Rani. I couldn't bear that,' Prasad worried, gathering her to him.

She adored it when he revealed the extent of his love for her. It made her feel empowered, able to take anything on.

'I will not be hurt. I can give as good as I get.'

During her escapades out of the palace, she'd come across a guard who thought a maid was fair play. When he'd tried to touch her, she'd aimed a kick right where it hurt and run away.

'I don't doubt that,' Prasad's eyes gleamed, mirth and admiration. But in the next instant, shining with anxiety, 'What if your father...?'

'My father wouldn't do anything to me.' This much she knew. When that man tried to touch her, she'd passed on a message to her father about the guard who had assaulted her maid. The very next day, that guard was gone. 'He wants to please me, get me on his side.' Their plan depended on it.

A huge part of her hoped that when they executed the plan, her father of before, whom she had looked up to and emulated, would be returned to her, instead of the distant man in his place who became more of a stranger every day. The father who had once looked at her with such pride, encouraged her outspokenness, praised her intelligence.

For her father of old would surely give his blessing when he learned of Rani's love for Prasad, especially once he found out Prasad was his childhood friend's son. He'd realise, like Prasad had said, that his daughter's union with his first ever friend's son was meant to be. And after all, hadn't he taken risks, staying on in Germany alone while his friends moved on, wooing Mama with his fledgling German, winning her disapproving father around? Hadn't he turned his back on his own father and the kingship for Mama, for love?

When Prasad and Rani pulled off their plan, Baba would come down from his power trip, become hers again, the royal blinkers falling from his eyes.

Wouldn't he?

22

ESME

'So, you're afraid of commitment like you believe your father was?' Sally prompts gently.

A sudden burst of laughter from outside. The receptionist chatting to someone. The merry tinkle of voices at odds with the solemn silence within this room.

Esme takes a breath. Shifts in her chair. Wishes she was on the couch.

'I... I've never been in a proper relationship until recently.' *Philip*, she thinks, experiencing a spasm of pain as his beloved face appears before her eyes.

'Ah.'

'My beautiful boy is the result of a fling with a married man. I'm grateful for Robbie but not proud of what I did. Sleeping with someone's husband, I mean. To be fair, I didn't know he was married at the time, although I didn't ask too many questions. I suppose on some level, I suspected he was lying.'

'Go on,' Sally says gently.

'Robbie's dad didn't want anything to do with him. I brought him up on my own. Until he left for uni, we were a tight-knit unit of two. I did not feel like I was missing out, to be perfectly honest.'

'You used your son as an excuse not to get romantically involved with anyone,' Sally says, matter-of-fact.

'Yes, I suppose so.'

'But things changed recently?'

'Robbie went to uni and I was suddenly on my own. I'm a curator at the local museum and there was this academic...'

Philip. The thought of him a throbbing wound.

'Yes?' Sally prompts softly.

'He... he's writing a book about our town – how it has changed and evolved through the years. We got to talking and I... we...'

'He broke through your defences.'

'Yes.' A whisper all she can manage.

'And?'

'We were very much in love.'

'Yes?'

'He... he proposed and I...'

Sally passes her a tissue from the now severely depleted box.

Esme blows her nose, manages to get the words past the huge, salty obstruction in her throat. 'I broke up with him.'

23

RANI

'You're sure you want to do this?' Prasad asks the afternoon before they are to set their plan in motion.

'I've never been more sure of anything,' she says. 'It *will* work. We *will* be together.'

'You're the bravest,' he beams, admiring, and she blooms in the accolade of his gaze.

She is in love, fired with zeal. Invincible...

At least, she is until she is apprehended by a guard, the exit to the moat and then the palace within sight. Her father's ceremonial sheathed sword, presented to him at his coronation, the sword that has been passed down through generations of Divanpur maharajas, their talisman, is hidden inside her borrowed sari skirt, bumping against her thigh.

* * *

'Stop,' the guard at the exit into the fort surrounding the palace calls.

She's so close. If she can just cross the moat, she will be free of the palace.

Has she been found out?

Should she make a run for it?

No.

She will be caught. She has many talents but sprinting at speed while wearing a sari, a stolen sheathed sword weighing her down, is not one of them.

'It will work,' she had promised Prasad.

'Don't worry,' she had reassured Priya when she set out on her escapades. 'We will not be caught.'

Now she wonders if perhaps she had been too glib, extremely overconfident.

Is the guard aware that she's hiding the sheathed sword within the skirt of her maid's sari? Is it somehow evident to him, although she'd made sure it was tucked away securely?

If she, daughter of the king, is caught escaping the zenana masquerading as a maid, that's bad enough. But if caught with this, the lucky charm of the Divanpur rajas, it is abominable. Unforgivable. The very worst.

24

RANI

Everything has gone strictly as planned.

Until now.

That morning, Rani had boldly walked up to her father's bedchamber, dressed, as ever, in Priya's sari.

She'd realised she could go anywhere, get away with most things, as a maid, and she made good use of this. They had such freedom, but it came of course with the caveat of very hard work, involving little reward, and if you were serving Uncle's wives, an abundance of insults and even beatings. Priya had recounted the stories of the abuse the maids employed by her uncle's wives suffered with a shudder, finishing with, 'All of them are jealous of those of us lucky enough to serve you and your mother. Please don't get caught; they will be only too happy to see my downfall.'

'I won't,' Rani promised. Again.

In contrast to the maids, who could flit about with ease, Rani, princess, had everything she could ask for except freedom.

Rani knew that her father woke early every weekday morning, and after breakfasting with his brother and courtiers, he attended darbar, the royal court, until midday. So she knew for a fact that he wasn't in his bedchamber at this time.

He'd informed Mama and Rani of his routine on one of his visits – Rani taking note although she pretended she wasn't listening, interested, bothered.

As expected, her way into her father's bedchamber was barred by a guard.

'You're not allowed inside.'

'But the maharani is ill and asking for her son. I was told he's in here and to fetch him at once.'

'I thought he went out with...'

'The maharaja told my mistress he was hiding in here. It seems he often does that,' she challenged, knowing the sentry wouldn't question the word of the king.

'I'll go. You wait here.'

'But he won't come with you. He knows and likes me. That's why I was sent. I will only be a minute.'

'Go on then,' the guard sighed.

It was just as Rani had promised the guard – the matter of a minute to steal the ceremonial sheathed sword, resting on a jewel-studded pillow in the ornate armoire beside her father's magnificent bed.

The armoire was locked, but the bunch of keys was in the lowest shelf of the chest of drawers beside Baba's bed. This had been his habit before – whichever house they'd lived in, the keys always resided in the lowest shelf of drawers on her father's side of the bed – and Rani had been banking on the fact that at least in this, her father had not changed. He also still favoured the right side she noticed, and Mama, in her lonely bed in the zenana – also ornate but not quite as choked by opulent silks as her father's – slept on the left. Rani had experienced a shaft of pain for both her father and Mama then. They'd been so in love, finishing each other's sentences, intuiting what the other was thinking without them having to spell it out. Now apart and yet, in their individual bedchambers, still following the habits of sleeping they'd adopted as a couple.

But she had no time to indulge her maudlin musings.

She tucked the sheathed sword inside her sari skirt and coolly walked out of the bedchamber, bold as anything.

'The prince is not in there, like I was told,' she said to the sentry. 'You were right, he must have gone out.'

He said nothing, his face impassive.

Shaking her veiled head, she walked away, anklets and bangles chiming a merry tune.

'Why keep the sheathed sword in the bedchamber, why not with all the other Crown Jewels and treasure?' Mama had asked, when, after the coronation, Baba explained the significance of the sheathed sword he had been presented with.

'It is for the exclusive protection of the present king. To defend himself from foes. It seems the very first maharaja of Divanpur was ambushed in his bedroom and he picked up the nearest thing to hand—'

'The sword!' interjected Arjun, who had been dancing around them.

'Yes, the ceremonial sword, of course.' Baba laughed. 'He attacked the intruders with it. They were overpowered; he won. Since then, the sheathed sword has served as lucky charm for reigning maharajas and rests beside their bed for their protection. Legend has it that if it is lost, then the king loses his life.'

'Better make sure you don't lose it then,' Mama had said, smiling gently, fondly at Baba.

Baba...

Her father, who had marvelled, so proud, when Rani read Marx and Shaw, Engels and Lenin. Who beamed when she embarked on one of her regular rants: 'The rich are brainwashed into thinking they are better, entitled.'

Her father. Angry about the rise of Mussolini in Italy and Hitler in Germany.

Her father, who had made her what she was. Shaped her. So it is inevitable, perhaps, that she is now plotting against him, the first step to which is using his own words, told in confidence to his family, to acquire the ceremonial sword which is his talisman...

25

RANI

Now, Rani peers through her veil at the guard looking her up and down.

She can't read anything in his expression.

She'd made sure to tuck the stolen sword securely against her thigh.

The tinkling, as she moves, of the jewels stabbing the sheath is masked by the ringing of her anklets and bangles.

The theft has not been discovered yet – her father is dining with his noblemen and will only retire to his bedchamber after. *Then* there will be a hue and cry.

So how has she been found out *now*?

* * *

Too fuelled by adrenaline to feel fear before, now, Rani experiences an all-consuming thrum of panic.

The plan. For it to work, she has to leave now.

She turns towards the guard, heart pounding, stolen sword pushing against her thigh.

Keeping her veiled head bowed, '*Huzoor*,' she says, meekly, in the dialect Priya uses.

'You dropped this,' he says.

She extends her hand, bangles clinking. She's ashamed that her fingers are trembling, but she can't seem to stop them shaking.

He deposits the paper containing the *peda*, milk fudge spiced with cardamom, that she packed to eat on the way; in all the excitement, she skipped breakfast. Her mother, the only one to care, wouldn't have noticed. She forgoes meals herself every day now, only eating at Rani's insistence, picking listlessly at her food.

Rani worries about her. *I'm doing this for you too, Mama, to get Baba back. The man you fell in love with, the father I remember, not the dictator he is now.*

'Thank you,' she says, again mimicking the coarse dialect of her maid, and hurries out of the palace.

The sun beats down incessantly, the air is gritty as she exits the fort, crosses the moat and walks past the village, through the market, the huts huddled together, so tiny after the vast claustrophobia of the palace, the labyrinth of streets spilling with humanity, packed and busy, vendors calling, hawking, cajoling, people cooking, arguing, laughing, asleep right there in the dirt, covered by a blanket of dust, sniffed at by animals, plagued by flies, the humid breeze that strokes her face spiced with chillies and angst.

The *peda* tastes honey sweet, of nectar and relief. She laughs, her father's sword pressing against her leg.

* * *

Prasad is at the peepal tree beside the river, his bullock tethered to it, listlessly chewing on the yellowing grass in the blistering sun, batting flies away with its tail.

Her love is sitting on one of the low hung branches arching over the riverbed, which is dry and cracked as the rains are late.

He jumps up when he hears her approach, the song of her anklets serenading him, his face lighting up in that wide sunbeam of a smile.

As always, at the sight of him, her heart blooms.

'You look so elegant and queenly, even in a maid's sari,' he whispers, gathering her in his arms, mango-scented breath hot in her ear, raising goosebumps. He is forever munching on raw mango dipped in sea salt.

She blushes.

'Did you get it?' he asks.

'Do you have to ask?' she counters and he laughs, burnished gold bells sounding out sparkling, bronzed cheers.

'I never doubted it.' Pride in his voice. 'You're braver than a lioness.'

'Turn around,' she orders and once he does, only his bullock watching with those molten toffee eyes, she pulls out the stolen bounty.

'Here it is.'

He gasps at the curved dagger, glinting deadly blue, the jewels on its hilt and sheath reflecting the sun's rays as they shimmer and dazzle, blinding gold.

'The theft will be discovered right about now,' she says, experimentally wielding the sword left, then right. The bullock emits a mournful bellow of complaint as the reflected silver rays enchant its eyes. 'This evening, when I go back, when they've searched the palace in vain, I'll send word to Baba that my maid knows of a brave young man who tackled the thief and took possession of the sword, which he will return to the king on condition he can meet privately with him. I'll tell Baba that the maid will meet the man at the entrance to the palace and escort him to his private audience with the king. That will be me, of course. And when it's just me, you and Baba, I will tell him that I love you, the brave man who wrestled his sword from the thief, and want to be with you. I will appeal to the Baba I know is inside the stranger who's been swayed by power, the Baba who fell in love with Mama and who denounced a kingdom for her.' She grins at Prasad. 'And then we'll live happily ever after. See, didn't I say my plan would work? By tomorrow, we'll be celebrating!'

Caught up in joy and excitement – she's done the hard part and it's worked faultlessly; the rest should be easy – she swings the sword too hard and it tilts, nicking her finger.

'Ow.'

'You've hurt yourself.'

'It's sharp.'

Prasad carefully takes the sword from her, sheaths it and then, very gently, taking her hand in his, oh so tenderly, his gaze holding hers, he raises her cut finger to his lips, his body shielding her from his bull and in the distance, the sadhu meditating and the women washing clothes, mere dots.

It feels like they are the only two people in the world as, his gaze boring into hers, he softly licks the blood clean from her finger, setting her whole body alight.

On fire.

26

ESME

'Esme,' Sally says gently when Esme has composed herself. 'It's completely natural to panic when faced with a life-changing decision.'

'I...'

'You love this man?'

'Philip. Yes.'

'Then you must tell him so.'

'I...'

'He laid bare his heart, made himself vulnerable by proposing to you. The ball is in your court now.'

'I know...' Esme shreds yet another tissue. 'I've messed up your floor,' she says, pointing to the debris of tissue scraps littered around her chair, confetti-ing the heavily discounted, bad-decision shoes that she's stubbornly wearing on bandaged feet.

'Don't worry about it. Hoovers were invented for a reason.'

She smiles weakly. 'I... I don't want to lose him. I worry... I worry that it's already too late.'

'He loves you. It's not too late. You just have to gather the courage to tell him you love him too.'

'I... it's so messed up in my head right now. I broke up with him and a couple of weeks later, I lost Dad. It all feels connected somehow. I... it doesn't make sense I know, but it's how I feel.'

Esme is defensive, but Sally is nodding, her eyes soft with understanding. It gives her the impetus to go on, try and put into words, as much for herself as for Sally, the confused welter of thoughts in her head. 'There's this big void within me of missing Dad, although we weren't close. And another part pulsing with questions about why he was the way he was, why he didn't talk about Mum. I'd like to know more about my mother, who she was, what happened between them. I feel it would help my own relationship if I had an insight into theirs, so I can avoid making the same mistakes. You see, I love Philip so very much. But what if, when we are married, if we are married, I push him away?'

'Your mother died, Esme,' Sally says gently.

'Yes, but there is this huge mystery surrounding her. No photos. No keepsakes.'

'None?'

'Nothing at all. I don't even know what she looks like. Something happened between them, Dad and Mum. We couldn't mention her, talk about her, ask anything. It was a taboo topic. Still is. Andy doesn't talk about her either. He doesn't remember her at all. Isn't it odd? He must have been around four when she died. Old enough to form memories. And yet...' She pauses, swallows. 'I worry about history repeating itself with myself and Philip if I marry him. But I don't know what the history *is*. I should have asked Dad. But now he's gone, and I'm left with all these *questions*, forever unanswered...'

'What about your brother? How is he coping with your father's death?'

'Oh, he buries himself in work. Research. That's how we deal with things in our family.'

'Are you close, your brother and yourself?'

'We talk every so often.'

'That doesn't answer my question,' Sally smiles. 'You said your brother doesn't talk about your mother. Why do you think that might be?'

'I... I'm not sure, to be honest. We don't venture into the personal during our conversations. We discuss our respective jobs. He asks after Robbie. That's about it.'

Sally nods. Waits.

Esme sighs, knots her hands, stares at her raised knuckles. 'We aren't close. We drifted apart as teenagers and stayed that way.'

'When was the last time you saw him?' Sally asks.

'At Dad's funeral. Dad had left detailed instructions, paid for it all. We went through his effects together. There wasn't much. Nothing pertaining to Mum. Although I was hoping...' Another tissue disintegrates almost without her noticing.

'Did you and your brother talk about your dad when going over his effects?'

'Not really. There wasn't anything to talk about, nothing personal among his things. He was not a hoarder. He'd got rid of much of his stuff when the doctors said there was nothing more they could do and he moved into the hospice.'

She pictures the box of her father's meagre belongings – she'd unpacked them carefully, her hands shaking with grief. Andy beside her, his face inscrutable, a mug of tea cooling in his hands.

Dad's clothes neatly folded. His books – non-fiction mostly, on finance, travel. Several language guides and workbooks, mainly Sanskrit and Mandarin, which he was teaching himself.

He was always reading, always learning.

And that was it.

Sally's voice intrudes into Esme's introspection. 'No photos of you, your brother?'

'He'd already given us the relevant memorabilia he'd kept over the years when he moved into the hospice. Very efficient, my father.'

'Does your brother have a partner?' Sally changes track.

'No. Robbie would keep trying to set us both up on dates – he was so thrilled when Philip and I became an item and very vexed with me when I broke up with Philip.' She sniffs, blows her nose, takes a breath, gathers her thoughts. 'He even tried setting up his grandad, before he became ill, with the grandmother of one of his friends. "You're all so solitary, set in your ways. You need to get out more," he urges us, all the time.'

'Robbie is different then?'

'Oh he is. A social butterfly, my son. I was determined he wouldn't be like me. I've been open with him. He knows all there is to know about his father. I've shared everything I know about my own family – not much given Mum is a huge blank. To be fair, both Dad and Andy have been good father figures to Robbie. Attending his games, plays, concerts when they could. Helping him with school projects. He has a great relationship with Andy and did with Dad too. They'd spend hours building models of ships, taking things apart only to put them back together again, rarely talking but the silence comfortable, companionable.' Esme takes a breath, smiling as she pictures her bright, outgoing son. 'One thing none of us could do was give Robbie advice on dating. He figured that out on his own. That boy has been playing the field since puberty...' As always when talking about her son, laughter dances through her voice.

'Ah Esme, he sounds a lovely boy.'

'He is.'

Sally sets her notebook down, looks Esme in the eye. 'Now, from what you've told me, I think what's holding you back from making a commitment to the man you love is that it appears you're stuck in the past. To embrace your future, you feel the need to resolve your past, find out more about your mother and her relationship with your dad. Isn't there anyone else, apart from your father, who might have known her?'

PART II

27

RANI

1938, Girton College, Cambridge, England

Dearest Mama, Baba and darling Arjun,
    How are you all?
    I am fine and settling in all right. Although, after the orange heat of India, the cold is such a shock!
    Michaelmas term has been postponed because of the Munich Agreement. Most here are incensed by what Churchill did, pandering to that man, who is causing such grief.
    Everyone in my debating society seems to think war in Europe is inevitable, myself included...

Rani sets her pen down, a relief after the effort of the sentences, which she's aiming to be cheery and upbeat but end up unbearably stilted, and looks out of the window.

A pigeon pecks at the frost-jewelled grass of the quad.

How do you bridge half a world of distance and everything that came before in a few words?

How do you write to those you love completely and unconditionally, and those towards whom you harbour a complicated amalgam of love and hate and rage and guilt, together in one letter?

But writing in this way, addressing Baba as well as Mama and Arjun, is the best chance of her letter being read at all. At least this way, Baba can see, if he opens the letter, that she's trying; she can hope that he will share it with Mama and Arjun...

A shaft of pain lancing her. Oh, how she misses them...

And him. Her love. Sweet kisses. Hot breath sealing passionate promises...

No, stop, she can't go there. It hurts too unbearably much.

She sniffs, turning her attention back to the window.

A lone woman sits on the bench outside the reading room, hunched against the biting wind, her head deep within the pages of a book. A lady in a red cape emerges from the chapel, flustering the pigeon, which flies away in a blur of white-flecked grey. The lady in red walks briskly towards the reading woman, taps her on the arm.

She looks up, her face blue and nose red from the cold. Upon seeing who it is, she smiles warmly, closes her book and tucks her arm in that of her friend's. They join the women in groups of two and three walking briskly across the quad to the dining hall. It is lunchtime but Rani is loath to leave her room yet.

She looks at what she has written.

Europe staggering beneath the imminent spectre of another war.

War.

'Of course there will be another war. Hitler will happily take whatever Churchill offers to appease him and go on doing just as he pleases. Europe will have to take a stance at some point, sooner rather than later,' she'd declared during the last meeting of the debating society and was surprised when, for once, instead of the exchanges that were wont to get very heated, everyone was in agreement.

She's joined the socialist society here at Girton too, attending all the lectures, listening to and participating in the often fierce debates, like Baba must have done at his college. It's wonderful, liberating, energising, her intelligence prized, her opinions courted like her father used to, once, before they moved to India.

Despite the mixed feelings her father engenders within her, more so now than ever, she misses such discussions about political and other matters with him. Although she hadn't had those since he donned his royal mantle.

But being here at his alma mater reminds her of him so much. The father he used to be.

Her college is women-only, but a world away, literally and figuratively from the zenana. No veils here, no covering up, hiding away. Here at Cambridge, which is a universe in itself, women's opinions are courted, their intelligence lauded. The ever-present guilt bites when she thinks of Mama at the zenana, coping on her own, fiery pain scalding Rani.

When she attends lectures outside of her college, she pictures Baba traversing these same streets as an idealistic young man and realises that she is walking in his footsteps.

The other day, as she was crossing the quad to the reading room, one of the visiting dons had stopped her. 'You are Prajanya Raj's daughter, I gather. Admirable young man. Very promising. He's king now I hear.'

She'd clenched her fingers to hold in the hurt. 'Yes, sir.'

'He'll make a good one. Very smart, as I recall. And you're a linguist.'

'Yes, sir.'

'Take after your old man, then. Apple doesn't fall far, eh. Enjoying it here then?'

'Yes, sir.'

'Very good.'

Deciding that she has dithered enough, she picks up her pen, writes on.

Arjun, I've joined the chess society as well. And I beat everyone here too, so you're in good company.

Her brother had sobbed, 'Didi, please don't go.'

He'd taken to calling her *Didi*, sister in Hindi, when they arrived in India, having picked it up from hearing the other children at the palace address their siblings, she imagined. She'd teased him about it but secretly she'd loved the way he said it, adored that lilt unique to his pronunciation of the word. Why hadn't she told him so? Too late now. She sniffed, roughly swiping at her eyes.

He had clung to her and Mama had to gently prise him off. Mama's eyes were shimmering as she gathered Rani close, placed a kiss on her hair. 'Take good care of yourself, *meine liebe.*'

She blinks, clears her head. Goes back to her letter.

There's even a society called ODTAA – One Damn Thing After Another. Yes Arjun, that word. Mama made you wash your mouth out when you proudly practised it on us after you picked it up at school, I know.

She thinks of her brother reading this, his eyes wide with cheeky wonder, that infectious guffaw that always set her off.

'Like a donkey braying,' she'd declare and he'd guffaw some more.

When visiting with Opa and Oma in Germany, on snowy weekends in the depths of winter, they'd have 'tent' days, when they fashioned tents out of bedclothes and lounged about within, telling each other stories.

She could picture him, her little brother, eyes full of mischief.

And now she sets her pen down, allows the tears to come.

How she misses him, misses them all.

Misses Prasad, their flare of fierce, intense love that burned at the altar of her father's throne...

She will finish this letter, post it, but she will get no acknowledgement that it has been received, read.

No reply.

Nothing.

And yet she writes, doggedly, religiously, every week.

A gentle knock on the door.

'Rani, are you coming down for lunch?'

Gertrude, who rooms across the hallway, reads Mathematics, the only one who comes close to beating Rani at chess, and who finishes the daily crossword faster than anyone else. Rani's aim is to best her at it one day.

She told Gertie so, and Gertie's response was, 'Ah, whether you'll ever achieve that is a matter of debate. What is not, however, is me beating you at chess, very soon.' Her eyes twinkling with mischievous determination.

Now, Rani blows her nose, wipes her eyes with her handkerchief, pastes a smile on her face and opens the door to her friend.

28

RANI

'What is the meaning of this?' Baba, who has never raised his voice, in all of Rani's nearly eighteen years, yells.

'Baba,' Rani, riding high on the success and faultless execution of her plan, is calm, her father's loss of cool having the opposite effect on her. 'I've tried telling you. I love Prasad, the brave man who rescued your sword, who is Murli's son, by the way – Murli, your childhood friend...'

'Rani, do you take me for an absolute fool?' her father roars. 'As soon as I saw you in here, instead of the maid I was expecting, I knew what you'd done. How *dare* you steal the ceremonial sword?'

Oh.

Rani and Prasad exchange glances. While coming up with the plan, Rani had failed to account for the fact that her father knows her only too well, that he might cotton on to what she had done. She had wanted him to think highly of Prasad. Hence the stealing of the sword and its heroic rescue and return by Prasad. She miscalculated. But Rani is confident that she can work around this. This is Baba after all, on his own, without his brother and courtiers to adversely influence him. And, despite being a little cowed by his unusually fierce demeanour – he has never been this angry with her, not even when she asked him whether he'd take on more wives, like his brother and father before him – a part of her can't help but be thrilled that her father can still read her, that he knows her so well. That same part of her hopes that when he cools down, he will appreciate her bravery, applaud her initiative, admire her fortitude and drive for coming up with and executing such a daring plan for love.

'I've had my men searching high and low for the culprit with the sheer cheek to enter my bedchamber and steal the ceremonial sword, with orders to chop his head off when found, when all the while my own daughter...'

Baba's face is an alarming puce, his eyes red veined and in danger of popping. Rani has never seen him like this. 'My brother was right. He maintained it was someone in our inner circle. He even implied it might be you.'

Ah so it wasn't Baba but Uncle who had zoned in on Rani. The small thrill Rani was experiencing at the thought of how well Baba knew her to divine her part in this, and her hope that he would appreciate what she had done once he had the chance to calm down, dissipates entirely.

'I... I blew up at my brother when I should have believed him. He said I am a fool when it comes to you. He is right.'

'Baba...'

'You are an absolute...' Baba sputters to a stop, apparently unable to find words strong enough to convey his disgust, his explosive rage.

He's always so very controlled. Gentle. Dignified. Even during those times he's provoked, he's always reined in his anger. But now...

She'd thought stealing the sword was the hard part. This,

talking her father round, she could do. That's why she'd requested a private audience. But now she is wondering if it was a mistake. For here, in place of Baba, is a complete stranger who, for the first time in her life, *scares* her.

Now Prasad speaks, 'Your majesty...'

Baba turns on him with the venom, spite and hiss of a serpent. 'Quiet. You have enchanted my daughter, corrupted her...'

'Baba...' Rani intercedes.

'Don't you dare. I'm ashamed to call you my child.'

She rears back, stunned. Shaking. Eyes brimming. It wouldn't have been worse if her father had hit her.

But it gets worse...

'You are a slut...'

And in that instant, even as Baba stops, knowing he's gone too far, the colour leaving his face the ashen cream of mortification, Prasad acts.

In a hellish instant, he has pulled the sword out of its sheath and is holding it to her father's neck.

Rani's eyes blur with tears and shock.

Her father's neck is pale and vulnerable as a newborn babe, except for a drop of burgeoning blood where the dagger, glinting like the wide-fanged smile of a thirsty vampire, kisses his skin, vulgarly festive scarlet against the anaemic pallor of stupefied flesh.

'Don't you dare call her that,' Prasad spits. 'She's brave, pure, true. She's worth a million of you, a whore to wealth, power, kingship.'

The sword pierces Baba's skin, the single drop becoming a glittering crimson necklace.

And although Rani has hated her father at times, wished for his downfall, stolen the sheathed sword which is now drawing blood from him, the dagger which is the talisman of generations of Divanpur maharajas, their lucky charm now poised to kill him, she can't bear it. She can't. Not this.

The two men she loves, one about to hurt, maim, kill the other.

'No,' she screams, 'no!'

At once, Prasad stops. Turns towards her.

It is enough for her father, who in one calculated action, grabs Prasad's wrist that wields the sword, twisting it away from him, at the same time as calling for his guards.

And in the next instant, Prasad is being apprehended and manhandled by a platoon of armed men, and the royal physician is being summoned for Baba.

As Prasad is pulled, wrestled, dragged away, as the sword is wrangled from him, his eyes fall upon hers. His gaze, love and despair.

No.

No, no, no.

* * *

She wakes screaming.

It takes her a while to come to. Make sense of her surroundings.

She's freezing. The fire is out, embers fizzled to smoky grey.

No relentless sunshine. Only the sizzling, dazzling, searing memory of heat.

She is in England, at Cambridge. Right where she wanted to be.

Rani is ambushed by guilt, devilish purple, that lances with frost-edged knives.

29

RANI

'You will go far away from here, where, hopefully, you can wield no more harm,' her father had cried. 'Cambridge, where you wanted to go, which is why, I guess, you did this. But you are dead to us.'

She was stunned for a moment as his words sunk in.

Cambridge.

Dead to us.

The hurt made her lash out. 'Just like you were to your father, history repeating itself. You are doing to me exactly what your father did to you, don't you see that?'

'I did not conspire to kill my father.' Her father's eyes glinted dangerously. 'By stealing the ceremonial sword, you stole our family honour. You should thank me; in sending you to Cambridge, I'm saving you from the wrath of my brother and kinsmen. If it were up to them...' His eyes shuttered, his body giving an involuntary shudder – whatever they'd planned was too much even for him.

And in that instant, she had a brief glimpse of the Baba of before. *Her* Baba.

She wanted to tell him she loved him.

She wanted to say she was sorry, that she hadn't meant for this to happen, for the two men she cared for most in the world to be hurt, wounded, devastated because of her actions.

She'd come up with her plan for she wanted to keep both of them, her Baba of before returned to her and Prasad, the love of her life, in her life always.

Instead, she appeared to have lost them both.

She wanted to say all this, but what came out was, 'I'm expected to thank you for it?'

Baba's eyes once more shot daggers at her. 'I thought it was what you wanted. To escape the zenana, study at Cambridge. Well you've got it, although the means by which you have...' He stopped.

This was not the man who had lost control before in front of her and Prasad. In fact, this man was the exact opposite. Cool and collected.

'Once there, you can reflect on whether it was worth it, the choices you made to get what you wanted, to betray your family for a lonely prize.'

'Is all this...' she waved her arms around at the luxurious furnishings, the ornate, gilded ceiling, the jewels sparking on her father's person, 'worth it for you turning your back on everything you believed in, Baba?' she'd cried.

'You will be dead to us,' her father repeated, his gaze hard in a way she'd never seen before.

'You taught me to be true to myself, to stand up for what I believe in and for this, you exile me, cut me off?'

'I could have *died*.'

'You didn't. And for that, you have to thank Prasad. I will go away to England. But please spare Prasad.'

'*Thank* him?' her father sputtered. 'Spare him? The man who held my own sword to my throat, cut me with it? He was about to *kill* me.'

'He didn't. He is young and impulsive, the son of Murli the royal milkman, your childhood friend, Baba.'

When her father didn't appear to be moved, she added, 'He is in love, like you were once. Tell me, if your father had insulted Mama, wouldn't you have done the same thing?'

'Have you quite finished?' Her father was impassive.

'Please spare Prasad, Baba.' For her love's sake, she swallowed her pride and begged.

'He was going to commit treason.'

'So was I. *I* stole the sword, gave it to him. But you are sparing me.'

And now, finally, her father lost his cool, shouted, 'Enough!' He took a breath, bunching his palms into fists. Then, his voice marginally softer, 'If you had an idea just how much I had to grovel to my brother and kinsmen on your behalf...'

He might say she was dead to him, he might be exiling her, but he loved her.

He loved her.

It drove her to try, one last time. 'Baba, Prasad did not kill you. He stopped. For me. Because he loves me. Please, will you spare him? For me. Because you love me?'

In response, her father turned away, dismissing her.

The conviction, the knowledge that despite everything, her father loves her, having interceded with his brother on her behalf, is why she writes, regularly, every single week despite never having received a reply.

Yet.

Where there's love there's always hope, isn't there?

She hasn't dared mention Prasad in her letters. But, she hopes, prays, wishes with all her heart that Baba took that last conversation with Rani to heart, that he will be able to convince his brother and kinsmen to let Prasad go.

They were so naïve, she sees now, she and Prasad. Blinded by love and the sheer rosy optimism of youth. Now that she has gained some distance both in miles and time from everything that happened, she can see that the thrill of escaping the claustrophobia of the palace, the ecstatic, heady joy of first love combined to make her think they were invincible, that everyone would come round to their (flawed) way of thinking. She did not see the loopholes in their plan at all. She was so very, very innocent.

Rani has resolved that she will always think before she acts from now on, twice, thrice, several times. And she will make amends for what happened with Prasad, somehow. She cannot do anything from here, she doesn't know his fate; although she tried so hard to find out before she left to come here, no one would tell her anything. She refuses to accept he's dead. She chooses to believe Prasad has been spared, *please let it be so*, and she will right the wrong done to him, imprisonment and torture – *please, no* – when his only fault was to love her, believe her when she said their plan would work and defend her honour when her father insulted her. If not now, then when she is able.

She will.

* * *

'You silly, silly child,' Mama had cried, holding her so very tightly, as if she could keep Rani with her by the sheer strength of her embrace, her rose perfume mingling with sorrow. 'You act first, then regret. Oh *meine liebe*. I will work on your Baba. It is not goodbye forever, I promise.'

Her mother kissed Rani's hair, her nose, each eye and cheek, her chin, anointing her face with her tears.

'Not goodbye,' Mama whispered.

Rani couldn't speak, undone by remorse, for her impulsive actions meant her mother was now alone in the zenana, with nobody on her side.

Mama didn't blame her, which made it worse, for Rani blamed herself.

'Don't go, Didi,' Arjun sobbed, clinging to Rani until Mama gently extricated him from her, all of them in tears.

Rani had tried, before she left, to gain access to the prison where Prasad was being held. She tried wearing Priya's sari. It didn't work – the guards were hyper alert and extremely thorough now.

Priya had kept her job – at least there was that. Her part in the deception had not been discovered, Rani claiming she stole the sari.

When departing for England, Rani gifted Priya all of her saris and jewellery, asking in return for Priya to please keep an eye on her Mama, help her if needed – it was all she could do to assuage her guilt at leaving her mother alone.

* * *

It is her little brother's cries she hears at night echoing the wind howling in the trees outside her window. It is Prasad's face she sees, that expression as she screamed, 'No!', his face turned towards her, the sword's sharp blade piercing her father's neck in that instant before her father overpowered him. The love and pain in his eyes as he was led away, screaming, fighting, the sword bloodying his hands as it was wrestled from him. 'I spared your father,' he was saying with that gaze, 'for you. I sacrificed myself, for you.'

30

RANI

She wakes up in her room at Girton, gasping, plagued by nightmares and regret.

Guilty.

Guilty even as she attends lectures – she's reading Modern Languages. Guilty as she absorbs knowledge, the sharp pleasure of learning, putting her brain to good use. As she makes friends, has spirited discussions with the other women scholars in the dining hall; as she signs up for and takes active part in all of the societies – and there are many – that excite her fancy; as she swims in the indoor pool, works in the reading room, the reverent silence, the whisper of turning pages, the sombre gravity of century-old books, the taut, amber musk scent of industry, the burnished gold pleasure of education, infused violet blue with guilt.

'*Once there you can reflect on whether it was worth it, the choices you made to get what you wanted, to betray your family for a lonely prize,*' her father had said.

Baba...

She experiences, as always, since the worst happened, a complex mixture of anger and guilt, remorse and pain and upset.

* * *

That week, the papers are full of accounts of the horrific violence against Jews in Germany. The headlines read:

Jewish Homes on Fire, Women Beaten

And:

Synagogues Burned and Shops Looted

The Archbishop of Canterbury writes in a letter to the editor of the London *Times*:

There are times when the mere instincts of humanity make silence impossible.

Nazi officials justify their actions as a response to the assassination of a German diplomat, Ernst vom Rath, in Paris by Herschel Grynszpan, a German Jewish refugee living in Paris.

Rani thinks of Opa and Oma, the wonderful times she and Arjun spent with them. The Germany Rani remembers, the repository of some of her happiest memories, is very different from the one making the headlines. Spoilt and adored by her grandparents, dining in the best restaurants, invited to exclusive events and concerts, fawned over at lavish parties graced by the country's elite, by virtue of being the granddaughter of the man who owned the largest and most exclusive jewellery store in Dusseldorf, Herr Alexander Cohen, frequented by anyone who was anyone. In fact, you hadn't made it if you didn't wear *something* – whether cuff-links, a tie-pin or a necklace – from Cohen's.

Rani had secretly loved the fuss everyone made of her when visiting her grandparents, although of course she complained that it was wrong – it went against her socialist views.

'Everyone must be treated equally. This is not right,' she would rail even as she helped herself to more *Kirschtorte* from the best cake shop in Dusseldorf delivered to them by Opa's friend Johannes Lindberg with a note which said:

For Rani – I know how much you adore these.

'It is kind of him,' she'd said officiously during their last visit, not knowing then that this would be their final visit ever with Opa and Oma for the maharaja's summons would arrive in a few months' time and Baba would pack his family off to India. Rani had asked through a nectary mouthful of *Kirschtorte*, unable to stop herself from digging in, 'But does he do this for everyone?'

'My opinionated granddaughter.' Opa had beamed. 'Johannes sends it for you because he is proud of you too. He'd been arrested alongside me because of our socialist views. We got off lightly because his relatives are in the top positions in government. So I suppose that defeated the purpose. But we can do more good by being free. Do better for the movement.'

'You be careful now,' Oma interjected. 'You know Hitler doesn't take kindly to Jews. Johannes isn't one but you are. And even he won't be able to save you.'

'Oh stop worrying, woman,' Opa said lightly. 'I'm always careful.'

If Rani had known she'd never see her beloved grandparents again, she'd have given them an extra hug. She'd have insisted on staying in Germany for longer...

Rani misses her grandparents immensely. Opa's eyes shining with love when he looked at Rani, calling her, '*Bubbale*', beloved. Oma's welcoming arms, her vanilla-scented embrace, the house blessedly warm and gloriously unchanged, each time they visited, just as in her memories, smelling of chicken soup and baked strudel, buttery dough, boozy raisins, cinnamon apples and caramelised sugar.

But, although she'd rather they were in this world, in a way, she thinks it's a blessing Opa and Oma have passed on. They would be so distressed by what is going on in their country. If they were still alive, their home might have been the one burned down, their shop looted.

Rani cannot bear to think of Mama, how she must be feeling, stuck in the zenana while her people are discriminated against, hurt and hounded, in her country oceans away.

Guilt bites, chilli hot, and with it sadness, stinging and pincering with sharp, taloned claws, for abandoning her beloved mother to the zenana.

The discussion when the debating society meets is understandably about what is going on in Germany.

'What was he thinking, that Herschel Grynszpan?' Sara, reading Physics, a Jewish refugee herself, asks. 'Storming into the German embassy and shooting the official like that. Didn't he think it through? That he was making things worse not only for his parents but for all Jews. That it would start something much bigger, more terrible than he could have envisioned in his worst imaginings...'

But Rani understands Herschel Grynszpan. He is but seventeen. Like she was a few months ago, when, fuelled by passion, she stole her father's sword and set events in motion that have led her here, exiled from her family, and condemned her love to prison and worse – no. No.

She knows exactly what was going through Herschel Grynsz-pan's mind when he pulled the trigger. He was fired by fury, avenging heat. Angry on his parents' behalf. Convinced what he was doing was right.

Oh, she understands all right.

'He was not thinking,' she counters, in response to Sara. 'When he read that letter from his parents stating that they were being deported from Germany and could he send them some money, when he understood, reading between the lines, what they were not saying, how much it had cost them to beg, he felt hot, red flames ignite, fury masking fear and worry at the total turning of tables – the parents he looked up to changing, becoming all too human and vulnerable. Just people. Not heroes as he had thought, as a child. Able to do anything at all. Transcend difficulties. Save the world. Now they were looking to *him* to save *them*. It scared him, terrified him. So he sought refuge in anger instead. When he took the gun, stormed to the embassy, shot vom Rath...' She pauses. Everyone is rapt, waiting on her. Listening intently. 'He was not thinking.'

They clap, even Sara, who raises her glass to her. 'You make a good point.'

Their admiration causes fiery heat to blossom in her stomach, paint her cheeks bright crimson, like the blood necklace wrought by the sword Prasad wielded upon her father's skin, these fiercely intelligent women who've become her friends, respecting her opinions, applauding them.

While she's beating them at chess, when they sit in the library reading and studying side by side, when they attend lectures, when she finds herself enjoying it all, the learning, the camaraderie, the company of these amazing women, she sometimes finds herself forgetting at whose cost she's here, and what it has cost her. She finds herself replying to her father's challenge: 'Once there, you can reflect on whether it was worth it, the choices you made to get what you wanted, to betray your family for a lonely prize', in her head.

If not for Prasad, Baba, and for Mama, whom I've abandoned in the zenana, I'd think it was worth it.

I love it here, despite myself, despite the imminent threat of war in Europe, and I would savour every minute if I wasn't aware of how much I've lost.

I know how lucky I am to be here, when my fellow Jews are being discriminated against in my mother's and grandparents' homeland.

I am aware of how fortunate I am to be alive even if I am shunned, ostracised, cut off, missing you all more than I can say. I miss Mama's gentle patience, her smile, the comfort of her touch. I miss Arjun's joy, how he found pleasure in every little thing, his innocence, the way he threw himself at me, flinging his arms around me and saying, 'I love you, Didi.'

I love it here even though I carry with me, every minute of every day, the terrible knowledge that because of my actions, Mama is even lonelier than before in a palace and country not her own, and Prasad, my love, might be dead.

But he isn't, please, Baba. He isn't. I'd know if he was. The part of my heart that beats for him would ache, wouldn't it? It would grieve.

And I do know that despite you changing in India, you haven't changed completely. You still sleep on the right side of your elaborate yet lonely royal bed. You still love me despite what I did.

I realised, during my last audience with you, that in spite of all that's gone on, I do have faith in you. That you will, when it matters, do the right thing.

So, Baba, I will believe that you've realised how alone and isolated Mama is in the zenana and welcome her proudly to sit beside you in court, to sleep beside you in your royal chamber.

I will believe that you have pardoned Prasad for you loved someone deemed unsuitable for you (Mama) too, so you do understand. I will believe that you've managed to persuade your brother and your kinsmen to let him go, that he's not being tortured in jail or dead because of me.

I persist in believing this. It is the only way I can go on.

Baba, when I first escaped the palace, saw how Prasad and his fellow villagers lived, on a few grains of rice a day, unable to afford medical help so young people, like Prasad's sister, with their whole lives ahead of them, died, I vowed to try and make a difference, bring about change.

But then I fell in love and my resolution fell to the wayside. Now, I have made a new vow: that I will use this education that I am attaining at great cost, for good. I will use it to help bring about change, make a difference and this time round, I will not be swerved from my goal. This way, my escaping lightly, as opposed to Prasad, will not be in vain. This way, I will be redeeming myself somewhat.

I feel guilty every single day, all the time, for while Prasad was captured, imprisoned, is paying a very high price for the plan we concocted together, the plan that was my mastermind – not with his life, please – I've got away scot-free. I've been rewarded, in fact, since I've received what I wanted: the gift of an education at Cambridge. It's exactly what I have, as a socialist, always riled against: the discrepancy, the chasm between the rich and the poor. Now I'm a beneficiary of this very difference.

This is why I will use it to make a difference. In this way, I will hopefully assuage my guilt a little.

I can't go back in time, protect Prasad, help him. But hopefully, I can help in other ways, other people. And in this way, make amends.

31

RANI

Dear Mama, Baba, and beloved Arjun,

It's happened just as most here predicted.

We were at lectures when one of the mathematics scholars burst in rather unceremoniously and announced, breathlessly, that we were at war.

We've taken suitable precautions. Corridor windows are now painted dark blue and blackout curtains are hanging in our rooms.

But it's been quiet thus far. What they're calling a 'phony' war. Although several of our male counterparts, some from your college, Baba, have rushed to sign up.

Hope you are all well.

Sending love and best wishes,

Yours,

Rani

Rani seals the letter and closes her eyes, wondering how Mama must be feeling about the war. Like Rani, she too, must be experiencing mixed emotions. Sadness that Opa and Oma are not here, but relief that they don't know that it's come to this – Europe declaring war, once again, upon their beloved homeland, now a Nazi state, annexing other countries, discriminating and committing horrific atrocities against Jews. What would Opa and Oma's fate have been if they were alive? Would they have fled their homeland in time, like Oma wished to? Would they have fled at all given they, especially Opa, were so proud of their German identity? Opa always maintained stoutly that although Jewish, Germany was their home just as much as the Nazis'. He believed that sense would win against insanity, that his friends, fellow Germans, would never turn on their compatriots who had fought beside them for Germany in the previous war.

'It's just a phase. We are living in a civilised country. This cannot continue. Most people are decent. They will see sense,' he'd said after Hitler passed the Nuremberg Laws in 1935 (prohibiting Jews and non-Jews to marry or have sexual relations, and forbidding the employment of German women under the age of forty-five in Jewish households or for Jews to display the national flag or Reich colours), after which the atrocities against Jews multiplied.

Oma had been so very upset. 'You fought in the war alongside your German brothers for the motherland. You earned your limp and an Iron Cross for it. We've dutifully paid our taxes year after year, contributed to the economy, are law-abiding citizens, and yet none of it counts,' she'd lamented to Opa. 'In our own country, we are made to feel like the enemy. We're being punished just because we are Jews. They're stripping us of our dignity, by their words, their actions, making us feel other. Less human. I think we should leave when we have the chance.'

'Why should we leave?' Opa had asked. 'We have every right to stay. Why should we be scared, run like cowards? Are we meant to hide and cower and act guilty, act the way an ignorant few have labelled us, as though we've done something wrong, as if we are a sin, for the rest of our lives? This oppression can't continue, not in the middle of Europe in the twentieth century.'

'But it is.' Tears had shivered in Oma's eyes, her hands clasped tightly together, knuckles bloodless. 'You always say we are a shrewd people. But the Nazis have stronger fists that they will not hesitate to use to control us.'

Her words would prove to be prophetic. Although Rani would give anything to reverse Baba's decision to go to India, now, she is selfishly glad her family are there, away from Europe at war. If they were in Europe, Baba would have most likely signed up and Mama, with her German Jewish identity, wouldn't feel safe, even as she worried for Baba. And Arjun... beloved, innocent Arjun would have had to grow up too soon, like the young boys here, watching their brothers and fathers sign up, even as their mothers, who lost their fathers and brothers to the First World War, will secretly agonise if they will see their beloved husbands and sons again while outwardly putting on a brave face.

32

RANI

Dearest Mama, Baba, beloved Arjun,

Hope you are all well.

Writing to you all is a bit like writing to loved ones away at war, I imagine. Writing into the ether. At least they have some hope of receiving a reply. I have long since given up.

No, I lie. I haven't given up – I won't. But... I don't even know if you read these letters.

However, I still write and will keep on going in the hope that you do.

In any case, I have come to depend on these letters. It is as if I am having a conversation with you all – very one-sided but needs must – once a week.

Arjun, if you were to visit my college today, you'd be forgiven for mistaking it for a farm. You'd go in search of your Didi, and you might find her digging in the garden which is now one great big vegetable patch.

Because of rationing, we've had to adapt, you see. Yes, we are now feeling the effects of war even in sheltered Cambridge.

At Girton, we have tried to be self-sufficient with our

veggies and we've succeeded – mostly. Mushrooms have proved tricky to cultivate (although they grow so frustratingly easily in the wild), confounding the botanists and biologists amongst us who've tried every experiment going. They're a dogged lot and are certainly not giving up yet.

We've grown onions and celery, carrots and lettuce, cauliflowers and tomatoes and hopefully we will be adding mushrooms to that list soon.

But guess what crop is thriving, a bounty of abundance? Have you got it yet, Arjun? Yes, potatoes. We have potatoes coming out of our noses. Potato soup. Potato pie. Even potato cake! Arjun, now don't you make that face. In the absence of the real thing – rationing woes – it's not too bad.

Rani sets down her pen. Wipes her eyes, blows her nose, takes a moment. How she misses her brother! But she is grateful every day that he is in India, far away from this madness. And that Mama is too, even trapped in the zenana, which is a different kind of madness. Rani hopes and prays that Baba sees sense soon, stands up to his brother and the nobles, and abolishes the segregation of women, allows them to live with their men.

And Arjun, if you don't find your Didi planting or watering or mulching in the garden, she just might be feeding the pigs. Yes! We keep pigs at college now.

We've also taken in women from Queen Mary College, London. For, as I've intimated in my previous missives, the phony war is well and truly a thing of the past – London is being bombed continuously and persistently. We are relatively safe here; we've survived unscathed so far. Hence the influx of evacuees from Queen Mary – we are 'doing our bit', helping out.

The unexpected but very welcome result of this is that my friend Gertrude is sharing with me. I must admit, it's fun having a roommate. We talk late into the night about various things and I can almost forget the incessant ache of missing you all. Almost. It is like those times you'd come into my room pleading nightmares, Arjun. I'd put up a token complaint that you absolutely saw through but it was great, having your company. If I'd known we'd be separated in India and divided by an ocean after, I'd have shared my room with you every night...

Again she has to stop, wipe her eyes to prevent her tears staining the page.

Anyway, now when I wake up in the night with a nightmare (yes, Arjun, your Didi who is not afraid of anything and who used to joke that nightmares are afraid of her now gets night terrors), the place absolutely dark because of the blackout curtains, it's nice to hear the gentle snores of Gertrude from across the room. Please don't let on that I told you she snores. It's comforting. It eases me back into sleep.

Before, when I couldn't sleep, I'd make myself hot cocoa. Now we have to make do with NAMCO, a cocoa substitute – the less said about it, the better.

We've handed in our ration books and we all chip in with chores now as most of the housekeeping staff have signed up. We are on kitchen, cleaning, gardening and fire-watching rota. I like fire-watching the best. Gertrude and I make sure we volunteer together. We chat as we keep watch and I must say it's very enjoyable and soothing, having a friend to pass the time with. We'd both like to do our bit for the war effort. Several others have left their courses to sign up but we'd like to finish ours as we're nearly there.

Rani stops writing to order her thoughts.

She *will* complete her course. And when she has, she will put her education to good use, doing her bit for this country, her refuge, to help win the war.

When she'd escaped the palace and seen first-hand how the poor lived, she'd vowed that she'd never become complacent, never expect things just because she felt entitled, that she'd work to earn her keep. She would not be like her father, principles pushed aside for the benefits of royalty. Forgetting the world beyond the unreal confines of the palace skewed to favour a privileged few.

In accepting her exile to Cambridge, escaping with the world-class education she'd hankered after, while Prasad no doubt suffered a much, much harsher fate, Rani has been extremely fortunate. Now it is her turn to give back.

The pictures in the newspapers of the bombing of London, children playing among mountains of rubble, reminds her of India, the village children scavenging in the rubbish heap alongside the rats, using it as a makeshift slide.

She's landed on her feet despite what she'd done, ending up at Cambridge – her father is paying for it, and at the time, devastated, upset, scared, she'd accepted it. But it grates. She wants the education, but she has no means of paying for it herself. Because of the lottery of her birth, she is able to have this education denied to those not blessed with rich fathers. She might have rebelled against Baba, mocked him, scorned him for turning his back on his principles but she was doing the same by taking his money. And so, she must pay her dues. Discharge her debt to society.

And she will. She *will*.

Now, the letter:

Gertie is impatient. She'd rather sign up now than wait to finish her course. But her parents are adamant that they'd rather she finished her studies before she did anything foolish – their words huffed angrily in the retelling by a very cross Gertie. Did I tell you that they didn't want her to come up here at all?

'They'd rather I made a suitable marriage,' Gertie had grumbled. 'They push eligible bachelors and wealthy widowers who "are open to bluestockings" – translate as wanting babysitters for their brood, more like – at me every time I go home. I'd like to stay with you here at college during the holidays. No meeting suitable men, just reading and wandering in the grounds. The college empty except for a chosen few, like you, Rani. Bliss.'

Every holiday, Gertie invites Rani back to hers. Rani had accepted and visited with Gertie one Christmas. But being with Gertie's family – her jolly brother, a year older than her, who went to Oxford and kept taking digs at Cambridge, who was so happy-go-lucky and so very kind to Rani, her proper parents, her boisterous posse of cousins – had hurt. It made her miss her own family, Mama, Baba, Opa, Oma and most especially Arjun, even more than before.

She'd gently rebuffed Gertie's cousin Jack's clumsy attempts at courting her, yearning for Prasad with his wild ideas, passionate kisses, mango-scented breath hot and spiced with love, sitting side by side on the branches of the peepal tree arching over the cracked, drought-harangued riverbed.

Gertie's lovely, sprawling home ignited memories of holidays in Germany at Opa and Oma's.

Arjun colouring at the kitchen table while Rani and her mother helped Oma bake challah buns, Opa's favourite, and *schnecken*, which was Arjun's as much for its snail-like shape as for its nectary stickiness. The kitchen warm and toasty and scented with sweet dough. Snow swirling lazily outside the window settling in starry cotton flakes on the sill, lending it a frosty, opaque sheen, making Rani glad to be indoors.

Mama and Oma reminiscing as they rolled out pastry, both in aprons, working in tandem, perfectly synchronised, their velvet voices, the occasional music of their laughter festooning the room in happy swirls. Arjun humming as he coloured – his tongue poking out of his mouth as he concentrated. He was very precise and did not like the colours to blend or swerve outside the lines. Opa and Baba returning from the shop, their coats and hair dusted with snow, silvery white.

Mama wiping her hands on her apron, a smattering of flour coating the floor mimicking the snow slurry building up on the windowsill, before kissing her husband. Oma offering steaming cups of herb-infused tea to her husband and son-in-law.

All of them sitting down to supper, warm soup and challah and *schnecken* for afters. The kitchen fragrant with risen dough and caramelised sugar, happy laughter and animated chatter, and cosy with love.

Being reminded of those happy times made the longing for her family all the more intense. It was too much.

She didn't go again, turning down all Gertie's well-intentioned invitations: 'Come on Rani, you're the only one who will make the holiday somewhat bearable.' Then, with a nudge, 'And, you can attract the attention of some of the men Mama insists on inviting over.'

'She didn't when I was visiting,' Rani said.

'That's exactly why, because you were there. Now do you see why I'd like you to come?'

And Rani had laughed while saying gently, 'The answer's still no.'

Gertie threw the pillow she was kneading at Rani. But she

said, kindly – Gertie was always kind and rarely took offence – 'I do get why you'd like to stay here.'

Holidays spent at Girton were peaceful. The college and university, emptied of most of its cohort, was quiet in a way it never was during term time. Rani's days spent reading and going on long, rambling walks down to the river, following its course. Past the locals going about their business. Gossiping swans unperturbed by sweaty punters, furiously working their boats. Canoodling lovers picnicking under the romantic cover of sweeping willows, sparking ache in her heart. The occasional student or don, dreamily distant – like Rani, in a world of their own.

She learned Cambridge, both the university and the town, by heart. And as she walked down the quaint streets, over winding bridges, through the glorious archways of the centuries-old colleges, she thought, *my father walked here too*. The music wafting from ancient churches, bronzed gold organ chords sombre and soulful, called to her. She sat in chapels and she listened to the music, her feet resting on tiles below which august Cambridge alumni lay in eternal rest. She looked up at the beautifully frescoed ceiling, angels taking flight, and she felt a great calm. The closest thing to pure, perfect peace.

And it was then that she understood a truth about herself. She would always miss her family, feel bad for abandoning Mama to the zenana, worry about, feel guilty about, and miss Prasad. But she could also discover bliss in solitude, joy in small things, wonder in the world.

She turns her attention to the letter:

Arjun, you know how you always say that when you grow up, you want to be like me?

She closes her eyes, tries to summon her brother's voice. The expression in his eyes. But it wavers. She can't quite see him, hear him, revel in the infectious, glorious sound of his laughter ringing in her memory, and it hurts.

How it hurts!

Well, my friend Gertie always wanted to be one better than her older brother. So when he went to Oxford, like their father, she set her heart on Cambridge. Her parents refused to send her, even after she'd won a place here at Girton. They considered a university education wasted on a girl; they'd much rather she went to the elite finishing school in Switzerland her mother had attended. Gertie, on the other hand, was of the opinion she'd rather die than go to finishing school where she maintains she'd have died of boredom. She argued her case (her brother taking her side which, she concedes, was jolly decent of him), and when that didn't work, sulked for days – and goodness, can she sulk when she puts her mind to it! You are not bad yourself, Arjun, but Gertie would beat you hands down. Anyway, her parents did give in, finally, and I for one am so very glad she's here.

Have I told you how we became friends? We'd bumped into each other of course, in halls, in the dining and reading rooms, and she was particularly incensed when I bested her at chess – she has confided since that I immediately ousted her brother from top enemy slot right then.

'What about now that we are friends?' I asked when she told me this. 'Am I still...?'

'Top of my list of people to better? With regards to chess, a definite yes.' She'd grinned, linking her arm in mine.

She's a character is Gertie. You'd like her, Arjun.

Anyway, we properly became friends when she organised

the protest at Cambridge, for degrees for women, rousing the scholars here at Girton and at the other ladies-only college, Newnham, into action. I was more surprised than anyone when she picked me as her deputy. I'd been very quiet until then, you see, still finding my way around.

'I'd seen you come into your own when debating. And that fierce spark when you play chess intrigued me. That fire to win... I knew there was more to you. I was right, wasn't I?' she told me later.

She was. She is. She reminds me of you so much, Arjun. I've tried to think of what you both have in common and the only thing I can come up with is that you both look for and bring out the best in me.

Sorry I keep digressing.

The protest, then.

'I can't believe our university is so antiquated,' Gertie fumed. 'Women are awarded degrees at Oxford and at the London universities. Why aren't we?'

She girded us all into action and oh! It was so liberating and absolutely wonderful, all of us women scholars at Newnham and Girton marching through the university holding placards, which had been designed by yours truly: The number of women allowed into Cambridge capped at 500 – shameful.

No degrees for women. Shameful.

Women are just as good, if not better. Let us prove it. Make the change. Be the change.

You get the idea, Arjun.

It had been brilliant, Rani muses, setting down her pen. The passion-fuelled drug of solidarity. The feeling of being part of something bigger. Important. Doing instead of taking what was happening passively, working to bring about change.

'Even if they don't change their antiquated rules in time for us, they will see that the tide is turning,' Gertie said. 'They will take notice and perhaps sooner rather than later, let's hope, they bring it into effect.'

Of course, now with the war, everything is different. Everyone coming together to fight a bigger enemy.

Rani's eyes are drawn back to her letter.

It is more of an exercise in writing for herself, talking to the family she misses. She highly doubts they read it. If they did, they would be very confused, as often the letters are as jumbled as her thoughts, jumping all over the place, a stream-of-consciousness narrative, knitted together and posted. She imagines her father throws the letters away unread – that is, if they reach Baba at all. She doesn't put it past her uncle to be gatekeeper, taking it upon himself to get rid of the letters rather than delivering them to her family. But it helps ease the missing and so she writes.

Do you know what happened today, Arjun?

Although we're growing vegetables and are self-sufficient in this way, it still isn't quite enough. I think I've said before – there are plenty of potatoes but not much else. Butter, sugar, meat and milk, especially, are in short supply. We are always hungry.

Mary, one of the few remaining kitchen staff (most have joined up), swiped the leftovers from high table and brought them back to share with us, the absolute jewel. We had a feast of bread – a toast finger each and even the thinnest sliver of cake! Something so blessedly sweet and not a hint of potato in sight. Heaven. We'll take any treats we get!

As I was saying, Gertie and I will sign up once we've finished our courses. Like the rest of the country, we want to get back at the man who discriminates against people just because of their race, the colour of their eyes, their hair. If we were in Germany, because of our Jewish heritage, we would be in the firing line.

I am so glad you are in India, Arjun, far from here. And don't worry, please, I will be safe. I want to see you, hopefully soon. That's incentive enough.

Mama, Baba I've ended up addressing this letter mostly to Arjun but if you are reading this, you know, I hope, that I write for and to you all.

Yours,

Rani

33

RANI

Baba, Mama and my dearest Arjun,

After years of writing weekly into a void with no hope of reply, so much so that I had come to terms with viewing it as a diary exercise, imagine my surprise, cautious hope and, I must add, suspicion when, at breakfast, Gertrude, who receives mail nearly every day from her parents, brother, assorted cousins and family, announced, 'A letter for you, Rani. I took the liberty of collecting it from your cubby.'

I never have any post waiting, except for the odd flyer. Certainly no letters. I must say, I choked on my (watery) porridge. Jane was on kitchen rota and she sticks to the measly rationing quota, scientist that she is, she's irritatingly precise to the last diluted fluid ounce.

Gertie was looking at me, right eyebrow raised. She knew what a big deal this was. Which is why she collected my letter – I never bother to check my cubby any more, but bless her, she always does. She's stubbornly held out hope on my behalf even as mine has dwindled over the years to the merest sliver.

My hand shook as I accepted the letter with a nod of thanks

– I could not trust myself to speak, you see, for as she handed it over, I saw the Indian stamps.

My heart jumped. I never understood the meaning of that phrase until it actually happened to me.

Finally. A part of me (the dwindled to just a sliver part) has been waiting for this since I came here.

I was fingering the envelope reverently, recalling that missive waiting for you, Baba, the summons that changed all our lives – was this what it was for me too? – and startled when I felt a hand on my shoulder.

'Do you want to take it up to your room?' Gertie, kind as always. She must have seen something in my expression, my lovely friend, as I stroked the letter with trembling fingers.

Do you know, whoever said mathematicians are odd and unfeeling have not met Gertie. She's a thoroughly understanding soul and so empathic too. I will admit she is odd. But I ask, who isn't?

Sorry to digress. I'm prevaricating. It hurts so much.

Your letter, Baba… it brought it all back. What happened, and my part in it. What was said. And what wasn't. Your silence for three long years.

Rani stops. She cannot continue. Instead, she picks up her father's letter, his first communication since he declared her dead to the family.

34

RANI

One curt paragraph is all the communication from her father after his long silence:

> We're worried about you, having heard reports of war and continued bombing, although Cambridge seems to have escaped for the most part. You are nearing the end of your course. Come home. Memories are long and forgiveness is thin on the ground. But... I have spoken to my brother – we will make sure you come to no harm.

The words shimmer before Rani's eyes. Her Baba's handwriting so very familiar. And yet that tone – so uncompromising. But... it is *something*, especially after the complete embargo of the last few years. He has reached out. It is a wonder he's capitulated at all. Mama's doing, Rani suspects. She did promise Rani she'd work on Baba, that his anger, their goodbye, was but temporary. It must have taken her this long because she only got to see him once a week, if that, when he visited with her in the zenana. The thought of Mama alone and lonely in the zenana hurts, a raw ache in her wounded heart. Arjun growing up without her hurts. He's nearly twelve now – he must have shot up in height. She cannot picture him as anything but the cheeky little eight-year-old she saw last, sobbing his heart out. And Baba...

Prasad...

Hurt upon hurt upon hurt.

Rani takes a deep breath, picks up her pen. So many years of writing blindly, putting her emotions down, very cathartic, as she had thought no one was reading her missives, and so she's been very open and personal, has revealed too much, perhaps...

This is the hardest reply.

She's yearned for this very thing – for Baba to invite her home, welcome her back. She's missed them all so. She wants to know what was Prasad's fate, whether her father let him go, like she pleaded.

The nib of her pen presses down hard on the paper. So much so that it tears. An ink blot staining the page. She sniffs, frustrated and upset.

Picks up a fresh sheet. Starts again.

Dearest Mama, Baba, Arjun,

I've waited for this. Longed for it. But...

Although I miss you all more than I can put into words, I have to say that I can't return home just yet.

She places a protective hand on the paper to prevent her tears ruining it.

I've promised to help with the war effort. I have to do this. Give back.

I hope you understand.

I will come back. But not just yet.

She wants to put her education to good use, even if it means not seeing her family – especially Mama and Arjun, and hopefully Prasad, if her father has been merciful and spared her love – for longer; perhaps, depending on what this job she has committed to do involves, forever. It is a risk she must take now she has joined the war effort.

Thank you for your forgiveness, Baba. I really appreciate it and I am grateful. I can just about imagine how much negotiating and grovelling it must have required you to do with your brother and his cronies on my behalf and how much you must have hated it.

She is formal now she knows that Baba is definitely reading this letter. Not at ease like before.

She sets her pen down, cradles her head in her hands and weeps, thinking of her little brother, whose face she can't quite recall, whose features waver at the blurred edges of memory no matter how much she tries to bring them into focus. But... his voice, crying, 'Don't go, Didi,' haunts her dreams. Mama cradling her face, kissing her forehead, her eyes, the tip of her nose, her cheeks, her chin, anointing them with her tears. Her butterfly touch. Her rose scent, sharp with sorrow. Her father, when she was a child and snug in the embrace of his arms, saying, 'Rani, our queen,' with such pride in his voice. The look Prasad gave her as he was led away, his eyes never leaving hers as he was forced into submission, dragged, manhandled...

She can't recall them all perfectly any more. They are snatches of wistful memory, brine-soaked nostalgia: her father's laughter. Mama's expression when she was tired. Arjun asleep, that angelic expression, a stillness to him that was never in evidence when he was awake. Prasad's eyes shining gold as he beamed at her. She treasures these precious gifts from her whimsical recollection. But she wishes she could remember more, recall everything in perfect, three-dimensional detail.

She will go back once her duty is done, if, when she survives the war. She will breathe them all in again, get her fill of them, her loved ones, learn them by heart.

Just not yet.

The hardest decision she's made so far.

Quite the hardest.

35

RANI

Rani was in the kitchen the previous morning, scrubbing potatoes, when Alison, also reading Modern Languages but taking a two-year degree under war emergency regulations, had popped her head round the door, breathless. 'Mistress Wodehouse would like to see you.' Her voice soft with fear-suffused awe.

A summons from the Mistress of Girton herself! In all Rani's tenure here, she could count on one hand the number of times their paths had crossed, always at college events that required the august lady's presence – and then, Rani had never interacted with her personally. Traditionally, the mistress of Girton also used to be tutor to the undergraduates, but Mistress Wodehouse changed all that, appointing Mary Duff to assist.

Until that day, Rani had not spoken two sentences with Mistress Wodehouse face to face, and she was perfectly content for this to continue, for like everyone at Girton, she was very much in awe of this amazing personality who so efficiently ran the college and was steering them so competently during wartime, in exceptional circumstances.

'Do you happen to know what she wants with me?' Rani asked, trying to steady her voice as her mind went through all manners of possibilities that might require this audience. As far as she knew, she was doing well and was on track to finish her course. Was it her father? Had something happened to him or Mama or Arjun? *Please no.*

'No,' Alison was saying. 'I was returning from the reading room when she accosted me and asked me to find you and send you to her. "Immediately please," she said.' Alison paused to take a breath and then, kindly giving Rani, who was standing there, stunned, a verbal nudge, 'Here, let me finish the potatoes for you.'

Rani wiped her hands, taking care to make sure no stubborn dirt flecks remained under her nails. She smoothed her hair into place, her heart thudding so loud, she was sure Alison could hear it.

* * *

The twenty-two steps leading up to Mistress Wodehouse's chambers felt interminable. And yet, despite this, Rani thought she arrived at her door too soon.

She wasn't ready. Her hand shaking as she knocked.

Come on, buck up, she chided herself. *You have faced worse. You stole Baba's ceremonial sword. You can do this.*

But what if it is bad news about my family?

From inside, 'Come in.'

The room Rani entered was vast but gave the impression of being much smaller than it was. And this was thanks to the books taking up every surface, spilling from bookcases, piled on and toppling from side tables, masking the plush carpet, even crowding the fireplace!

Mistress Wodehouse was sitting at a beautifully polished

walnut desk which was, in contrast to the rest of the room, remarkably free of books. All it held was a pen stand. Light pooled from the window behind her, golden honey, setting her hair on fire. The window looked out onto the quad, framed by a morning that was bright and cloudless, the sky the white of purity, the garden – neat furrows of veg plants – clothed in a serenely sparkling frost fleece.

Was that...? It *was* Gertie going into the reading room. Perhaps in search of Rani. They were supposed to meet in there after Rani's kitchen duties. Rani had not had time to tell her friend of her sudden, urgent assignation. She suppressed the urge to call to Gertie: *Help me. Save me. I don't know why I am here.*

For she still didn't have a clue.

Mistress Wodehouse had, apart from asking her to enter, not acknowledged her presence, nor given any indication whatsoever of knowing she was there.

She was serenely reading a letter in front of her on the desk, beside the pen stand.

Was the letter to do with Rani's family?

Rani cleared her throat.

And now Mistress Wodehouse looked up. 'Ah, Miss Raj, please take a seat.' Indicating the chair opposite. 'Just move the books. Set them anywhere. On the floor will do nicely.'

Rani did as she asked, moving the tomes on philosophy and education out of the chair, adding to the already precariously teetering piles on the floor.

'So Miss Raj, you're coming to the end of your course and you've done admirably well, as all your tutors agree.'

Ah. Rani released the breath she'd been holding. It wasn't to do with Baba, Mama or Arjun. If it was, Mistress Wodehouse would have said so immediately, wouldn't she?

Her tutors were pleased with her progress. So why was she here?

'What are your plans for when you finish?' Mistress Wodehouse looked keenly at Rani.

Why was Mistress Wodehouse interested in *her* plans? 'I'd like to do my bit for the war effort—'

Mistress Wodehouse didn't let her finish. 'Good, good. I've heard you're the best at college, possibly even one of the best at Cambridge, at chess.'

Not a question, so Rani waited.

'Do you like crosswords?'

'I enjoy doing them, yes. But I have to admit my friend Gertrude is faster and better at them.'

'She's the mathematician.'

Again, not a question, but Rani said, 'She is, yes.'

'Well, I have a letter here from my friend who's involved with top-secret work for the war office. They're looking for linguists and mathematicians who are also good at chess and crosswords. They've asked me to put forward some names and I'd like to recommend you, and also your friend Gertrude.'

Oh. Rani felt awe and gratitude, both at once. The Mistress of Girton felt it right to recommend *her*, Rani. And even better, Gertie too!

'I can't tell you much about what it involves; as I said, it's all hush-hush. But you will be helping to win this war that's been going on for far too long.' Mistress Wodehouse looked right at her. 'Is this something you'd consider?'

Work that was top secret, that would help win the war, that required people with the skills she possessed? This is what she'd wanted, what she was hoping to do, after she finished her course. What better way to put her education to use than this? It was like a message from the gods. And to think she'd been so worried when she was summoned here...

'Yes, I'd very much like it,' she said.

'I was hoping you'd say that.' When Mistress Wodehouse smiled, she looked much younger, her eyes twinkling pleasingly. 'And jolly good going, Miss Raj, at your course and at chess. Well done. Please could you send Gertrude in to see me?'

'I will. Thank you.' Rani beamed, relief and happiness at knowing, suddenly, what she would do next. It had all worked out so serendipitously. And to be chosen for recommendation by the mistress of Girton herself!

* * *

Gertie, when she came back from seeing Mistress Wodehouse, could hardly contain her excitement, throwing her arms around Rani. 'We're doing it, we're saving the world!'

Rani laughed as Gertie danced her around the quad, expertly manoeuvring through and sidestepping the rows of veggies. 'I bet Mistress Wodehouse is watching – her window looks out onto here, you know.'

'Well, she'll be dancing too as she knows just as well that together, we are invincible. That's why she's chosen us. Right then, Hitler better watch out.' She viciously stepped on and squished to earthy death a rotting potato. 'There, he's gone. Victory is ours!'

Rani threw her head up to the bright white heavens and laughed.

And the very next day, she had received her father's letter.

36

ESME

The nursing home is a modern building, state-of-the-art facilities, ramps for wheelchairs.

Esme is led past a dining room, clatter of cutlery, a tremulous voice chanting, 'No, no, no.' The inviting scent of bacon and coffee, the patient murmur of nurses interspersed with aged voices raised in plaintive query.

Past a room packed with bookshelves, tables dotted with newspapers, the odd resident or two ensconced in armchairs, squinting at the papers, rustle of sheets held up to faces, peering short sightedly over glasses that are falling down noses.

A squeak of slippers. A shuffling wanderer, bare dome of head, still in his bathrobe, gaping open slightly to reveal sparse silver wisps of hair glinting on the wrinkled flesh of his bony chest, being asked gently, by an approaching nurse, 'Edward, my dear, are you coming down to the dining room for breakfast or would you like me to bring it up to you as usual?'

He blinks, uncomprehendingly at the nurse, 'What's that?' as Esme walks past.

'Ah, here we are.'

The nurse escorting Esme opens the door to a wide, bright room, floor to ceiling glass doors facing undulating, green lawns, a lake shimmering beyond, ducks waddling up to the doors, inviting smiles.

It is a long room, residents engaged in carefully monitored activities with their carers. The nurse accompanying Esme leads her to the older lady reclining on her own in an armchair facing the garden.

'I must warn you. She's deteriorated quite a bit since you saw her last. Gets agitated very easily and is more confused than ever. I'll be over there,' indicating a group gathered around a table, playing cards, 'if you need me.'

Esme nods, smiles her thanks.

Esme doesn't do commitment; she runs away from it. But if she is able to love at all – *Philip*, her heart laments – it is thanks to this woman beside whom Esme now pulls up a chair. Her mothering of Robbie is also, in large part, thanks to the example set and the firm love dished out by this woman, who is the only mother figure Esme has ever known.

She doesn't turn to look at Esme. She appears unaware of her. She is absorbed in gazing at the pigeons pecking at the grass, unperturbed by the ducks waddling up from the lake in a fluster of quacks. She has shrunk since Esme saw her last, when she'd visited just after her father died. Her hair is thinner, pink scalp visible, so nakedly vulnerable.

Esme is pierced by a sharp stab of guilt.

Like with her father at the hospice, she'd vowed to visit more often but, again like with her father, it hurt too much, seeing the heavy-set woman she knew and loved reduced to this small, bird-like creature, papery skin coating fragile bones, confusion clouding those bright eyes that used to soften with affection, glare with reprimand when necessary, shine with love and glow with pride, sometimes all of these at once, when they looked at Esme.

Robbie visits Mrs Lewes more often than Esme does.

He's a favourite with everyone in the nursing home, doctors, carers and residents alike.

Mrs Lewes doesn't remember who he is much of the time but he takes it in his stride and charms her anyway, the two of them having a laugh, so much so that, the nurses tell Esme, she asks after the 'young chap' days after he's been and gone, and given her deteriorating memory, that's a miracle and a half.

When Esme visited last, it was with the intention of informing Mrs Lewes of her father's death. Together, they would grieve for him. For Mrs Lewes had loved Esme's father as she would a younger brother, she the protective, bossy, older sister. She had had no children, no close relatives. After her husband died, she'd adopted William, Esme's father, as her family. And she'd loved his family as fiercely as her own blood.

When her dementia – which she'd dismissed as forgetfulness due to her advanced age – got so bad that she proved a danger to herself and others (she forgot the pan on the stove – if a neighbour hadn't smelt the fumes and intervened, the whole street would have caught fire), William had arranged her move to the best nursing home in the area and when he was diagnosed with stage 4 bowel cancer with no hope of recovery, had made provision in his will for her nursing home bills to be taken care of.

Esme and Andy were listed as her next of kin.

At her previous visit here just after her father's death, Esme had tried telling Mrs Lewes that William was gone, but she was having a bad day. She hadn't recognised Esme, and when Esme had mentioned William, she'd rocked back and forth, ululating so violently that two nurses had to subdue her.

As Esme drove back home, having to stop every so often for

her eyes were too blurred to see the road, she'd wondered if Mrs Lewes had somehow intuited what Esme had been going to say, that this was her way of warding off the inevitable bad news. She'd always been so perceptive, knowing when Esme or her brother were in need of a hug or a kind word without them ever having to spell it out.

Mrs Lewes was the one Esme turned to when she found out she was pregnant. She had been practical and down-to-earth, as was her wont. It was just what Esme needed.

'Do you want the child?' Mrs Lewes had asked.

'Yes.'

'Is the father in the picture?'

'No.'

'Then you'll do it yourself, like the many women widowed by war had to do. And you'll do a wonderful job.' Mrs Lewes' eyes softening as she said this. 'In any case, I will be there, to show you the ropes.'

And true to her word, she had been, every step of the way, until her memory failed her.

PART III

37

RANI

Bletchley, 1941

Rani smooths down the skirt of her smartest dress, which is, nevertheless the worse for wear – they are at war; dresses, as with everything else, including morale, are fraying, tired, make do and mend – and adjusts her hat as she gets off the train at Bletchley station.

To her right, fences topped with barbed wire.

To her left, a vast expanse of green stretching as far as the eye can see.

At first glance, it doesn't appear as if this quiet, dozy place is where she and others like her will help win the war.

'You'll be working with the best brains in the country,' she was told when she was assigned to Bletchley Park, the nature of what she was going to do a secret even to her, even after she'd agreed. She still doesn't know, but whatever it is, she will give it her absolute best to justify the sacrifice she has made – postponing her long-awaited invitation to reconcile, reunite with her family.

There has been no response from her father – early days yet

she hopes and not anger at what he might see as her stubbornness, her contrariness. She trusts the reconciliation will only be postponed, not cancelled, that Baba will understand. That she won't die, another casualty to this interminable war, before she sees them again. Surreptitiously, she crosses the fingers of the hand not lugging her trunk. Prays, *please.*

She'd eagerly eyed Bletchley as the train slowed down to a stop, small and quaint, the quintessential, bucolic English country village. Awnings advertising local shops, the butcher's with cuts of meat in the window – a paltry showing due to war shortages, a line snaking outside, women with baskets, their heads covered by scarves and hats.

The greengrocer's with a selection of vegetables and fruit, meagre but beautifully displayed. A church, tall and stately. Village children playing under the trees, hopscotch in the road, jumping out of the way of the odd carriage, cantering horses, while their mothers scuttled between shops. Veterans of the first war too old to sign up for this one sharing pints and memories outside the public taverns, one at each end of the high street.

No obvious sign of the war here. No ruined buildings nor craters splintering the road, no debris and rubble and dust lending a heavy orange tint to tired smog. No keening engines, and billowing smoke, nor the crisp, burned, yellow reek of death. Idyllic country life, albeit rife with scarcity, lack, which the villagers seem to accept with cheerful resilience. Rows of redbrick cottages haloed fiery vermilion in the early-autumn sun.

Rani wishes Gertie was with her; she'd have made some wry observation, eased the nerves Rani can't help but feel, despite the setting for her war work being so deceptively unassuming, perhaps because of it.

She's already missing her friend fiercely. 'Keep safe,' she whispers, her fingers still tightly crossed.

After their respective meetings with Mistress Wodehouse, where Rani and Gertie had jumped at her offer, the chance to put their skills to good use, Gertie rather more enthusiastically than Rani herself, Rani presumed, they'd both been summoned to the war office. At the interview, after testing their various skills, Rani was assigned to Bletchley Park while Gertie was placed elsewhere. They weren't to tell each other where they were going but Gertie, on the day they were to part, began, 'I know you won't tell anyone, Rani...'

'No don—'

But before Rani could finish, 'I'm with the SOE, Special Operations Executive. I'm commencing training tomorrow to be a spy!'

Gertie's voice rising in excitement, even as Rani's heart pounded with fear on her friend's behalf. Even as she mused that before India and everything that happened, Rani would have been just as daring as her friend, fearless, embracing risk with no thought to caution or consequences. Rani looked at her friend, starry-eyed at the thought of being a spy. She wondered if she would ever see her again and if she did, would she have changed like Rani herself had done, by her actions, what she'd faced and endured. She'd always thought she gravitated to Gertie because she reminded her of Arjun. But now, suddenly, Rani understood that Gertie reminded her of *herself* before India: passionate, completely daring and uninhibited, afraid of nothing at all, willing to do anything for her ideals, take on the world.

After India, Rani, on the other hand, was altogether more restrained and reserved, approaching everything with caution, thinking twice, sometimes thrice, and she wasn't entirely sure if that was a good thing.

Gertie was saying, rubbing her palms together, 'It's jolly good. I'm actually going to be doing something worthy. You know? Not only making a suitable marriage. But I do wish we were together. I'll miss you.'

'Me too,' Rani whispered, her eyes shimmering like her friend's were doing.

Gertie reached across, squeezed her hand, 'Rani, wherever you're going, they're very lucky to have you. With our joint efforts, we *will* win the war.'

'I hope so. I don't know what I'm going to be doing, just that I'm to report to Bletchley Park.'

'You'll find out soon enough. Now, Rani, we must promise each other not to get killed.'

They chuckled sadly, knowing the difficulty of keeping this particular vow in the midst of war.

'I will promise to stay safe,' Rani said, wiping tears from her eyes.

'I will too.' Her friend's sweet breath hot on her cheek. Flavoured with friendship, respect. Love. 'We will meet when our leave coincides.'

They hugged like they'd never let each other go. Wondering when or if they'd ever have the opportunity again.

The poignant, honeyed, nectar memories of their years together at Cambridge, talking late into the night in a room nightmare-dark with blackout curtains. Growing together from gawky girls to accomplished women. Gardening. Cooking. Fire-watching. Cleaning. Reading. Debating. Swimming. Learning.

She waved until her friend was but a dot, wavering, blurring, disappearing.

Whispering, 'Stay safe,' long after she was gone, into the empty air.

And then it was time to pack her own bags and heed the call of duty to England, to give back to the country that had offered

Rani refuge, education, solace, friendship, companionship, belonging.

* * *

Rani drags her trunk up the lane and when she comes to a driveway leading to an RAF sentry post – *ah, this is more like it* – she knows she's in the right place.

The sentry on duty bars her way.

'Miss?'

She stands up straight and tall. 'I'm here to see the commander.'

'Letter of invitation, please.'

She digs around in her bag, produces it just as a car drives up the lane, its growling engine sounding vulgarly out of place in the quiet peace of the countryside, birdsong and the occasional lowing of cows grazing in the fields adjoining the gates, a train whistle in the distance. The sentry looks past her at the sleek car then, with a cursory glance at the letter gives her a quick nod.

She falters as the car vrooms past in an acrid gust of diesel and smoke.

And then, Rani walks into Bletchley Park, her place of work for the duration of the war, fixing her hat with one hand, her trunk in the other, on slightly trembling legs, curious, excited, nervous, as she begins this new chapter in her life.

38

RANI

A lake shimmers in the weak sun, reflecting golden rays from within its depths, lending a glittering, festive sheen to the circle of trees standing guard around it, willows sweeping its banks with graceful bows.

Rose gardens that Rani can picture in summer, vibrantly gloriously ablaze in a host of riotous colour. Prefabricated huts mushrooming around the vast grounds, chimneys puffing out clouds of smoke. The house itself – Bletchley Park Manor – hidden, coyly offering tantalising glimpses, sun-burnished gables peeking out from behind a huge tree. Grounds stretching beyond, these too dotted with huts and concrete blocks. The smoky sweet scent of berries and autumn-frost-harangued earth.

The house is not vast by any means; in fact, it appears rather haphazardly put together. But it carries a dignity, a sense of grandeur, red bricks glowing bronze, lending it an impressive, rather intimidating air of secrecy. Its very facade appears to declare: *important work goes on here.*

Perhaps Rani is reading too much into it but she feels excited all the same, along with fear, a thrill of possibility, anticipation.

She marches smartly up the drive, past the lake twinkling with secrets.

Groups of men and women, well wrapped up, making the most of autumn sun, scattered about the grounds chatting, sharing picnics, a determined and intrepid few playing tennis in their coats and mittens in the courts across from the lake.

Girls giggling, coats pulled snug around them as they lounge on benches set about the bank, others with their hatted heads thrown up to the slices of sky, tawny blue, visible through the awning of branches above, as ducks shimmy up to them, eager to share in their gossip.

A cluster of men, some in suits, others casually dressed amble past, head down, deep in discussion.

'Code,' Rani hears. 'Bloody complicated.'

A woman comes past on her bike, her bell twinkling merrily, coattails flying behind, hair secured in a scarf tied with ribbons under her chin.

She elegantly jumps off the bike, leaving it carelessly by the door to the manor atop a heap of other bikes, and skips inside.

From what Rani can see, the women far outnumber the men. Is it because the men are all away fighting at the front?

It appears idyllic, peaceful, looking for all the world like a house party. And again her impression of earlier, when she got off the train, reinforced. You couldn't say there was a war on.

Well, apart from the scarcity in the shops in the village, and here, the sentry at the gate and the high walls, of course.

How can these merry, languid people giving off student vibes be involved in top-secret work?

But then she recalls what she heard the men who passed her just now saying. Something about codes.

As Rani passes one of the many huts dotted around the grounds, a woman rushes out carrying a sheet of paper.

Ah, now here's evidence of the urgency Rani associates with defeating Hitler and stopping the war.

'Sir, this needs to get to the commander, pronto,' she says to a well-dressed man who was strolling ahead of Rani, hands in pockets, head down and about to enter the hut.

The man scrutinises it. 'Ah thanks, er...'

'Victoria, sir.'

'I'll see that it gets to him.'

Rani follows the man into the mansion – he'll lead her to the commander.

He is preoccupied, perusing the sheet of paper, even as he opens the door and steps inside.

As he turns to shut the door, she intercepts him. 'Excuse me, please.'

He's younger than she'd judged from the way he walks, shoulders hunched, head bowed, with the gait of a much older man. His face is grave, expression, solemn, as if he carries the weight of the universe on his shoulders. Worry lines scrimp and scurry about his eyes.

'I have a meeting with the commander,' she says.

He folds the piece of paper the woman from the hut gave him to pass on to the commander that he was looking at, drops it into his pocket.

He clears his throat. 'And you are...?' His gaze meets hers for a brief moment before slinking away – she's left with the impression of eyes the smoky grey of broody autumn sky storming a tantrum in opposition of rapidly approaching winter.

And Rani is struck by the realisation that this serious man is shy. She was feeling slightly overwhelmed but this sudden understanding makes her bold.

'I'm Rani Raj. I was invited to join the team here at Bletchley Park because of my skill with languages,' she says, crisply.

He nods, and again that quick, fleeting glance. 'Pleased to meet you, Miss Raj. I'm William Strong. Please do follow me. Commander Travis's office is this way.'

39

RANI

Mr Strong escorts Rani past rooms whose grandeur is enhanced and accentuated by the buzz and thrum of pulsing energy, their partially open doors affording her a tantalising glimpse within of unsteady piles of haphazardly stacked books, desks piled high with paper.

The punching of typewriter keys, the whirring of odd-looking machines – some veritable beasts taking up the whole room and dwarfing the men and women standing beside it – the likes of which she's never seen before but which look exciting and modern, pistons and levers and drums, churning and revolving, with spools of wires, a mess of plugs spouting from them like entrails of masticated prey from a giant's mouth.

The low hum of breathy conversation. Busy-looking men and women, the women's heels clacking in urgency, the men's eyebrows puckered as they rush in and out of rooms, clutching paper, chewing on pencils.

Rani notes the officious hum of bubbling activity, the under-lying conviction that this is important work they are doing. Here is concrete evidence of the 'best brains in the country' galvanised in their machinations, their concentrated efforts to best the enemy.

And she will, later today, after this meeting with the commander, be one of them!

Every single person they pass appears to know Mr Strong, raising their hand, hello, if deep in conversation, some nodding and others cheerily greeting him, their gazes curious, inquisitive as they take her in.

And her nerves recede in the wake of eagerness, the desire to join this cohort, and start working to make a difference.

Outside the ornate, panelled door to the commander's office, Mr Strong once again clears his throat, before saying to Rani, even as he raises his hand to knock, 'I'll let the commander know you're waiting.'

Before she can reply, he's knocked, there's a faint, masculine, 'Come in,' in response. As he enters, Rani is afforded the merest glimpse of a vast room with glass windows offering a view of the grounds, green grass dancing to the frisky wind, a typewriter on a polished wooden desk, a hand setting a telephone receiver back down.

As she waits outside the door, sounds drift up to her, laughter, snatches of conversation: 'bomb', 'cribs', 'Enigma', 'Prof', 'code', 'Dilly', the music of keys dancing on typewriters, the clanking of machines, the quacking of ducks outside, the scent of tea being brewed and ink and polish, people walking past, the swish of their clothes, the tang of their sweat, the rustle of the papers they are holding.

A woman, tall and reedy, everything about her formidable, from her clothes to the hair pulled back tightly into a severe bun, enters the commander's office with a pot of tea and biscuits on a tray.

The low rumble of voices wafts out of the room before the door closes behind her.

After a bit, the woman emerges, nods at Rani. 'They won't be long.' Her voice too, like the rest of her, is crisp, straitlaced.

But she is right, for before long, Mr Strong appears, biscuit crumbs dotting his suit and tie, saying, still too shy to meet her gaze, focusing on the wall above her head, 'You are to go straight in.'

He is holding open the door courteously for her and she breathes in his scent of woodsmoke and pine as she walks past him and inside.

Mr Strong closes the door softly behind her and she is alone with Commander Travis, sitting behind his desk, his piercing gaze taking her in from behind dark-rimmed spectacles, missing nothing.

He says, benignly enough, 'Ah, you're the girl who has the German.' And then, with a quick smile, 'Helen recommends you very highly indeed.'

Helen? Rani wonders.

'Your mistress at Girton,' Commander Travis prompts. Her face must have given her confusion away.

Mistress Wodehouse. Helen to this man. He must be the friend she referred to, who was looking for linguists good at chess and crosswords, whose letter she was holding when she invited Rani to her office and offered her the chance to do work in service of the country.

Enough wool gathering. The commander is waiting, his hands crossed, his face solemn.

'Thank you, sir. I'm eager to do my bit.'

His voice when he speaks is grave as he enunciates every word. 'Now, Miss Raj, this is a top-secret operation we run here, crucial to national safety. I'm sure I don't need to impress upon you the need for discretion.'

Has he divined somehow that she shared with Gertie where she was going to be based? She wouldn't put anything past this man with his all-seeing gaze.

Behind the commander, in the slice of gardens of this great house framed by his window, girls walk, arm in arm, shiny blonde heads aglow. A man cycles furiously. Weeping willows sweep the waters of the lake that ripple and glimmer silver gold in the weak but welcome October sun. Ducks, their green feathers burnished gold, traverse calmly through the water.

Two girls shiver on the lawn, drinking tea – she assumes – from thermoses, sharing sandwiches, ducks waddling up to them for crumbs. One of them throws her head up to the sky and laughs, her mirth sparkly silver, Rani imagines.

The gesture reminds Rani of Gertie. A sharp pang of missing. *Keep safe.*

'I am very discreet, sir. I'm a hard worker and I want to help win this war.' She injects all the passion within her, the drive to give back in order to make up for what happened in the past, into her voice.

The commander steeples his fingers and his gaze pierces her with the potency of a javelin pinning flesh.

Permeating the solemn silence of this room, the thrumming murmur of people involved in important work, crucial work, the whirring and clattering of machines, the ink and paper smell of busyness.

'Miss Raj, you will be working as a codebreaker.'

A codebreaker! So that's what they do here. Intercept enemy messages and try to decipher them.

Now this is true war work. This is the reason why it's all hush-hush. This is why they are recruiting people with language skills.

Rani experiences a thrill of pure adrenaline. And now she also understands why they were interested in her chess ability. In chess, every piece has a specific movement, and the game requires one to remember not just the movement of one's own pieces but that of one's opponents too. One has to read one's opponent to understand their strategy, and adapt to their moves, all within a specified time limit. The game requires you to be supremely strategic and logical, and think in patterns, which Rani imagines are all qualities that lend to codebreaking.

Commander Travis is saying, 'You will be dealing in intelligence of the most crucial nature alongside the best minds in the country, perhaps the world. Our work has the potential to win us the war. Secrecy is paramount to what we do here. I cannot stress this enough. You will not discuss what you do with anyone outside the hut you're assigned to.'

'I assure you, sir, I can be trusted.' She meets the commander's gaze with an unswerving one of her own. 'I will give it my very best. I will not let you or this country down.'

'You will sign the Official Secrets Act.' Then, twirling the pen in his hand. 'Are you colourblind, by any chance?'

She blinks, taken aback. 'Er... I'm not, sir.'

'Good.' He nods. 'The German messages you'll be tasked with trying to decode are colour-coded depending on where they were intercepted from, which part of the army or Air Force they were sent from and where they were going to.'

Ah, now his question makes perfect sense.

'No telling family or friends what you do and where you're based. For all they know, you're packing parachutes for airmen. All incoming personal post to be addressed to a London PO Box, details of which the supervisor at your hut will give you when you report to work in the morning, 8 a.m. sharp.'

She swallows, pushing down the worry and angst at the

thought of her family. The question mark hanging over whether her father will reply at all, keep the tentative line of communication open when she has asked that his invitation to return home be postponed. In any case, she will write to her family again, once she has details of where they are to send letters. Behind her back, she crosses her fingers.

'Now as to where you will stay, William Strong, whom you just met, also a codebreaker, one of our best, has a room spare. He has kindly agreed to accommodate you, so you will be billeted with him.'

Oh. She'd assumed she'd be staying in dorms like at Cambridge. *I'm no longer at school. I'm working now.* 'Thank you, sir.'

Commander Travis nods and flashes that brief smile again. 'Welcome to Bletchley Park, Miss Raj.'

And just like that, she has the job and a place to stay.

She is part of the Bletchley Park community, soon to be engaged in work paramount to the country's safety, the world's defence.

40

ESME

Esme sits beside this woman she loves, so reduced. A bare shell.

'I've survived the war, lived to a grand old age, outlived your much-younger father. Don't you go feeling sorry for me,' Mrs Lewes would say if she could, Esme knows.

Ever practical, their Mrs Lewes.

'Do you love him?' Mrs Lewes would have asked if she was hale and well and Esme confided in her about Philip's proposal.

'Yes.'

'Is he kind, caring, dependable?'

'Yes.'

'Then why did you let him get away, love?' Mrs Lewes would have shaken her head and tutted. 'Don't you know men are thin on the ground after the war and a good man... well, my love, when you find him, you keep hold of him.'

I didn't, Mrs Lewes. Instead I ran from him.

Gently, Esme takes her fragile hand in hers.

Now Mrs Lewes turns away from her perusal of the garden, towards Esme.

Her eyes, cloudy with incomprehension the last few times Esme was here, are clear and brightly sparkling.

'Esme,' Mrs Lewes smiles, and Esme feels as if a great weight has lifted off her chest for the first time since she received the call informing her of her father's death.

Here is the woman she loves, returned briefly to her.

A gift.

'Where's your brother?'

She peers behind Esme.

'He got held up. But he'll come to see you soon,' Esme says, resolving to call Andy as soon as she leaves here, ask him to visit.

And then, taking advantage of these precious moments of lucidity, knowing how ephemeral they are, Esme prepares to ask the question she queried of this woman often as a child, only for her lips to disappear, her mouth morphing into a hard, uncompromising line, to be told to, 'Shush, it will upset your father, child; he's suffered enough.'

Half expecting the same now, Esme says, tentatively, 'Mrs Lewes, I'd like to know more about Mum.' *Something. Anything.* 'Would you tell me about her, please?'

Mrs Lewes blanches, visibly. She grasps Esme's hand with surprising strength, her fingernails digging into Esme's palm. 'Rani.' She spits with a vehemence that surprises Esme.

41

RANI

Bletchley, 1941

'It's a bit of a way,' Mr Strong clears his throat, 'at the very edge of the village. But it's a pleasant ride by bike.'

Rani has signed the Official Secrets Act and now Mr Strong is introducing her to her billet.

'I don't have a bike,' she says.

'Ah you can use my wife's.'

'Won't she be needing it?'

'No.'

He turns away, abruptly signalling the end of the conversation.

He might be one of the best codebreakers at Bletchley Park, as endorsed by the commander himself, but he is a very strange man, Rani decides.

* * *

Mr Strong lives in a tall, thin house, a bit similar to himself, in a street of small, squat, two-up two-down houses. It is as if the house is looking down its nose at its neighbours, from its superior vantage point, while also discreetly snooping on them.

The door is opened even as Mr Strong digs around in his pocket for his key, by a large woman, wearing a worn apron and a frown as her gaze, which was indulgent as it settled on Mr Strong, indeed rather motherly, hardens when it lands on Rani.

She sets her hands on her hips, blocking the doorway, left eyebrow raised slightly at Mr Strong, who clears his throat – he does it often, Rani has noticed. A nervous gesture? she wonders. What has he got to be nervous about?

But, as she turns her attention to the stern woman at the door, feeling like a schoolgirl awaiting the results of a particularly challenging exam, she understands why he might be.

They'd walked past the railway station, where she'd arrived just that afternoon, a train pulling out as they approached in a gust of steam and high-pitched whistling, between fields snuggling down for the night under a blanket of shadows, and into Bletchley village, past the pub, vinegar and cheer, and the church, its steeple splintering the gloomy grey awning of sky, past the greengrocer and the butcher and the other pub at the end of the high street, bawdy laughter and a fug of sour smoke.

They turned right at the pub and as they approached the street that led to his house, standoffishly spying on its shorter, stouter neighbours, Mr Strong had spoken at last, after a bout of throat clearing. 'My wife is away.' And, after a pause, 'I left my bike at Bletchley Park to walk with you, show you how to get to and from work. I'll pick it up tomorrow.'

That was the sum total of their conversation.

And although Mr Strong was taciturn to the point of rudeness, Rani found that she didn't mind. There was so much to take in. Her work, what she would be doing at Bletchley Park. Code-breaker! The sheer thrill of it. She was also memorising the route to and from work. And quite apart from that, there was something comfortable about the silence. Mr Strong did not require her to fill it – he seemed content to walk in step beside her. When they'd started off, she'd struggled to keep up with his long strides – although he walked with the weary gait and hunched shoulders of a much older man, he was tall, and the span of one of his steps equalled two of Rani's. But within minutes of setting out, he'd realised she was lagging and had slowed his pace to suit hers.

It had been a long and eventful day. And this walk to her new lodgings, a sombre man keeping her quiet company, daylight fading in streaks of mellow pink at the edge of the fields where they merged into the horizon, was, she mused, just what she hadn't known she needed.

Now, as the scowling woman blocking the doorway huffs, 'Mr Strong, I was not expecting guests,' Rani is all the more grateful for the restoring walk as questions and apprehension ambush her.

What have I got myself into?

Mr Strong seems a shy, retiring sort of man. He told her his wife was away. So who is this woman? She referred to him as Mr Strong so she must be staff. But she is acting very familiar. And why is she regarding Rani in such an unfriendly manner?

The practical side of Rani is already making plans to talk to the commander, ask for somewhere else to stay if it is too awkward here. Surely there have been instances when the Bletchley Park cohort have not been happy with their billets? She does not want to give the impression that she's rigid, unable to adjust, make compromises, so early on, and especially given they are at war. But...

The woman is ranting, 'I've only enough soup for us, and that's meagre enough, what with the rationing.'

Mr Strong goes bright red as he fumbles with his glasses, pushing them further up his nose.

Rani feels sympathy for this strange, reticent man thrust into an awkward situation he, obviously, judging from the rapid clearing of his throat, doesn't know how to deal with.

Finally, he comes up with, 'I'm sure we'll manage, Mrs Lewes.' Then, in a hurry to get the words out so they appear to stumble into each other as they exit his mouth, 'This is Miss Raj. She started work today and the... er...'

More clearing of his throat. Rani is starting to feel sorry for it – it's awfully abused.

'Erm... the commander suggested she billet with us, as I'd... um... mentioned we had a room spare. Doing our bit, you know.'

'You already do your bit.' The woman is unimpressed. 'Working all those long hours.'

'I... It all happened quickly so I... I couldn't get word to you.' He sounds apologetic, his head bowed, as if awaiting punishment.

'Well, there's nothing for it now.' Abruptly, she capitulates, her tone softer, much less strident. 'The soup will have to stretch to three.' She sniffs, her punishing gaze pincering Rani and finding her wanting.

Mr Strong visibly perks up now the woman is agreeable. He turns to Rani, as ever not quite meeting her eye. 'Miss Raj, this is Mrs Lewes, our housekeeper.'

Housekeeper! Tyrant more like, Rani thinks.

The woman is formidable and it appears that she rules this particular roost.

Rani opens her mouth to lie politely that she is pleased to meet her, but before she can...

'Do you speak English?' Mrs Lewes asks, looking Rani up and down.

'Mrs Lewes!' Mr Strong interjects, his colour high.

'Just as well as you,' Rani says sharply, in her most cutting tone of voice. *If not better*, she just about stops herself adding.

Mrs Lewes is unimpressed, sighing as she finally moves away from the doorway and into the house. 'Very well, come in then. I'll heat up the soup.' At the last a truly unnecessary, grudging sigh, in Rani's opinion.

'I'll give you my ration card so we can pool rations,' Rani says, still sharp.

Mr Strong nods gratefully in her general direction, some of the tension leaving his shoulders.

'That will help,' Mrs Lewes concedes in a tone that projects: *it's the very least you can do.*

Rani steps into the dark, narrow passageway which smells strongly of cabbage and leads into what she surmises from the settee and the armoire visible within the slightly open door is the drawing room. She is glad to be indoors at last. She was getting rather cold, standing at the door, both by Mrs Lewes' frosty unwelcome and the evening air that, even though it is only early October, blustered with a quite definite bite, portending an icy winter...

'Who are you?' a little voice suddenly pipes up.

Rani startles, blinking in the direction of the stairs where the voice came from, even as Mrs Lewes and Mr Strong call as one, 'Andrew!'

Mrs Lewes follows up with, 'You're meant to be in bed, young man.'

'I was waiting up for you, Daddy,' the little boy addresses Mr Strong. 'I only pretended to be asleep when Mrs Lewes checked.'

'Now then...' Mrs Lewes begins, hands on hips, voice stern,

but the boy interjects, once again addressing his father, 'You missed our walk.' Although his words are petulant, the little boy delivers them expressionlessly, in a staid monotone, sounding old beyond his years.

'I'm sorry, son, I got held up.' His voice is completely different when talking to his boy, softer, the stiffness quite gone, gentleness in its place.

Rani realises with a pang that he got held up because he'd waited for her long after his shift had finished, and then walked with her instead of cycling home, slowing his pace to match her smaller stride.

'I promise I'll try and make it home in time for our walk, but there will be some days, like today, when I can't.'

The boy nods solemnly, his curls flying, and turns his attention to Rani. 'Who are you?' he asks again.

His tousled head and arms dangle from the banister. His upside-down face peruses her curiously, and in that sombre gaze, she recognises Mr Strong, although *he* has not yet looked at her as directly and unapologetically.

'I'm Rani Raj. And you are... let me guess, Master Upside Down?'

His lips part in the tiniest flicker of a smile. Blink and it's gone, replaced by that serious appraisal. She notices Mr Strong and Mrs Lewes exchange glances.

Although he's once again unsmiling, that sudden, solemn, starburst smile stabbed Rani's heart for it recalled her brother so sharply. It so briefly lit up his face that she could easily have conjured it up – she'd be excused in doing so as this little boy brought to the fore her missing and yearning and ache for the very dear boy she longs to see, even more so now she's denied herself the opportunity, postponed it, *please, not forever.*

Rani pushes away her pain and turns her attention to this child,

Mr Strong's son, who is now righting himself and coming down the stairs, trailing a dog-eared, very chewed bunny, his face too grave for his years; to look at him now, that he smiled at all seems impossible.

He is wearing worn, stripy pyjamas. He is a few years younger than her brother when she saw him last, about five she'd guess.

He holds his hand out formally and says seriously, 'I'm Andrew Strong. I'm nearly five.'

Mrs Lewes snorts, 'You've a way to go yet.'

Rani ignores her, focusing on the child.

'Pleased to make your acquaintance, Master Strong.' Rani takes his precious little hand, so warm and tiny and vulnerable, in her own. 'Can I just say, you're very handsome the right side up.'

Again, that sudden flash of a smile, there, then gone, so quickly it's almost a mirage.

Almost. For the skewering of her heart, the pain and the gratitude to be afforded a visual recollection of her brother, the impression of Arjun's smile in this little boy's, is real.

Again, a quick exchange of looks between Mrs Lewes and Mr Strong.

Now, Mrs Lewes glances from Rani to Andrew and back again.

'Miss Raj will be staying with us for a bit, son,' Mr Strong says. 'Now come on up to bed.'

And once again, Rani notes how tender he is when speaking to his boy, so very different in tone to his shy, abrupt manner with Rani and his deference to Mrs Lewes.

'Is she to be my new mama?' the child queries.

Mr Strong stops, looking dumbfounded, his arm, which he was going to wrap round his son, hovering in the air, suddenly purposeless.

It is Mrs Lewes who breaks the stunned silence. 'What's this silliness, child? You should be in bed. Miss Raj works with your father and needed somewhere to stay. We have a room spare and since it is wartime, we all have to chip in, so she's stopping here for a while, that's all.'

Andrew nods solemnly.

'All right. Up to bed with your father. I'm showing Miss Raj to her room. Goodnight, Andrew, sleep well and no more night-time excursions, mind.' Mrs Lewes remonstrates in a brisk, no-nonsense tone.

'Goodnight, Master Strong,' Rani says to the child.

'Goodnight, Miss Raj.' And with this solemn declaration, the little boy meekly follows his father upstairs.

'This way,' Mrs Lewes sniffs once they've disappeared up the stairs, leading Rani past the drawing room and dining room, both shrouded in darkness, to another set of stairs at the back of the house. 'These lead directly to our rooms. You're opposite me. Once you've freshened up, supper will be ready.'

Rani's first impression was right. This matronly woman clearly rules this particular roost with an iron fist.

* * *

Her room is one of the two in the attic. Comfortably furnished. Self-sufficient. The bed surprisingly comfortable.

'If you need anything, I'm in here,' Mrs Lewes says, knocking on the door of the room opposite, and this time, Rani can see she actually means it.

She is warmer towards Rani now. Somewhere since their frosty introduction in the doorway, there has been a noticeable thawing of her cold, unimpressed reception of Rani; Rani suspects it is to do with Andrew.

Supper is a silent affair, which suits Rani just fine. She's too tired to make conversation, the events of the day having caught up with her and work to look forward to tomorrow.

The soup is nothing to write home about. There is, as Mrs Lewes warned, precious little of it.

Mr Strong, who came down after putting his son to bed around the same time as Rani, silently wolfs his down, Mrs Lewes watching indulgently.

'That was delicious, thank you, Mrs Lewes,' he says when he's finished every last drop and Mrs Lewes beams.

And to Rani, politely, 'Goodnight, Miss Raj.'

'Goodnight.'

As she drifts off to sleep, Rani wonders what exactly the setup here is with her taciturn colleague, his grave child, his housekeeper who acts nothing like a servant and everything like his mother and his son's grandmother, and his wife, who is away.

42

RANI

The next morning, when Rani comes down to a grey morning, foggy with a nippy chill – but she's ready to face it and her first day at work, having slept surprisingly well – Mrs Lewes is bustling about the kitchen. It is warm and cosily inviting and smells fragrant enough, of spiced oatmeal but even this can't quite disperse the underlying miasma of cabbage that permeates the house.

'Ah, Miss Raj, good morning. Do sit down.' Mrs Lewes even goes so far as to offer Rani a smile as she gestures at one of the stools at the table with a gloopy ladle.

This woman is an entirely different being to the ogre who scowled at her while barring entry into the house the previous evening.

She places a bowl of watery porridge and a mug of chicory tea in front of Rani, talking all the while. 'Mr Strong has already left as he is walking to work. He said you can use his wife's bike.' She sniffs disapprovingly at the last and Rani isn't sure if it is directed at Mrs Strong or at Rani for borrowing her bike. 'He's made sure to check it's in order. You will find it propped up against the wall just outside.'

'That's very kind of him. I'll be sure to thank Mrs Strong for the loan of her bike too when she gets back. And until then, I'll take good care of it.'

Mrs Lewes' demeanour changes, her lips disappearing completely as she frowns.

What a moody so and so, Rani thinks. But out loud, she says, meekly, 'Thanks for breakfast.' Hating herself a little for pandering to this woman.

But Mrs Lewes is unbending, her voice tight as she says, stiffly, 'Eat up. You better leave soon if you're to be on time for the 8 o'clock watch.'

Rani must look as puzzled as she feels, for Mrs Lewes says, her voice marginally less harsh, 'You do know they call the shifts watches at Bletchley Park, don't you?' And, shaking her head, as she realises Rani doesn't know, churning the porridge on the stove with more force than necessary, 'Secrecy is all well and good but it is taking it a bit far if the people they've got working there don't know anything.'

Rani opens her mouth to protest that she's not even properly started yet, but Mrs Lewes beats her to it, 'Go on, finish up. Mr Strong usually leaves at seven-thirty sharp and he's a strong cyclist. It's a quarter past already.'

'Yes,' Rani agrees, spooning porridge into her mouth, stopping herself just in time from adding 'ma'am', wondering what it is about this woman that inspires instant obedience, from Mr Strong, his son, even herself. Is it the fact that she's bossier than Rani's tutors at Cambridge?

There's a patter of little feet down the stairs, and soon enough, a tousled head appears. Andrew, rubbing sleep from his eyes, one hand clutching the much-abused bunny with the chewed ears. He comes to a stop upon seeing Rani, suddenly shy, bringing the raggedy rabbit up to his face and peering at her from behind its ineffectual camouflage.

'Good morning, Master Strong. Did you sleep well?' she asks.

Sombre eyes regard her from behind the floppy rabbit's dirty, bedraggled body, even as he nods silently.

'Come on then, child, sit down,' Mrs Lewes says. Her voice is stern but eyes soft as she places a bowl of porridge in front of the boy.

'Porridge again!' He sighs heavily.

'Now then, eat it all up if you want to grow tall like your father,' Mrs Lewes pats his head fondly.

'I'm already Strong,' he says, quite seriously.

Rani suppresses a smile while Mrs Lewes tuts, 'Don't be cheeky now.'

The boy toys with his porridge.

Rani spoons the last of hers into her mouth, endures the tea, cold now, gulping it down like punishment, and says, as she takes her bowl and cup to the sink, 'Right, I'm off to work. Goodbye, Mrs Lewes, Master Strong.'

'You may call me Andrew,' he says shyly.

She'd like to ask him to call her Rani in return – she'd quite like that – but she knows, intuitively, that Mrs Lewes would disapprove. And in this household, she's already learned, although she's hardly been here two minutes, Mrs Lewes' word is law. And so she says instead, with a warm smile, 'Thank you, Andrew, I will.'

He regards her seriously, no hint of a smile.

* * *

The bike is propped up against the wall outside the kitchen window, just as Mrs Lewes said. The seat is perfectly matched to her height – she and the elusive Mrs Strong must be exactly the same size. Or Mr Strong must have estimated and adjusted the seat to suit Rani, which is thoughtful and kind of him, but which, now she has spent some time with him, Rani muses, is something he *would* do. He is shy and quiet, but empathic, she noted, judging by how he was yesterday in the face of Mrs Lewes' recalcitrance, not wanting to hurt or upset anyone, hoping for the best outcome for all.

As she straddles the bike, she is afforded a glimpse into the kitchen, through the window, right in time to see Andrew jump off the table and come to the window, dragging his bunny by the ears, even as he mouths something at her.

She can't hear what he's saying.

She will likely be late – not a good look on her first proper day – if she doesn't leave right away; it is going on 7.30 a.m. But Andrew looks so forlorn, nose pressed to the pane. He reminds her of her brother, whom she misses with all her heart, who had held on to her and cried, 'Didi, please don't go.'

And so, she gets off the bike, leans it against the wall again, goes up to the door, calls, 'Is something the matter, Andrew?'

His eyes are large and wet as he says, 'That's my mummy's bike. She's dead.'

'Oh.' Rani is confused. She's sure Mr Strong said his wife was away. Her gaze meets Mrs Lewes' over the boy's head. Her eyes radiate caution and warning even as she frantically wrings the tea towel she holds in her hands. The woman Rani had down as indomitable looks upset as she shakes her head ever so slightly over the child's tousled mop.

What's the story here? Rani wonders. *Why does the boy think his mother is dead if she isn't? Why do they allow him to think so?*

'That's why Mrs Lewes is staying with us. To look after me when Daddy is working. Mr Lewes died too in the other war,' Andrew says earnestly. 'But I suppose you can use Mummy's bike as she doesn't need it any more.' His eyes shining with the sheen of tears.

'Thank you, Andrew. I will take good care of it, I promise,' Rani says, her heart going out to the child.

Andrew nods in that serious way of his, so like his father.

Mrs Lewes lays a hand on the boy's shoulder. 'Come on in, my dear, your porridge is getting cold.' Her voice as gentle as Rani has heard it. 'And Miss Raj is going to be late.'

The boy waves from the doorway, clutching his sorry rabbit with the stuffing hugged to rags, until she is out of sight. Rani cycles furiously even as she ponders the mystery of this cobbled-together family into which she has arrived, the image of the child's liquid eyes chasing her all the way to Bletchley Park.

43

RANI

Rani makes it to Bletchley Park with a few minutes to spare, albeit in a dishevelled state as she's pedalled frantically and without pause, as if Hitler himself is after her. Instead of flinging her bike into the pile by the door like she sees others doing, she props it carefully against the wall, mindful of her promise to a little boy mourning his mother.

She's breathless by the time she arrives at Dilly's cottage, where she's been assigned, at the dot of eight.

Dilly is bespectacled, giving him an owlish look.

'You're the new girl,' he says, looking briefly, absently at her, but it is obvious that his mind is elsewhere. 'Good, good. Ursula here will show you the ropes.'

The tall, beautiful blonde beside Dilly tuts. 'I'm Harriet, Dilly.'

'Sorry, my dear.' Dilly mumbles, wandering away, his attention on the piece of paper he's peering at.

'He's like this much of the time,' Harriet sighs. 'Too busy solving complex problems in his head to pay attention to mundane things. But I prefer this to his temper tantrums.'

'Oh?'

'Don't look so afraid; they don't last long. He has tantrums at any change of routine. But he is also fiercely intelligent. What we do here is hugely important, as I'm sure you know. So we forgive him anything. But his wife must have the patience of a saint, is all I can say.' Harriet shrugs and grins.

The cottage is near the stables, across the courtyard from the main house. It is, in actual fact, a series of interlinked rooms, functional and messy, windows with blackout curtains, basic desks and chairs and filing cabinets overflowing with books, machines, files. Papers piled haphazardly everywhere, even on the floor, giving an impression of chaotic urgency.

It is busy, machines clanking, a host of women, heads down, fingers flying as they clatter away on typewriters, some with ink-stained fingers jotting things down. The scent of cigar smoke and industry.

'Our job,' Harriet says, 'is to decrypt the fiendishly difficult German Enigma machine encrypted messages. Before, we would do it all ourselves, which was incredibly painstaking work – it is painstaking now too of course but it was harder before the bombes. At least now the bombes help reveal the possible Enigma settings used to decipher a message, which gives us a head start, given we've only twenty-four hours to break the code.'

Bombs? Enigma? Racing against time to break code? Rani is as intrigued as she is puzzled. But, again as when the commander briefly gave her a short overview, she is beginning to see why her chess skills might come in handy.

Harriet is saying, 'Enigma uses rotors to scramble messages into unintelligible cyphertext. The standard three rotor Enigma machine is capable of producing 159 million million million combinations of ciphers,' Harriet sighs. 'And each one of the machine's possible combinations generates completely different cyphertext. Our challenge is to find the key settings for each network – what makes it even more complicated is that they are reset at midnight every day.'

'Oh,' is all Rani can think to say, the phrase '159 million million million combinations' reverberating in her mind.

'Alan Turing, whom we've nicknamed the "Prof" and who is head of Hut 8...' Harriet pauses. Then, 'You've seen the huts, haven't you, dotted about the grounds?'

'Yes.'

'Each has a function. Hut 4 and Hut 8 are connected and so are Huts 3 and 6. I'm assuming the huts are similar to our cottage – comprising a central passageway and rooms branching off it. That's as much as I know. We're not supposed to discuss what we do outside our respective cottages or huts; you know that, don't you?'

'I do.'

'Of course you do. You signed the Official Secrets Act like all of us. I'm such a dolt sometimes,' Harriet smacks her forehead. She's so chatty and friendly – Rani can see why Dilly assigned her to show Rani around. But Rani wishes she wouldn't jump around from one topic to another quite so; she's committing all the information to memory in neat little boxes as is her way and it makes processing it all something of a challenge. Although from the sounds of it, work is going to be even more of a challenge, Rani thinks, feeling a flare of excitement ignite in her heart. She's definitely up for it.

Harriet points to a huge, noisy machine. A clique of men, interspersed with an odd woman or two, are collected beside it, noting something. Mr Strong is among them and as Rani and Harriet pass, he nods at Rani without quite meeting her gaze.

'This is one of the "bombes",' yells Harriet above the whirring and clanking of the rotors on the machine. 'Spelled with an e at the end and so not to be confused with the dreaded death and mayhem causing cargo ambushing London nearly every night for the past many months of war. There are several of these bombes dotted around Bletchley Park. They're monstrously huge, aren't they? But they do the job, mostly, give us a head start with the code. Thanks to these, we're able to decode many of the messages and pass on the intelligence with enough time for it to be acted upon. Stella, who's billeted with me, works in Hut 11 operating those monstrous machines. She's not quite sure what they do and I can't tell her, which is all for the best of course. Careless talk costs lives. Anyway, she's a little thing, like you, and not tall enough to reach the top of the machine; she has to stand on a plank of wood to operate it! She was most upset the other day for she lost her only lipstick, a gift from her beau, from before the war, down the side of one of the machines. Gone, *poof*. And lipsticks are like gold dust now, what with rationing and shortages.' Harriet giggles, even as she purses her bright-red lips into a cherry bow. 'I'll let you in on a secret,' she points to her lips. 'Beetroot. I swear by it. Keep one in my pocket at all times.'

Ah that explains the sweet, slightly organic scent wafting from Harriet.

'One must look good, to boost morale, you know, especially one's own.' Harriet winks. Then, 'But where was I? Ah yes, the bombes were invented by Alan Turing, *Prof*. You'll see him around, on his bike, if you haven't already. He's hard to miss, never without his gas mask. I doubt I'd recognise him if I were to see him without it.'

'It must be awfully uncomfortable. Why does he do it?' Rani asks, curious.

'The gas mask apparently helps with his breathing. He is afflicted by asthma, you see. But you will soon learn that there's usually no rhyme or reason for some of the things our colleagues do. Codebreakers are an eccentric lot, apart from yours truly, of course.' She giggles again, infectious mirth.

Rani has to agree about codebreakers being eccentric, taciturn Mr Strong, who shies away from eye contact, coming to mind.

'Prof apparently chains his mug to the wall, worried someone will steal it,' Harriet is saying. 'Edna, who works in his hut, said that he does take that horrid gas mask he's never without off once inside, but a fat lot of good it does as he never looks anyone in the eye.'

Just like Mr Strong, Rani thinks.

'And then there's our Dilly,' Harriet's voice fond even as she sighs. It's like she's talking about her favourite uncle. 'Never a dull day with Dilly, that much I can assure you. He calls us all by our first names, but invariably mixes us up. And well... you'll never believe what happened just yesterday!'

'What happened?' Rani asks dutifully.

'Well, the code has been especially difficult to crack these last few days, no cillies, no give at all. The Germans are upping their game.'

'Cillies?'

'Ah, you'll soon learn all the terms. And you'll be grateful for cillies, I can tell you that much. They are a boon for us codebreakers.' And noting the puzzled frown still gracing Rani's face, Harriet chuckles. 'Cillies are the predictable message keys, repeated or left unchanged from one message to the next. We look out for them in the coded messages and once crossed out, the rest of the message is easier to break. Well...' Harriet rolls her eyes, 'easier to try to break if you see what I mean given the 159 million million million possible combinations. It's just so ridiculously complex. Just as you think you've got it, they change it, make it more difficult. And their changing over of the keys at midnight doesn't help either. They're always one step ahead. Even Turing's bombes are struggling. If it wasn't for the cribs, we'd have no chance at all. Although Dilly would rather we not rely on either cillies or cribs...'

'Cribs?' Rani frowns, scrambling to set it all to memory. She recalls hearing the word bandied about the previous day and wondering about it.

Harriet laughs. 'You'll get there, I promise. Cribs are patterns to intercepted messages but they are notoriously difficult to spot and have stumped experienced codebreakers.'

'Is *anything* about the job easy?' Rani jokes.

'No,' Harriet is quite serious. 'This is why it requires the concentrated efforts of the best minds in the country, perhaps the world. But while it's often frustrating and no two days are the same, when we do break the code and prevent a German offensive just in time, that's quite something. What we do makes a real difference, never forget.' And now she smiles. 'Now, I was telling you about what Dilly did last night but got side-tracked. As I said, the code has been especially difficult lately but Dilly thought he was nearly there and so, rather than waste time going home, he decided to stay over at Bletchley Park Manor, share with some of the other codebreakers from the cottage billeted there. Talking of eccentricities, Dilly believes steam and soap help focus his brain, aid it to arrive at connections not immediately obvious, so, when late last night, the code was still proving elusive, he said he'd take a bath after supper.' A chuckle in Harriet's voice. 'The others were waiting for him to join them at cards, make up the four. But when an hour had passed...'

'An hour?' Rani is surprised.

'They were worried then,' Harriet's voice grave. 'You see, he has been looking peaky lately. Rumour is that he's seriously ill but won't stop working.'

She pauses. Rani leans closer, holding her breath. This woman does know how to tell a story.

Finally... 'They knocked on his door.'

Another pause.

Rani is on tenterhooks.

'What happened next?' she asks.

'They knocked again. No reply.'

'Oh.'

'Then they looked at each other and understood that they were all thinking the same thing.' Harriet narrates as if she was right there while all of this was taking place.

'And what was that?' Rani whispers, not knowing why she's doing so.

'They broke into his rooms.' Harriet says, matter-of-fact.

'They *what*?'

Harriet's eyes twinkling. 'They broke the door down. It's not been fixed yet. If you go upstairs in the manor, into the rooms reserved as billets, you'll find one of them without a door. More important things to do, a war to win, you know?'

Rani couldn't care less about the door. 'What happened next?' she asks.

'Dilly was most annoyed. And not because of no longer having a functioning door. "I say, I was just arriving at the answer. My mind was about to make the connection," he yelled, stark naked.' Harriet, clocking the blush Rani can't keep from staining her face, grins cheekily. 'My apologies, but I have it on very good authority that this is how it was. Dripping soapy water all over the floor, Dilly pointed at the hole where the door once stood, asking the interlopers to leave. And then he climbed back in the bath, oblivious to the fact that the water was quite cold.'

Harriet pauses, smiling at Rani, 'So now you've been introduced to the codebreakers, foibles and all, let me tell you a bit more about what you're going to be doing.'

'Yes please,' Rani says.

'Well, the intercepted messages all have similar formats: letters, followed by numbers, followed by letters. Now we've also noticed that multiple messages have the same few first set of letters; we've ascertained that they are means of distinguishing where they came from, so, for example, a batch of messages with the same initial set of letters came from the same operator. The set of numbers is the time they were jotted down. Now, if we also find cribs and cillies, that takes us even closer to solving the code, do you see?'

Rani nods eagerly.

'That's about it then. The rest is just hard graft. So, are you ready to get to work?'

'As I'll ever be.'

'That's the spirit, my dear.' Harriet beams.

And so begins Rani's foray into codebreaking.

As she works, the sounds of machines whirring, typewriters clacking, codebreakers conferring, the kettle whistling, the giggles and chatter over weak cups of tea, ducks quacking outside her window, the wind soughing through the trees, her worries about whether Baba will accept her need to do her bit, allow her back into the fold on her terms, her guilt with regards to Prasad and Mama, her missing Mama and Arjun with an ache that is now part of her, a yawning wound that bleeds constantly, persistently, her concern for Gertie's safety, fade away, her mind grappling with complex code, wondering if this is the message that will, when decoded, change the course of the war, turn its tide.

It is so very exciting, like chess or a particularly challenging crossword but with very high stakes, her brain completely engaged.

Being here is a revelation. It is illuminating, invigorating, being within touching distance of making history, breaking Hitler. Supremely, exquisitely thrilling.

It is like those heady times with her father when he would teach her maths, philosophy, Mandarin, a whole new world unfolding, beautiful, mysterious, wondrous, hers for the discovering.

44

RANI

That evening, when she gets back from work, Mr Strong is already home and sitting at the kitchen table with his son, Mrs Lewes bustling about getting supper ready.

Andrew, his little face serious, waves earnestly from the window, with the hand clutching the raggedy rabbit, chewed ears bobbing, as she rests the bike against the wall, beside Mr Strong's.

As she gets in the front door, Mrs Lewes calls hello, a real improvement on the previous evening, when she'd barred Rani's way in.

The house smells of dough with just a hint of cabbage.

Rani pops her head in the kitchen, 'Hello everyone.'

Andrew says solemnly, 'Good evening, Miss Raj. Daddy reached home before you.'

'Yes, he must be a strong cyclist, unlike me. I'm only just passable, I'm afraid.'

'He is,' Andrew agrees. 'And I will be too when I'm grown up.'

Mr Strong smiles at his son, and Rani feels a stab right at the centre of her heart at the expression on his face, unguarded for the first time since she's met him: it is that of almost painful love.

He looks up, catches her watching, flushes with colour, his gaze flustering as he glances away, down at his hands.

'You will be so only if you eat all your supper,' Mrs Lewes says, waving her oven glove at Andrew, her smile belying the stern nature of her words. And, to Rani, 'If you'd like to freshen up, Miss Raj, supper will be ready in half an hour.'

Supper is potato pie – not that much different from Cambridge, the travails of rationing – but to her credit, Mrs Lewes has tried, with the addition of cabbage and liberal seasoning of pepper, to add some flavour to the stodgy potato.

It is a quiet affair. Just the gentle song of cutlery on plates.

But, as she has observed when with Mr Strong thus far, it isn't uncomfortable.

Like Mr Strong, his son too prefers silence, it appears. But it is a soothing silence, not a seething one.

It is Mrs Lewes who queries, 'So then, how was your first day, Miss Raj?'

Andrew looks up at her with his serious gaze. So does his father.

'It was good. I like the work.' She really, really does. It taxes her brain. She loves the challenge of it, enjoys working with the brightest minds in England and the world, towards a common goal, knowing she's doing something productive that will change the course of the war. And it's not only the work. It seems very social too, from what she's seen so far of the manor, the cottage, the grounds. It thrills her to be one of the posse of predominantly young people lounging by the lake, seemingly unmindful of the weather, feeding crumbs to the ducks, joshing each other, eating lunch on the grounds followed by a game of rounders. Apart from the very serious nature of the work, it feels like an extension of university life. She even saw a notice about a tennis party.

'Very well. I know you can't say any more than that,' Mrs Lewes nods, collecting the plates.

'Yes,' Andrew says gravely. 'It's top secret.'

'That it is,' Rani agrees.

'If you say anything, you will be shot.'

She smiles at that. 'Well, not quite. But even though your daddy and I are working in the same room, it's best if we don't talk to each other about what we're doing. It's that secret.'

'Oh.' Each of his eyes as wide as his supper plate. 'One day, I'm going to do top-secret work like you and Daddy, Miss Raj.'

When she looks across at Mr Strong, he is looking at his son with that same expression of painful, overwhelming love as before. It is intensely personal – he must not be aware of it, for the man is usually so guarded; he keeps his emotions so tightly reined in. She looks away before he catches her watching again. A pang in her heart for this reserved man and his serious son whom he appears to care for so very much.

'Come on then, son,' he says gently, his voice different, the timbre of it softer when conversing with his child. 'Let's go for our walk.'

The boy slides off his chair, which is bolstered by pillows so he can sit at the table, his palm dwarfed by his father's, the other holding the ubiquitous bunny.

Mrs Lewes observes Rani looking at it as they walk away, tall father and small son.

'His mother gave it to him. He's never without it. Needs it to sleep.' She sighs heavily, the dishes clattering as she scrubs them.

Rani stands beside her, drying without being asked, watching through the window as father and son disappear down the street, the evening sky pinkish grey skeined with clouds, swallows fluttering restlessly on rooftops, chimneys billowing navy balloons of smoke, trees dancing in the nippy, apple-scented breeze.

'They go every day. Up to the meadow and back. A ritual established after...' She sighs again deeply, her hands immersed in soapy water. 'Mr Strong doesn't like to talk about it and won't enlighten you so I'd better since you're staying here for the time being.'

She takes a breath even as Rani holds hers.

'He married a flighty girl. I don't quite know what she saw in him myself. She didn't much care for Andrew – he was an inconvenience if anything. She was bored. Wanted fun. Even with a war on. Mr Strong was too serious for her, Andrew an encumbrance. She found someone to have fun with. An American at the embassy. Was going on for a while I suppose, even before they came here. Their marriage had ticked along while they were in London. It was when they moved here that it went wrong. She was too far away you see, from the restaurants, the parties, from her lover. Domesticity was not for her. She upped and left one day. Just like that. Only a small note to say she was leaving and never coming back.'

Ah. This is why Mr Strong was so short when he said his wife was away. His voice discouraging further comment as he turned away from Rani. It also explains...

'The spare room. My room...'

'Mr Strong was occupying it. Nominally. He spent almost all of his time, when not working, in Andrew's room, overcompensating for the fact that the poor child's mother ignored him.' Mrs Lewes takes a deep breath. 'They took separate rooms after Andrew was born.' She sniffs.

Rani experiences another sharp lance of pain for her quiet colleague and his little cherub. 'But Andrew...'

'Andrew.' Once again, Mrs Lewes sighs deeply, looking out the window at nothing at all, her eyes glazed over, hands suds deep in the now cold water. 'He hasn't laughed since his mother left. Smiles only very rarely.'

Ah. Now she understands the look that had passed between Mrs Lewes and Mr Strong when Andrew smiled – very fleetingly – at Rani's quip last night. Why Mrs Lewes' demeanour towards her had changed between her cold introduction and showing Rani to her room.

It's obvious this woman beside her cares very much for Mr Strong and his son, and is very protective of them. And on the heels of this thought, she recalls what the child had said to her this morning when she borrowed his mother's bike, how Mrs Lewes' expression had changed from stern to pleading silently with Rani...

'Andrew said that...'

'He assumed she was dead.' Mrs Lewes sniffs again. 'And Mr Strong... he doesn't like to talk about it. His way of dealing with it is to ignore it.'

'So Andrew thinks she is dead?'

Mrs Lewes' silence was Rani's answer.

'But...'

'She's not coming back. She doesn't want the child. She made it clear in her note. She's in America. Gone for good.'

'Ah.'

Between them, they've cleared up. The plates are clean. Put away.

'You're a bit of all right,' Mrs Lewes remarks.

'You're not too bad yourself,' Rani ventures.

Mrs Lewes laughs, a surprisingly dirty guffaw from the staid, matronly woman.

By the time Andrew and Mr Strong return from their walk, Mrs Lewes and Rani are tentative friends.

45

ESME

'Rani?' Esme is puzzled. Has she lost Mrs Lewes to the wandering pathways of her broken mind?

But the old woman's eyes are sharp, her gaze boring into Esme's.

'Who's Rani, Mrs Lewes?'

'Your mum.'

'Wha...'

'She broke William. Destroyed him. Finished what the other one had started.'

Other one? Esme barely has time to ponder – Mrs Lewes isn't finished.

'He never recovered from her perfidy. Never trusted anyone again,' Mrs Lewes lobs each word with fiery force. 'She thought her letter would be enough. As if... as if *anything* would excuse what she did.'

She sounds so lucid. Her eyes very clear, not even slightly milky with confusion like they usually are. And at least some of what she says makes sense.

'Her letter?' Esme asks, going along with her.

'He couldn't bear to keep it. Wouldn't throw it away either. He gave it to me for safekeeping.'

'Where is it, Mrs Lewes?'

'Where is what, dear?'

Oh no. Has Esme lost her? Was she ever *with* her? What she's said might all be nonsense. And yet... in a strange way, it rings true. Her father was a broken man. He had issues and she's always suspected it was to do with Mum. Rani? The name sounds so exotic.

And Mrs Lewes said something about 'the other one'. Is there some truth to what Esme has always suspected but never acknowledged: that she and her brother might be half-siblings? People are taken aback when they find out Andy and Esme are related: 'But you don't look anything alike!'

This is true. Esme is dark, Andy fair. Andy tall, Esme not. Esme could pass for mixed race – so it wouldn't surprise her if her mother, Rani, if Mrs Lewes is to be believed, wasn't white. But Andy appears, looks and build wise to be from pure English stock through and through.

Now she's started, Esme needs to get to the bottom of this. If there is a letter, that's *something*. And so she says, 'Rani's letter.'

'Ah, that letter.' Again, anger thrumming through Mrs Lewes' aged voice, fiery red. 'In my Bible. I keep it with the Ten Commandments. Thou shalt not lie. Ha!'

'Mrs Lewes, can I have a look at it, please?'

'Have a look at what?' Her eyes clouding over. Confusion colouring them murky grey.

'Rani's letter,' Esme tries.

'What are you talking about? Who are you?' She's getting agitated now.

Then the nurse who brought Esme over is there, kneeling beside Mrs Lewes. Placating her with soothing murmurs, 'Now, Mrs Lewes, shall we go back to your room? It's time for your medicine.'

And with that, Esme is dismissed.

46

RANI

Bletchley, 1941

When Rani gets home at the end of her second week at work – how quickly she's started to think of the Strong residence as home – Mr Strong says, 'A letter for you, Miss Raj. It was redirected to your billet here from the London PO Box where all the Bletchley mail goes.'

Gertie, she thinks, heart blooming. At last, correspondence from her friend. Hopefully containing an address where she can write to – a PO Box that gives nothing away, like her own, Rani suspects, but she doesn't care. It's a means to connect with her friend.

How she's missed her!

Rani imagines the letter she would write Gertie:

My dear friend, I'll end up saying nothing much at all, because of the need for secrecy at all times and this letter from you will also be chock-full of cheery platitudes and not much else no doubt. But if I could talk freely, my dear friend, I'd have so much to tell you!

I work at Dilly's cottage – he's so intensely bright, it's such a privi-

lege to work with him. He's prone to temper tantrums when things don't go his way, but he's so inspiring, Gertie. He's ill, we can all see it, but his devotion to work is paramount. He's an example to us all.

The other codebreaker whom I really admire is the man I am billeted with: Mr Strong. He's a quiet, shy man – he's yet to make proper eye contact with me – but he's so very good at work. Focused and just brilliant. One of the fastest codebreakers around and he's known to solve code without the aid of cillies and cribs even.

For instance, today, one of our fellow codebreakers complained, 'None of my messages have cillies. Don't tell me the Germans have finally cottoned on!' And to the room in general, 'Do any of your messages have cillies?'

'Mine do,' someone called from the other side of the cottage.

'That's capital. We've a chance yet. And mine I'll just hand to Strong. He'll break it. He's our secret weapon.'

Mr Strong blushed but he said, 'Let me have a look.'

'We've more than a chance, cillies or not,' Dilly growled.

'But the cillies help.'

Scowl darkening, Dilly mumbled, 'They do, for now. But the Germans will realise soon enough about the predictable message keys, repeated or left unchanged from one message to the next.'

So that's what cillies are if you were wondering, Gertie.

Dilly was saying to the room, 'I know we often try cillies when looking for the day's Enigma settings, and they prove extremely useful. But we should also learn to do without them, try not to rely on them quite so. We should all aim to be like Strong.'

Mr Strong blushed again even as he cleared his throat and said, 'Er... I think I've found the pattern to this one.'

And he had, without the aid of cillies too!

Like I said, an inspiring man.

Gertie, I'm only talking to you in my head so I might as well throw caution to the wind and tell all. Women outnumber men three to one here. *There are two distinct communities. The debs: sisters and cousins and friends of the Oxford and Cambridge dons and graduates – I suppose I'm one of these – and the girls, eager to do their bit, recruited from the WRNS, the WAAF and the ATS. We all get on well enough, as we all are working towards a common goal and since none of us can talk about the work we do, we find other things to natter about. Gossip, mostly, of which there is plenty, I tell you.*

For instance, this is what happened yesterday.

We were all working frantically – a 'jumbo rush' job had come in, which meant absolutely urgent, no one to do anything else until this was done – when there was a huge outcry outside.

A loud splash, followed by human exclamations and loud honks from startled, outraged geese and ducks.

'I say!' came the alarmed shout. 'Someone's gone into the lake.'

Everyone breathlessly rushed outside, arm in arm.

I couldn't get to see much to be honest. I'm short, as you know, and there were all these tall heads craning in front of me. Even Harriet, standing next to me, who I'm close to but not as much as you, don't fret, who's at least a head taller than me, couldn't make out what was going on. By the time we got closer, the crowd was dispersing and there was nothing to see.

I learned what had happened from the feverishly circulating gossip, once we were back at our desks.

'Mr Wilson, one of the senior codebreakers from Hut 8...'

'Is he the one with the colourful bow ties and hair as long as a girl's?'

'The very one. You can't miss him. Anyway, he was all het up; he's as much of a one for losing his cool as Dilly, Sarah who's worked with both, says. He threw a bottle of ink at her once – she ducked just in time, but they couldn't get the ink stain off the wall.'

'Oh my!'

'She swears it changes shape every day.'

'But why did Mr Wilson go in the lake just now?'

'Ah, he was in a state and some of the others said they'd dunk him in the lake, to which he replied, "I'll do it myself!" And he did! Clothes and all! Set the geese aflapping!'

Giggles all round. Then, sobering, 'The others jumped in after him, dragging him out wet, bedraggled and limp, all his blustering washed right out of him. He's been ever so down. They say he might have, you know...' voice lowered to a whisper, so we all had to angle forward, the better to hear, '...tried to kill himself.'

Gasps all round.

I stabbed the point of my pencil into the soft flesh of my palm to stop my own gasp escaping, Gertie.

'The pressure got to him. It's so intense, isn't it, what we're doing...?'

'What is it we're doing exactly?'

More giggles.

'Get to it, team, jumbo rush job, no time to waste.' Dilly.

And with that, we got to work.

Not a very nice story I know, Gertie, but it is how we cope, through camaraderie, impromptu tennis matches when the weather cooperates. Yes, tennis, me! I'm getting rather good at it, and only a fortnight in, too. When we meet next, I'll be able to beat you at it! Jokes aside, we mainly cope by trying to make light of things. Otherwise it's all too easy, like with poor Mr Wilson, for the pressure to get to us.

When I first arrived and saw all these young people laughing, chatting, smoking, taking lunch and playing tennis and rounders and winding the birds up by the lake, on the lawns, even in frosty autumn, I wondered about the jovial, university-like atmosphere, when there was a war on and supposedly very important work going on here. Now I understand. The work is so very intense that if we didn't have these moments of light-heartedness, we'd all go crazy. I'm sure you understand. It must be the same for you too...

But having said that, I do absolutely love the work. It challenges and invigorates me. They were spot on, assigning me to Bletchley Park.

And I have absolutely no doubt you're being an excellent spy, my friend. But promise me you're not taking unnecessary risks. Please do keep safe...

Oh Gertie, I do so wish we could talk. Really talk like we used to at Cambridge long into the night, the darkness heavy with our secrets, while we ourselves were lighter, unburdened, cushioned by the warmth of friendship.

Those were the days...

'Miss Raj?' Mr Strong nudges gently.

Rani blinks, coming out of her head and back into the present.

It's been an eventful few days and she loves the work. The buzz she gets when trying to find a pattern to the code – there's nothing quite like it.

But she finds she also likes and looks forward to returning to the billet with the cobbled-together family of which she's very much becoming a part, serious little Andrew, who reminds her of the brother she misses, claiming a piece of her heart.

Now his reserved father is handing her the letter which she's sure is from her friend.

'I will write as soon as I'm able,' Gertie had promised during their last conversation when she shared that she was to be a spy.

And as soon as Rani was told where letters to her were to be addressed, she'd posted two letters herself with the details, one to her family and one to Gertie, care of the Foreign Office, hoping they'd forward it on to her, wherever she was, her dear, dear friend.

'My parents think I'm with the Foreign Office. They're not wrong. It's not my fault they've assumed I've a safe, sit-down job,'

Gertie had said that last morning before they went their separate ways.

'But is it fair on them, Gertie, when their son is already missing?' Gertie and her family had only recently heard that Gertie's older brother was missing in action.

Gertie's eyes clouded at the mention of her brother.

'But you understand, don't you, Rani, that I *have* to do this, for him and all our brave lost. And in his case, there's some hope. He's only missing, not...' She couldn't go on.

'You do know the chances of you finding him while on one of your missions are minuscule?' Rani said gently.

'Of course. I completed the supposedly fiendishly difficult maths tripos, you know,' Gertie joked but in her raw eyes, Rani read the truth: Gertie's defiant hope of finding her brother no matter the odds stacked against her.

Rani has not heard from her friend since. But if she has written a letter, does that mean she is back home? If so, Rani wonders if they can meet – she has the day off on Sunday. She was planning to catch up on sleep – the work is rewarding but the shifts long. They take it out of her. In any case, if Gertie is back, she can travel up to London on the train and meet her friend. They will carefully skirt around what they are doing – both not allowed to share details. They will instead talk cheerily of nothing of any consequence and simply enjoy each other's company. Perhaps they'll have coffee at Lyons, if one is still standing, given the bombing London has endured. It's Gertie's favourite, although the coffee will most likely be made with chicory and powdered milk. And who knows if there will be cake? But, if, by some miracle there *is* – and here Rani's mouth waters – well, then they deserve to treat themselves to it. No matter if it isn't to pre-wartime standards; it will still be heaven after Mrs Lewes' 'puddings' bulked up with potato which Rani eats dutifully even though they cause her stomach to spasm during the night.

But, to Rani's fantasy...

She and Gertie will savour each moment in the other's company, not knowing when they will next see the other.

All these thoughts skitter through her head as she reaches for the letter.

* * *

When she sees the Indian stamps, she pauses, her hand trembling as she clutches this communication from her family to her chest.

'Are you all right?' Mr Strong is moved to ask.

She can only barely manage a nod before she escapes upstairs.

Once in her room, she shuts the door and sits on the bed, taking several deep breaths.

Gently, she strokes the envelope. And, in a moment of weakness, giving in to the strange but seemingly uncontrollable impulse, she smells it, wondering if it carries the scent of India.

Bizarrely, she thinks she detects the spice and baked earth scent that is uniquely India, and breathes deeply of it even as she chides herself for her foolishness.

As she carefully opens the flap and takes out the paper inside, embossed with her father's seal, she fancies she can smell the perfume of rosewater and jasmine.

Her father's missive is short and to the point.

Rani,

She notes the lack of endearment and it hurts even though she was expecting it.

You've stayed on in a war-torn country putting yourself wilfully in danger to pack parachutes for airmen?

Rani can sense her father's incredulous anger coming off the page in waves. She could not tell her family the truth about what she is doing. She will never be able to tell them or anyone at all, having signed the Official Secrets Act. She recalls what the commander said, as she was putting pen to paper: 'This contract is binding. You won't tell anyone ever. Not your family, not anyone. Are you sure you want to go ahead?'

'Yes,' she'd answered firmly, 'I'm sure.' Her gaze unwavering.

The letter.

In what way does this make use of your education? What skill does a linguist bring to the packing of parachutes? You are once again worrying your mother and brother needlessly. I'm only going to say this one more time. Come home.

It is not my home, she thinks in a burst of angry defiance, recalling the old, pre-Cambridge Rani. *I didn't choose it. You did. For all of us, whether we wanted to or not.*

Her father's letter:

If you insist on staying there then consider us dead to one another, this time for good.

The paper falls from her suddenly weak hand onto the bed.

She stands up on jelly legs, tucks loose strands of her hair behind her ears with trembling fingers and in the process, tucks the hurt away, hidden behind memories of family: Baba, Mama, Arjun, and love: Prasad, each a sorrow-soaked lament.

Then, decisively, she wipes her eyes, pushes her head back and goes downstairs to join the Strong family for supper.

'Miss Raj, it's pie. My favourite,' Andrew says, as always solemn in expression and tone of voice, as she takes her seat at the table next to the dear little child. He's more chatty with her now, although everything he says and does is relayed with the same grave expression and monotone.

'Very good.' She conjures a smile for him.

'Woolton pie, recommended by the ministry,' Mrs Lewes says officiously.

Rani nods.

'All right, Miss Raj?' Mr Strong is gentle as she has ever heard him, for once looking directly, assessingly at her as he passes her the pie dish so she can help herself to a slice.

She meets his enquiring gaze, this opaque man for once transparent, with another determined smile. 'I'm all right, thank you.'

'Oh dear,' Mrs Lewes sighs between mouthfuls, 'I forgot to season the vegetables.'

Rani finds her portion very salty even though she hasn't seasoned it, passing on the salt pot to Mr Strong when Mrs Lewes offers it to her, even when the others liberally season theirs.

After supper, as Mr Strong and Andrew prepare to go on their walk, their daily ritual, Mr Strong says, 'What do you think, Andrew: shall we ask Miss Raj to join us?'

She looks up at this man, who is so remote and closed up and yet quite perceptive too, perhaps. Is this just an impulsive invitation or has he somehow understood that she does not care to be alone just now, with her maudlin thoughts?

Or perhaps it's not so surprising that he'd intuit that she needs the distraction of innocent, uncomplicated company, given how bright he is, unfazed even by the hardest of codes, figuring out a way to solve them.

'Yes,' Andrew says, and then turning to Rani, in his serious way, 'Would you like to come along, Miss Raj?'

'I'd like nothing better,' she says, taking Andrew's little hand in hers. And, to Mrs Lewes, 'I can help you with the dishes when I get back, Mrs Lewes?'

The other woman waves her dishcloth at Rani. 'You go on. They only take a few minutes.'

It is a pleasantly mild evening, the sky glowing rose gold. The smoky crisp and sizzle scent of frying potatoes from neighbouring houses mingling with nectary honey of ripe apples. They are even serenaded by birdsong.

Andrew takes it upon himself to educate her on their route, his father keeping step beside them, a quiet, calm presence.

'We go this way, past the pub, which is always noisy, and into the meadow. It is very peaceful at this time of the evening.'

He takes an abrupt detour off the road and leads her along the path that cuts through the meadow behind the pub. 'Look at the grass, Miss Raj. It appears black, doesn't it, although it's actually green. And look how it makes waves when the wind goes through it. Or when I ruffle it with my bunny.'

Outdoors, the boy is different. Almost animated.

Rani steals a glance at Mr Strong. This multifaceted man. So bright at work. So closed up in his personal life. And yet he unfailingly takes his boy for a walk every evening, instinctively understanding how much he needs this communing with nature.

'Look at the sky, Miss Raj. It looks like...'

'Mrs Lewes' chicory and carrot cake?' Rani asks, making a face. Mrs Lewes had saved rations and made it for a treat and Rani had dutifully eaten it but it wasn't very sweet and really rather tasteless if she was being honest.

Andrew turns to her and smiles.

A proper, wide, toothy smile.

It is a gift.

And in the gathering dusk, a steam train whistling in the distance, the scent of dew-soaked grass, this little boy by her side, small hand tucked trustingly in hers, his reserved father beaming at both of them because his son has actually truly smiled, she feels some of the melancholy that has tormented her since she read her father's letter ease a tiny bit.

47

RANI

Rani blushes as she jots down the message she's just decoded.

She's learned all her swear words here. An entire cache.

If her brother were to see them, he'd be impressed, Mama scandalised. She pushes down the swell of pain ambushing her, concentrates instead on checking, one last time, that she's got everything right.

She has.

She blushes again at the obscenity – this one, particularly, leaves nothing at all to the imagination. And as she often has before, she wonders at the German men writing these. Boys really. Not much older than Arjun. Adding swear words in as a joke, lightening the burden they carry, looking death in the face, in this way.

Oh, she laments, the futility, the sheer waste of war. These boys, smirking, she imagines, as they create the messages, with mothers who are waiting for them to come safely back. Will they get to grow up? Go home?

For the umpteenth time, she's happy Arjun is in India. Even as she misses him, aches for the time she has lost and is losing, not watching him grow, change. But he is *safe*. Unlike Gertie's brother, who is missing in action.

And Gertie. Where is her friend? How is she?

'Keep safe,' she whispers, her mantra, chant, prayer with regards to her friend.

'Something the matter, Miss Raj?' Mr Strong, who is in charge, that day, of collecting the decoded messages, asks in his grave voice.

'Oh, not at all, Mr Strong.' She keeps a straight face as she hands over the message.

He looks at it and his mouth is just as implacable, face as rigid as ever. But when he looks up at her, there it is: a thawing in his serious gaze. A sparkle to the eyes. A lightness.

A shared moment of conspiracy.

In that moment, he looks very like his young son, who has inveigled his way right into her heart, bagged a permanent place in there.

Andrew.

Rani thinks of his expression that morning as she rushed to make it in time for work – Mr Strong had already left; she was running late as usual. She'd have to bicycle extra fast. Andrew was at the table, sighing as he reluctantly spooned tiny portions of his watery gruel into his mouth under Mrs Lewes' unflinching gaze.

Out of the blue, he said, 'I wish I was old enough to fight in the war.'

'No, you don't,' Mrs Lewes and Rani said, both at once.

They shared a look even as Andrew looked from one to the other of them. 'But I want to do something important.'

'Time enough for that. Now the important thing for you is to finish your breakfast so you get to be strong in body as well as name.' Rani said.

She felt rather than saw Mrs Lewes' approving glance directed at her.

Andrew had sighed again like an old, weary man as she ruffled his hair, bid him goodbye, and rushed out. As she bicycled away, she waved at him, framed in the kitchen window.

He was slumped upon the table, cheek resting against the wood, hands raised in the air, both waving vigorously, one clutching his rabbit, the other the spoon dripping gooey gruel.

Her last glimpse was of the spoon falling onto the table before Mrs Lewes swooped in and he disappeared from view, camouflaged by her rather large back.

48

RANI

The daily evening walks with Andrew and Mr Strong now include Rani as a given, even as winter draws in and at work, the lake freezes over, the ducks and geese huddling down in the icy blast of knife-edged wind. A daring few young men and women attempt to skate over the frozen lake, the others, Rani and Mr Strong among them, cheering them on – well, cheering is a strong word in the context of Mr Strong. He smiles and nods while Rani and her feistier colleagues hoot and egg on the ice skaters.

After supper, Andrew jumps off his chair, puts his coat and mittens and shoes on without being pressed and comes up to Rani and tucks his hand trustingly in hers.

'Ready, Miss Raj?'

'As I'll ever be.'

'Your hand is wet. I can feel it through my mittens.'

'It was my turn to wash the dishes today. Mrs Lewes dried. I think I'm guilty of not drying my own hand properly.'

'Come over here, Miss Raj; I've finished with the dishes. I can do your hand.' Mrs Lewes brandishes her tea towel.

Andrew smiles.

Mrs Lewes and Rani laugh in shared joy at the boy's delight.

'How is Miss Raj at work, Daddy?' Andrew asks once they're outside.

It is dark already. Every so often, a pulse of amber gold, laughter, chatter, a baby's wail, and as they pass the pub, the warming, sour-sweet scent of hops, murmur of conversation, a burst of rowdy chuckling, permeates the absolute blackout darkness.

They walk the path from memory, as they can't see much, one of Andrew's mittened hands in hers, his bunny snug inside his coat – 'He's cold too you know, Miss Raj' – only its head peering out from under Andrew's small chin, his other hand secure in his father's.

Now in answer to Andrew's question about Rani at work, Mr Strong says, a hint of apology in his voice, 'You know I'm not allowed to say, old chap.'

'I just want to know how Miss Raj is getting on, that's all.' Andrew is petulant. His voice is gradually getting more animated now, less robotic.

'Have you tried asking her? She's right next to you, you know.'

A smile gilding Mr Strong's voice. In the darkness, Rani fancies it glows; it is that sort of voice, bringing to mind mellow honey, bronzed amber.

Andrew tuts in exasperation and Rani smiles. Every expressive gesture from this boy is a gift, not to be taken lightly, considering how he was when she first arrived. 'I love it, Andrew. It's very challenging, but what I love the best is seeing great minds, like your daddy's, in action.' She smiles brightly at father and son – her eyes have adjusted to the dark now enough to see Mr Strong's cheeks burn red as he blinks rapidly.

He clears his throat. 'Ah Miss Raj, it's a team effort really,' he manages.

'I think you're being modest.'

He grins at the same time as ducking his head to hide his flush.

Watching him so discomfited by her compliment makes Rani absurdly happy for some strange reason.

'Now then, Daddy,' Andrew says, his stern voice and words mimicking Mrs Lewes, making both Rani and Mr Strong smile, 'your turn.'

'Well,' Mr Strong clears his throat again. 'I think Miss Raj is really rather good.'

The admiration, affection and pride in his voice as he delivers the compliment makes Rani's heart glow and *her* cheeks flush.

She looks up, over his son's head, to find him watching her with soft affection on his face, the look usually reserved for his son. Her face on fire even as she breaks eye contact. This time, it is she who's unable, too shy, to meet his gaze.

Afterwards, as Andrew is running in the meadow, surefooted and nimble, hands stretched out, Bunny peeking from the top of his coat, tousled mops dancing, calling, 'Look at me, how fast I can go, even Bunny is scared but I'm not,' and Rani is clapping enthusiastically, marvelling at how he's now sounding his age, a happy, enthusiastic, active little boy, and feeling thrilled at the thought, Mr Strong says, quiet but firm, 'I meant what I said you know, Miss Raj.'

'I'm sorry?' Rani pauses in her clapping to look at him.

'You at work. You're very good. A real asset. You spot patterns to the messages that have stumped experienced codebreakers, the best minds in the country. Only very few, highly trained cryptographers accomplish what you do so regularly. We're all quite impressed.' Awe in his voice.

And again, Rani's whole body is alight from the heat of his compliment.

49

RANI

'Miss Raj, over here.'

Rani startles, peering blindly into the darkness, even more potent after leaving the cheery brightness of the cottage.

The voice, although soft, sounds disproportionately loud in the unremitting gloom of the blackout.

She's just finished the late watch – 4 p.m. to midnight – which most try to get out of but which she really doesn't mind.

'Miss Raj.' The voice again.

She knows the owner of the voice. But it can't be.

He should be at home asleep.

She must be imagining it.

The night is pulsing with shadows, and very cold. She shivers, pulling her coat closer around her.

The others on her shift have left – and those doing the grave-yard watch are already inside the hut. She had lost track of time, caught up in the challenge of breaking the code she was assigned – and she'd managed to do it just after her watch finished and the others streamed out. Harriet, who was also on the late shift, had offered to wait but Rani had waved her on. 'I'm almost done. You go on.'

The high of solving the code – it had been a particularly difficult one – means she doesn't mind too much that she'll have to walk back tonight instead of cycling, which would have been so much quicker. She's tried taking good care of the loaned bike, keeping in mind her promise to Andrew to look after his mother's property, but despite her best efforts, she had a fall lately. The bike cushioned her, but sadly, it had therefore fared worse and is being repaired.

'I'm sorry, Andrew,' she'd said.

'It wasn't your fault, Miss Raj.' The boy was gracious. Then, throwing his arms, Bunny included of course, around her, 'I'm glad you're all right.'

She smiles at the very thought of him.

He's stolen her heart. Filled, to some extent, the Arjun-shaped hole in there.

Now, as she tries to find the path in the intense blackout dark, again that voice. So very familiar. 'Miss Raj.'

Surely she's dreaming it?

And now a gleam in the darkness as her eyes adjust, finally, to the pressing velvet, brilliantly icy but sweetly fragrant night. The tip of a match being struck. Red gold. Highlighting eyes the glittery opaque of well-concealed secrets.

It can't be. But it is.

'Mr Strong, what are you doing here?'

He clears his throat. 'It's the middle of the night, and you've to walk all the way home. I... I thought you'd like some company.'

She's touched, overwhelmed, lost for words.

It's bitingly cold. He has to wake up early as he's on the day shift. And yet, he's left his warm bed to come here so she won't have to walk back alone at night.

He misconstrues her silence. 'I won't intrude; you won't even know I'm here.'

And now she finds the words. Looking up at him, her eyes having adjusted to the dark somewhat, she says, 'Thank you. It's really very kind of you to come out when you have your own shift starting in a few hours.'

He colours. Even in the dark, Rani can make out the bright red of his face.

'I... Andrew cares about you. He was worried, you see, of you walking home in the dark.'

'I care about him too. He's a wonderful little boy. He reminds me of my brother.'

'Ah. How old is your brother, Miss Raj?'

'Twelve,' Rani says, experiencing a sharp pang of missing. Another birthday Arjun has celebrated without Rani, another milestone reached without his sister cheering him on.

'What is he like?'

And Rani finds herself talking about her family, sharing anecdotes and memories, and it is painful joy. She is estranged from them but speaking about them, sharing their stories, makes them feel very near, brings them back to her.

Mr Strong is a very good listener, patient and interested, asking the right questions, giving her time to collect her thoughts.

When she is silent, overcome, he seems to understand, walking quietly beside her, smoking, the lake glinting seductively, a sequinned mirror rippling with the heady promise of silver-tipped gossip.

A squelch beneath her feet. She startles, nearly colliding with Mr Strong.

'What's that?' he asks, concerned.

'I... I stepped on something.'

'Definitely not a bomb as we are still standing.'

'A bomb?' She stares at him, although she can only just about make out his silhouette, the pale glow of his skin.

'We were bombed last November.' He is matter-of-fact. 'Hut 4 took a hit. Another bomb landed yards from the cottage.'

'*Our* cottage?' She shudders.

'The very one. Luckily, that one failed to go off. A couple of others fell on the grounds and failed to go off as well. No one knows where; for a moment there, I thought you'd solved the mystery.'

His voice does not change but she can detect the gentle smile gilding it. Then, softly, 'You stepped on a frog, Miss Raj,' Mr Strong says. 'They're abundant by the lake and daringly venture out at night, foolish things, and are, of course, notoriously hard to spot in the absolute dark of the blackout.'

'Do you think I... hurt it?' She can't bring herself to say 'kill'.

She senses rather than sees him shrug. 'We are at war. There will be casualties.'

She bites her lip to hide her smile – foolish, as he can't see it. Like her, he's concentrating on finding his footing in the inky dark, but, like before, she can sense *his* smile and it warms her heart.

Mr Strong accompanies her home every night until her bike – on loan from his absconding wife – is fixed.

She enjoys his company. He appears to instinctively understand when she'd prefer silence and when she wants to talk. He seems to have overcome his shyness with her, easier as they can't really make eye contact – which is what he struggles with – in the dark. Since they can't discuss work, they have to find other things to talk about but the conversation flows easily. As she's observed before, he's a great listener and she finds herself sharing more about her family and her past than she means to.

When he discovers her father is a king, he takes gentle digs at her, persisting in addressing her as 'Your Highness' or 'Your Esteemed Majesty'. She gets her own back by making fun of Oxford and its alumni, both greatly inferior to Cambridge, of course. He defends his alma mater and fellow Oxonians spiritedly and she finds herself disappointed when they arrive home and he bids her goodnight – the walks feel shorter each day – and even more so when her bike being repaired coincides with her shift changing to days and their midnight sojourns come to an end.

50

RANI

One cloudless, gloriously sunny and mild winter day, an impromptu tennis game is declared at lunchtime between Mr Babington, who is the reigning champion, and anyone willing to take him on. There are plenty of contenders, Mr Strong among them, the cottage emptying in a matter of minutes.

Rani sits on a bench by the lake close to the tennis court so she can watch her colleagues at play – well, if she is honest, her gaze is drawn to one particular codebreaker – while pretending to be reading her book.

'Mind if I join you?' Somehow, that codebreaker is beside her, smiling. He's lost his shyness completely with her now, daringly maintaining eye contact even during daytime.

'But you were playing...'

'Ah, you noticed. I thought you were reading.'

She colours, looking down at her book.

'Interesting, is it?' he asks, his eyes sparkling even more.

'Yes,' she mumbles.

'Must be a heavy read as I haven't seen you turn a page for the last ten minutes.'

She looks up then, his merry eyes inviting a reciprocal smile, and says, archly, 'I think I preferred it when you were shy and couldn't meet my gaze.'

Now it is his turn to colour. She realises that she likes very much how his cheeks glow, bright crimson beacons advertising that he still is at heart the shy, awkward man she first met – like his son, he's come out of his shell with her, which she also likes.

'I'm only joking,' she says. Then, 'A shame you lost. Perhaps it was because you were too busy keeping an eye on who's reading what and how much to concentrate on the game?'

And now he laughs. It is a beautiful sound. Wholesome. Infectious.

She can't help joining in.

When she stops, he is looking at her, an odd look on his face.

'What's the matter?'

'If you'd permit me to say so, Miss Raj, you have a wonderful laugh. Glorious. Like a celebration.'

Her cheeks afire once more, her heart light. She looks down at her book and very deliberately turns a page.

And again, he laughs. It is sunshine after a winter storm. Flowers blooming in kaleidoscopic colour. Rain after months of drought.

It is divine.

* * *

He takes to cycling back home with her when their shifts coincide.

One day, as they are walking through the grounds from the cottage after work to collect their bikes, they come upon a photographer, assembling a motley group into a pose in front of the entrance to the main house, Dilly, 'Prof' Turing and Harriet among them.

'Ah,' Dilly calls, 'Will and... er...' Predictably, Dilly has forgotten her name.

'Rani,' Harriet supplies.

'Join us, do.'

Mr Strong escorts Rani along and the group budges up as they join, Harriet grinning widely at Rani.

The photographer, who had walked to his machine, pops his head out from under the dark cloth through which, Rani assumes, he was critically eyeing the group, and sighs.

He comes up to them, pushing them closer.

Rani stumbles.

Mr Strong puts an arm around Rani to steady her, his touch igniting a tingling glow that reverberates through her body, surprising her into rigid shock.

'Smile for the camera,' the photographer instructs, his head shrouded by the black cloth once more.

Flash.

Rani blinks.

The group disbands, Harriet calling a cheery goodbye as she clicks past Rani in her high heels – she's always well turned out is Harriet, coming up with all sorts of ingenious hacks to get around rationing and shortages. She uses boot polish for mascara, beetroot for lipstick, and, yes, Rani notes that she's drawn lines up the back of her legs to give the impression of stockings.

'Mine have all been darned one too many times and are falling apart,' she'd confided in Rani. 'This is the next best thing. Needs must, my dear.'

Harriet is also a dab hand at sewing and a staunch devotee of 'make do and mend'. Once Rani had complimented her on a dress she was wearing: 'It's beautiful. Is it new?'

'Oh no.' Harriet looked shocked. 'I wouldn't waste my clothing coupons on this! I made it myself with fabric from blackout curtains.'

Mr Strong is chatting to Dilly and 'Prof' Turing, who's wearing his mask and turning his pockets inside out, searching for the key to his bicycle which he keeps locked to the railings, Rani surmises. Prof finds the key, twirls it in his hand, looking increasingly uncomfortable, clearly wanting to leave – he adheres to a strict routine, Rani has heard.

I want to leave too. Come on, Mr Strong, she thinks.

And as if he's heard her silent plea, Mr Strong says his goodbyes, turns towards her and smiles.

And again, like his touch of before, it sparks a fiery glow in her heart that warms her whole being.

51

RANI

That evening, on their walk, Andrew is full of beans and once they reach the meadow, turns to his father, 'Will you race me, Daddy?'

'No, I'm sorry, son, I'm too old.'

'Miss Raj?' Andrew looks hopefully at her.

Rani shakes her head. 'Sorry, Andrew, no can do.'

'Are you too old too?' Andrew asks in his serious way.

Mr Strong smiles.

'I'm not!' Rani cries in mock outrage. 'I'll have you know I've only a *very* few years on you, young man.'

'Then race me,' Andrew challenges.

With a pang, Rani is reminded, once again, as is often the case when with this child, of her brother with whom she had had several races over the years, only some of which she'd let him win. If she'd known then that her time with him was scarce, she'd have let him win them all...

'Well, I'm protecting you by refusing,' she says to Andrew.

'How?' He scrunches his nose in that endearing way.

'Because I'll win, of course.'

There's a chuckle from behind her. Mr Strong.

'*I* will win,' Andrew is firm. 'Daddy, you be the referee.'

'Yes, sir.' Mr Strong salutes his son.

'All right then.' Andrew is officious. 'Miss Raj, we run up to that giant tree over there, touch it and race back to Daddy. Agreed?'

She nods. 'Agreed.'

Andrew gets into position. Rani does too, taking her cues from the boy.

'Ready, Miss Raj?'

'I'm ready.'

'On your marks. Get set. Go!' Mr Strong calls.

And they're off.

The boy is fast, she will give him that. Faster than Arjun.

And very, very determined.

By the time they reach the tree, they are neck and neck but she is genuinely flagging.

By the time they're getting to Mr Strong, he's gaining on her.

She tries.

But he's nimble and focused and full of stamina, thanks to Mrs Lewes' bossy nagging at every mealtime to finish the food on his plate, Rani guesses, and reaches his father first.

'I win! I win! I win!' As animated as she's ever seen him.

He has just run up to the end of the field and back and yet still he has the energy to perform a little victory dance.

'Give me a minute,' she pants, holding her sides, 'to get my breath back.'

He laughs.

Mr Strong's head swivels towards his son in surprise, as does Rani's.

He is still laughing, tumbling rollercoaster giggles that go on and on.

Sheer, unadulterated joy.

It is the sweetest sound.

A festive celebration of glorious, unrestrained mirth.

Mr Strong's gaze hungrily takes in his son, as if to record every moment of this very rare, completely unexpected, happy, happy occurrence, his eyes shimmering.

As they walk back, Andrew skipping ahead, impatient to tell Mrs Lewes of his victory, Mr Strong turns to Rani. His face soft with emotion. Eyes alight with gratitude. 'You're good for us, Miss Raj. Thank you.'

She is touched. *You're good for me too*, she thinks. But somehow, when she goes to say the words, they evaporate on her tongue. It appears that Mr Strong is not the only one who is shy at times.

So instead: 'Just so you know, I didn't lose the race on purpose,' she says.

He laughs.

It too is as gloriously wonderful as his son's joy.

Right now, I'm perfectly happy, she thinks.

When they reach home, Andrew races inside, right into Mrs Lewes' open, welcoming arms, saying brightly, breathlessly, 'Mrs Lewes, I beat Miss Raj! We had a race and I won!' And he laughs, once again, heartily wholesome, as easily as if he has always done it.

Mrs Lewes looks up at Rani and beams, eyes shining, even as she holds the boy close, dropping kisses onto his hair.

And Rani goes to bed smiling, her dreams of an earnest little boy and his serious father. Both chuckling with kaleidoscopic joy.

* * *

She wakes up smiling.

Happy.

Lighter somehow.

She realises why when she sees Andrew at the table and he smiles at her. Easily. As if it is the most natural thing in the world. As it should be but hasn't for this child.

Until now.

'Good morning, Miss Raj. I woke early today.'

'You're beating me even at this now? Waking up? Please don't make a habit of it.'

Andrew giggles.

Mrs Lewes swivels from the stove, spatula in the air as she looks at the boy, tears shining in her eyes.

As Andrew spoons porridge into his mouth, she turns to Rani, mouths, 'Thank you,' swiping roughly at her eyes with the edge of her apron.

And Rani understands that she feels lighter because the ache of missing in her heart that she has got used to, a burden she always carries, has eased.

And it is thanks to this little boy and his father and the woman who is like a mother and grandmother to them.

She realises then that not only Andrew, but his father and even Mrs Lewes, have claimed a part of her heart now. Somewhere along the way, she has begun to care for them. She wants them to be happy.

And she is happy when with them.

52

ESME

The house is dark. It smells stale.

It needs a good clean – in her grief, Esme has neglected her small slice of this world that she had carved for herself and her son, their home, place of belonging – she sees now.

The cheery, sunshine-yellow curtains patterned with daisy 'smiles' as Robbie had observed when she first hung them up, are opaque with dust.

She opens all the windows, lets in the warm, gold light and the cavorting, smoke and nectar flavoured, late-spring breeze, which, once inside, flirts unashamedly with the dust motes, making them swirl dizzily as if drunk on sunshine.

And then she picks up the phone. Her instinct is to dial Philip's number, which she knows by heart.

I miss you. I love you. I'm sorry. I don't know what came over me. Will you forgive me? Can we start again?

But she loses her nerve and instead, calls her brother.

'I went to see Mrs Lewes today.'

'How is she?' Affection softening her brother's voice.

'She was lucid for a fair bit. And asking after you.'

A pause. Then, 'I'll go see her soon.'

It occurs to Esme then that perhaps her brother feels the same hesitation she does when with Mrs Lewes that she also experienced when visiting Dad. The pain to see them so ravaged, so different from the people they loved. Perhaps he too, like Esme, wanted to remember them as they had been, not the frail facsimiles they were now.

Today, Esme had visited Mrs Lewes with firm purpose, but nevertheless, she'd sat in the car once she reached the nursing home, gathering the strength to face whatever version the woman she loved would be that day. When visiting Dad, she'd do the same, rehearsing the words she'd say, preparing to breach the uncomfortable silences that inevitably characterised their meetings as she came to terms with the father she had admired looking so ill and beaten, no matter how hard he tried to disguise it.

It is only now that with sudden understanding Esme realises that perhaps it is not so different for her brother, which is why his visits to Dad and Mrs Lewes were even less frequent than hers.

There was a time, so very long ago now, when Esme had looked up to her big brother, studied him thoroughly in her abject admiration, and been able to correctly identify his every expression, read his mind, intuit his thoughts.

How, when, did they become strangers to each other?

Gently, she says, 'She's not looking good, Andy. She doesn't have long.'

Her brother sighs.

Is he too recalling how Mrs Lewes used to prepare a packed lunch for them every single day of their school lives, remembering their likes and dislikes (oh the irony, for now age, cruel thief, is wreaking havoc with that formidable memory), careful not to include the egg sandwiches Esme loathed in her lunch but making sure Andy was supplied with several, for he adored them, packing honey sandwiches as a treat their first day back after the holidays? How she administered to them when they were ill, fretted when they were late back home, gently tended to the many wounds and bruises, both physical and emotional, accumulated during their journey into adulthood?

Esme talks past the lump in her throat, tasting of the sea. 'She said something today. About Mum. How she broke Dad's heart and his trust.' She swallows. Continues. 'She mentioned a letter Mum wrote to Dad.'

'Ah.'

'Said she had it. Dad had given it to her for safekeeping, apparently.'

'What did it say?' A note of curiosity entering her brother's usually placid voice.

'I didn't see it. She was getting quite upset and the nurse took over. I'll ask to have a look the next time I visit.'

Esme vows not to leave it too long. She wants to know if there *is* a letter – Mrs Lewes was very specific about where she kept it – so it, or *something*, must be there, surely? If this letter exists, and if it *is* from this Rani – her mum? – then at last, something tangible exists relating to the past, hers and Andy's. Something linked to their mother! Excitement and nervous anticipation bloom rampant in Esme's chest, like they have been since Mrs Lewes mentioned the letter. It may just be an old woman's ramblings. Or it may not. Esme means to find out.

And what did Mrs Lewes mean by 'the other one'? Is there some truth to Esme's clandestine suspicion that she and Andy might have different mothers?

She decides not to mention this to Andy until she knows more. But... she does mean to put him on the spot. He's always maintained he doesn't recall their mother or anything to do with her. Well, she's going to test that right now.

Esme takes a breath, asks her brother, 'Do you remember someone called Rani?' Knowing full well that if her suspicion is right then Rani may not have been Andy's mother. Which is why she worded the question this way.

'Rani... Rani.' Her brother is quiet for the longest time. Esme is just about to nudge him, when: 'Do you know, Esme, that name does ring a bell.'

'It does?' She's startled. She wasn't expecting this, although a part of her couldn't help hoping.

'Yes. It's very... familiar. I... I can't tell you why but it... it evokes... *something*.' Her brother's voice sounds strangled, which is very unlike him.

Her brother the scientist. Someone who deals in facts. Not feelings.

It's been a strange day but Esme has the strong conviction, now more so than ever, that she's on the cusp of something.

53

RANI

Bletchley, 1942

When Rani comes down to breakfast – she has the day off so she is later than usual – Andrew is slumped at the table, his bunny floppy by his side. Although his face is flushed, he looks wan and great dark circles ring his eyes.

Mrs Lewes bustles about him, trying to get him to eat. But the child is listless.

He looks up as Rani enters, and says, sadly, 'Miss Raj, I'm not feeling well.'

'Oh dear,' Rani says. 'That's not good, is it?'

'Daddy had to go to work but he's going to come back as soon as he possibly can, he's promised.' The boy sniffs.

She feels his forehead. It is shockingly hot.

'Mrs Lewes already took my temperature. She nearly swore when she looked at it, so it must be very high.'

'It *is* sky-high,' Rani agrees gravely, biting her lip to hide her smile at his description of Mrs Lewes, who has her hands on her hips and her eyebrows raised in reprimand, but can't quite hide the worry crowding her eyes and dragging her mouth down in deep furrows.

'I feel hot and uncomfortable,' Andrew says. 'And here, feel my chest. Can you hear the crackle?'

'What?' Rani stares at him in mock horror. 'Your chest is cracking? Oh my, I've never heard of it; you *are* extraordinary even when you are ill, young man.'

He smiles then, a weak little imposter of one, but a smile nonetheless.

Mrs Lewes' worry lines ease a little. She hands him a hot water bottle. 'To bed then, child. I will tuck you in.'

'Can Miss Raj do it, please?' he asks.

Mrs Lewes looks to Rani. 'Will you, Miss Raj?'

'It is my great privilege to do so,' Rani says. 'And tell you what.' She takes Andrew's hot little hand in her own and allows him to lead her upstairs. 'We'll have a tent day. I guarantee it will make you feel better.'

'What's a tent day?' Andrew asks, and, despite his illness, he is inquisitive and curious.

'You'll see. When I was little and ill, it is what my own daddy and I used to do.'

A pang as she remembers tent days with Baba and later with Arjun, Mama keeping them supplied with snacks and succour.

But she squashes it. For now, an ill child needs her.

Rani deftly fashions a tent out of bed clothes, keeping her fingers crossed that Mrs Lewes doesn't barge in any time soon, or if she does, that she allows them this one day of desecration of Andrew's bed that she has so carefully made up, his sheets so beautifully laundered.

Once done, they both lie on his bed, his hot little body beside hers, and he looks up at the billowing, white cocoon they're enclosed within and claps with delight.

'This is our magic place,' she says. 'Where we can be whoever we want to be, where we can share stories and secrets. They stay in here, you see, swallowed by the special enchanted air. *Poof*.'

He claps, feverish, red-tinted eyes glowing. 'This is capital, Miss Raj.'

'It surely is. Now, would you like a story, young man?'

'Yes please.'

'Once upon a time, in a magical land, there lived a boy called Andrew who had many superpowers.'

'He did?' His eyes, so like his father's, glowing even brighter.

'He absolutely did.' She smiles at him. 'And do you know what his most special superpower was?'

'What?' He's agog.

'He could run super fast. So fast that he could beat very speedy adults, especially a really, really fast woman called Runny.'

He laughs.

And although dulled by fever, interspersed by coughing, it is still the sweetest sound.

* * *

They lie side by side, looking up at the gently undulating waves of dreamy cream, the impression of being on a ship going nowhere, Rani remembering tent days with her brother and father, Mama coming every so often with a feast of sweetmeats: apple cake, cinnamon strudel, matzo fritters, *kartoffel klausse* and, of course, everyone's favourite, *schnecken*.

Andrew's cheeks flushed and eyes heavy with the languor of rising temperature, he says softly, 'I miss Mummy so much.'

This beloved child's solemn confession lances Rani's heart.

She holds him close, breathing in his lemon and fever scent. Whispers, 'I'm really sorry, love. I know you do. Shall I tell you a secret?'

He nods trustingly.

'I miss my mummy too.'

He scrunches his nose. 'But you're a grown up.'

'You're never too old to miss your mummy, my darling.'

She holds him while he cries. Great big sobs. Such sorrow. Too much for a little boy to bear.

She strokes his back. Murmuring, gently, 'Let it all out, love. That's better. There. There.'

Afterwards, when his sobs have quieted to the occasional whimpering hiccup, he says, earnestly, 'You are my friend aren't you?'

'I am,' she says. His big, trusting eyes adorned with pearl-drop tears reminding her painfully of her brother sobbing the day she left.

'Friends tell each other secrets, don't they?' he says softly, playing with the pillowcase on which he is perched.

'They do,' she says, carefully. 'Is there something you want to share with me?'

'Promise me you won't tell anyone.' His gaze soulful.

'Hand on heart, I won't. And in any case, this tent is magic, remember? What we talk about in here is top secret.'

'Like the job you and Daddy do?'

'Exactly so. What we share in here stays in here in the enchanted air.' She smiles reassuringly at him, this child she loves so very much. She wishes with all her heart this tent was magic and could somehow heal his sorrow. She can't give him his mother back but she can listen. 'Now then what did you want to tell me, dear heart?'

'My mummy is not dead. But she's gone far, far away forever and ever and she's never coming back.'

'Ah.' Her heart once again breaking for this sweet, sad child. She wishes she could carry his hurt. As she deliberates what to do, she thinks she hears a sound just outside their tent.

But Andrew is biting his lower lip, which is trembling suspiciously.

So she ignores the sound and gathers the boy to her. He smells of freshly laundered sheets and festering sorrow and hot hurt, too old and burdensome for his years.

He snuggles against her and she feels his little heart frantically beating out his pain.

'How did you find out?' she asks.

'I overheard Mrs Lewes telling the new neighbours.'

Mrs Lewes. She thinks of the plump, blustering woman who loves both Mr Strong and his son so devotedly. Who had been so suspicious of Rani when she arrived, protective of the broken little family she was trying and failing to mend. Who has come round to Rani now she has realised Rani is on her side, now she's understood with her – motherly? womanly? – instinct that Rani cares for them too.

And Rani on her part can't help caring for the prickly Mrs Lewes. She is so because she is intensely protective of this father and son duo, both so serious and yet strangely vulnerable. Yes, even Mr Strong. For behind his reserved exterior, Rani senses he is a man as hurt and broken as she is herself. He is, like Rani, very carefully holding himself together.

Oh Mrs Lewes, she thinks now, as she holds the little boy close.

Mrs Lewes. Whose heart is in the right place but the same can't be said of her wandering mouth, forgetting to take into consideration little eavesdropping ears.

Another sound from just outside their cocoon. Again,

although tempted to check, Rani ignores it, focusing on the sorrowful boy in her arms carrying such a heavy load.

'Did she hate me? Was she angry with me? Is that why she left?' Andrew asks, his voice an anxious whisper.

'No, she loved you very much, I promise,' Rani says.

'Then why did she leave?'

It hurts Rani deeply. This child asking this question. How to explain the intricacies and follies and foibles of human beings, the fallibility of adults who, in the eyes of children, are perfect, meant to do no wrong, be above it? How to explain the foolish mistakes and impulsive choices they make in the name of love, caught up in the moment, unmindful of the consequences, not thinking about who they might hurt? How to tell him that there are several different kinds of love, some more potent and explosive and addictive and selfish than others, and that in the pursuit of one kind of love, other loves are the casualties? How to say that sometimes, we hurt the ones we love the most the deepest? And the flip side of that – oftentimes, we are hurt the most by those we love the best. How to tell him that we think we know the ones we love but we can never really know what is going on in someone's mind, what they are feeling, going through, even, especially, those we love the most? And so, when they do something we don't expect, we take it personally, although it perhaps wasn't meant that way, and is thus hardest to forgive by those it affects.

Why did Rani do what she did? She loved her father. And yet she stole his sword. She did not think at all, caught up in the flush headiness of first love. She did not stop to consider what might go wrong, who it might affect and how.

Why did her father exile her when he loved her so? Why did he choose to be king? Why do we do anything at all? Why did she say no to her father's letter inviting her home although she missed them all so much?

This boy is looking to her for comfort, succour, and so, although she feels out of her depth, she says, 'Sometimes, in life, we have to make very difficult choices, my love. Your mother loves you very much and it hurt her so very, very deeply to leave you. If she'd been able to stay with you, she would have, I promise. She misses you very much. So much so that there is an Andrew-shaped hole in her heart.'

Andrew considers, head cocked to one side, then nods gravely. His lip no longer trembling. Tears have dried on his lashes, leaving salty tracks on his beautiful, heart-breaking little face.

'I promise you this much, my love. Nobody who is lucky enough to know you will voluntarily leave you. How could they? You are the loveliest, most wonderful little boy.'

Now a very slight uplifting of his lips. A ghost of a sliver of a smile, even as he says, 'But Mrs Lewes says I'm sometimes cheeky.'

'Agreed,' she says, 'you're sometimes cheeky.' She plants a kiss on his springy, apple-scented curls. 'But always loveable,' she adds.

Now he smiles. A tiny smile but one all the same. She'll take it over his heart-rending sobs any day.

'Even when I'm being cheeky?' he asks.

'Especially then. But shhh... don't tell anyone.'

'This tent is magic, remember?'

At that moment, the sheets part and a head peeks in. 'Room for one more?'

'Daddy!' Andrew scrambles off Rani's lap and throws his arms around his father. 'Did the tent magic you here from work?'

'Perhaps it did,' Mr Strong says.

'Do you like it?'

'I love it.'

'I do too. It's magic,' Andrew says seriously. 'You can say

anything in here and it keeps it a secret. And it got you home from work early too.'

Mr Strong's gaze meets Rani's over his son's head and in the shimmering depths of those eyes so like his son's, she reads immense pain and sadness and love and gratitude. It comes to her then that the rustling she'd heard outside the tent was Mr Strong, home early to check on his son, and that he'd been party to their entire conversation. So much for top secret, enchanted tents.

54

RANI

The next day, when Rani comes down for breakfast, Mr Strong is still at the table, reading the newspaper. Although they are on the same shift, he likes to leave early while Rani leaves with minutes to spare.

He is silent, only the rustle of news sheets giving him away, while Mrs Lewes chatters away as usual: 'Andrew is much better. I checked on him during the night. No fever. Just the chesty cold, which will linger on stubbornly for a few weeks, no doubt.'

Andrew arrives halfway through Rani's breakfast. He still looks peaky, but his cheeks are no longer feverishly flushed, although he's sniffling mightily.

'Daddy!' he exclaims, 'Why haven't you left?'

'I wanted to see how you were.'

Andrew smiles. 'I'm feeling better but I do still have a bad cold.' He blows his nose noisily to emphasise his point. 'Bunny thinks so too.' He cuddles the sorely bedraggled stuffed toy – well, *stuffed* is a gross overstatement, in Rani's opinion.

'Even Bunny was worried yesterday. He said he burned when

he touched me.' Andrew is saying. Then, looking at Rani, 'Did you, Miss Raj?'

'I definitely did.' Rani agrees.

'Mrs Lewes nearly swore because I nearly died...'

'Don't even joke about that, young man,' Mrs Lewes brandishes a gloopy ladle at Andrew.

But the child is unfazed, cheekily pointing out, 'Mrs Lewes, you tell me not to make a mess but you're doing so – look, a porridge puddle.'

Mr Strong hides his smile behind his newspaper.

'You're getting too big for your boots, young Andrew,' Mrs Lewes grumbles as she mops up the gloop.

'Not yet. But I will be if I eat up all my breakfast,' Andrew says seriously.

This time, Mr Strong can't hide his chuckles behind his newspaper. He folds his boy in his arms, even as he laughs, Andrew perplexed at first, not sure what he said that was so funny, then caught up in his father's laughter, giggling along.

Rani can't help joining in the infectious, wonderful, starburst mirth.

'You're the limit, child.' Mrs Lewes rocks on her creaky knees as she laughs, wiping her eyes with her apron.

* * *

As they cycle to work, side by side, the morning air cold but fresh, the fields shrouded in mist, creamy gold, Mr Strong clears his throat. 'Thank you, Miss Raj, for being so kind to Andrew.'

'He is a delight,' she says, sincerely.

'I...' He clears his throat again. 'I owe you an explanation.'

'Mr Strong...'

'William, please. My son considers you his friend. And I...' More clearing of his throat. 'I do too.'

Friend. His shy admission warms her heart. 'Only if you call me Rani,' she says.

He smiles. His hair blowing in the wind as he cycles, his smile crinkling his eyes pleasingly, he looks young and unburdened by responsibility. This serious, vulnerable man she has come to care for. Whose intelligence she admires. Whose love for his son makes her own heart melt.

'Rani,' he says.

Her name in his bronzed, honey voice, uttered so carefully, as if it is precious treasure. 'My... um... my wife... er... ex-wife... she...' He pauses. Swallows. His Adam's apple bobbing.

Rani does not want to give Mrs Lewes' confidence away. But she can see how hard it is for him to speak of his ex-wife. So she says, 'You don't have to tell me anything.'

'I want to,' he says. Then, 'Can we stop for a minute?'

They will be late for work. She cannot imagine this man has ever been late for work before. He's so very proper and precise and meticulous and hard-working and diligent. But when it matters, he's willing to be flexible. Like how he came home mid-shift the previous day to check on his son. Again, the fact that he is willing to be late to explain about his wife to Rani touches her.

They stop.

They are at the meadow where they walk with Andrew, the regular ritual she is now part of.

The grass, nearly as tall as her, dancing in dawn-burnished, dew-speckled furrows.

'I'm sorry I didn't do it earlier. I...' He rubs his eyes wearily. 'We were neighbours. Our parents, family friends. It was never explicitly stated but it was understood that we would marry. Barbara, she... always wanted more. She loved parties, socialising.

She was beautiful. But she did not take to domesticity; mother-
hood was not for her. It irritated her. Held her back. I held her
back. We weren't suited, I see that now.'

He says it all in a rush as if he had been rehearsing it. Perhaps
he has, all night, Rani thinks, her heart going out to this man like
it had to his son the previous day. Both of them hurt so badly by
the thoughtless, selfish actions of one woman.

'It is Andrew who is the casualty in all of this. I didn't realise
he...' Mr Strong – *William* – stops, unable to go on, his jaw
working busily as he kneads his hands. She is overcome by the
urge to touch him, hold him, offer the comfort of an embrace.

She folds her hands across her chest to hold in the impulse.

This man and his son, both so serious and yet with such depth
to them. Both so broken. She can empathise with their ache, their
pain, their sorrow. They are getting by, trying to endure it, but it is
hard, some days worse than others. She can relate. For she is
doing the same.

'I worry about Andrew,' Mr Strong – she really must think of
him as William – is saying, his voice a throbbing wound.

This man. A grave, sombre carapace hiding a broken, vulnerable heart. Amazing intellect. A first-class brain. Steadfastly loyal
to those he cares for: his son – Rani has seen the expression on his
face in unguarded moments with his son, such love as to almost
hurt; Mrs Lewes, whom he respects with a fearful awe.

She wants to touch him, offer comfort, so badly. She hugs
herself tighter.

A horse and carriage clip clops past. A train whistles in the
distance.

The frost-speckled wind ruffles the grass blades, making them
cavort friskily.

The air tastes of ice and apples for some reason.

And then, suddenly, unprecedentedly, almost as if he has seen into her mind, the urge she's stopping herself acting upon, he reaches across, takes her hand.

Again, that thrill at his touch like when he'd put his arm around her to steady her when the photographer came to Bletchley Park.

'I'm glad Andrew has you now.' He smiles. And in that sweet smile, she sees his son. 'Thank you for being his friend.' A pause. Then shyly, 'And mine.'

As suddenly as he had reached out to take her hand, he drops it.

And she feels unaccountably bereft.

55

ESME

When the phone rings, startling her out of sleep – tortured, nightmare-plagued, but sleep nonetheless, an improvement on insomnia, counting out the wakeful, anguish tormented hours of night – Esme knows it's bad news.

It's only just gone six. The sky outside a murky, cloud-hounded grey, the barest hint of pale gold from rays of rising sun struggling valiantly to pierce through.

Another call prefacing, 'I'm so sorry.'

Too soon after the last, Esme thinks, the receiver going slack in her hands. Much too soon.

A pause in deference to the sad news about to be relayed, the knowledge, the certainty from which there is no going back. 'Mrs Lewes passed away last night. She went peacefully in her sleep.'

Grief stabs, harsh, no less potent for being expected. The woman who'd brought her and her brother up is no more.

She runs her fingers across her palm where Mrs Lewes' nails had dug grooves when she spoke about Rani, only a few days ago.

She'd meant to visit later this week, ask to see the letter.

'She doesn't have long,' she'd said to her brother, her words strangely prophetic.

56

RANI

Bletchley, 1942

Like with the daily walks, Andrew instigates tent days as a ritual on Rani's days off.

They spend entire afternoons lounging in bed under softly swaying sheets telling each other stories, playing games, laughing, talking, sharing.

Andrew loves to hear about Arjun and in recounting her brother's antics, he comes vividly alive.

It is a gift.

One afternoon, there's a tell-tale rustle and clearing of throat outside their tent.

They have been inventing great adventures featuring Andrew Superboy and his sidekick Runny. They fall silent, Andrew Superboy poised mid attack on an enemy warship, Runny inside the warship, disguised as one of the enemy, spying on them.

'Who is it?' Andrew asks, grinning cheekily at Rani.

'May I join you? I bring snacks. Andrew Superboy and his loyal friend need sustenance after all.'

Rani can't help but smile upon hearing the grin in William's voice.

She beams even wider when Andrew pushes open the sheets at the word 'snacks' and mouths in awe, 'You got chocolate!'

'I raided Mrs Lewes' emergency stash. Don't tell her, please; she'll be very cross.'

'I won't,' Andrew promises, gravely. Then, he throws his arms around his father. 'Thank you, Daddy.'

They have a glorious day.

They invent adventures galore.

They have a story-making competition. A story-completing competition.

And at the end of the day, as Andrew drifts off to sleep, he puts one arm around Rani, the other around his father. 'Can we do this every Sunday?'

Rani and William's eyes meet over the boy's head. Rani has enjoyed the day more than she can put into words. 'If your daddy and I both have the day off, I don't see why not,' she says.

William smiles, widely. Like his son's smile, it lodges right in Rani's heart.

'Daddy,' Andrew says, 'can Miss Raj be my new mummy?'

And now, William's flustered gaze drops away from Rani's even as colour rushes to his face.

'Andrew that's... umm...' He clears his throat vigorously.

When his father is not forthcoming, William opening his mouth, but no words making it out, Andrew turns to Rani and repeats his question, 'Miss Raj, will you be my new mummy?'

His father finally finds his voice. 'Andrew, son, that's not for you to ask.'

'You ask Miss Raj then, Daddy,' Andrew says, innocently.

William's face suffuses more red even as he once again clears his throat vehemently.

Andrew yawns loudly and William's eyes once again meet Rani's over his son's head. His face is flushed but there is something in his eyes, an intensity that makes Rani's body ignite with a fiery glow.

She thinks of how she'd thrilled at his touch the other day, how bereft she'd felt when his arm dropped away.

Rani is suddenly shy, his son's words echoing around the room, his question sitting between them.

She looks down at Andrew's tousled mop and notices that he is asleep, tired out from their packed tent day, made all the more special thanks to William's unexpected but very welcome addition. Andrew's mouth is slightly open, soft purrs escaping it.

Rani is just about to gently dislodge the boy's arm and make her way out of the room when William clears his throat. 'Rani?'

She looks at him and again, that depth to his gaze, and something else: a warm tenderness.

She cannot look away. She is mesmerised.

He swallows. She watches his Adam's apple bob up and down. His throat is blotchy with the effort to get the words out but he does, finally, find them. 'I have begun to care for you, so very much.' His eyes upon hers filled with emotion. 'Andrew, what he said... I... I'd like that too, for you to be my wife and his mother.'

She thinks of how when with Andrew and William, she does not miss her family as much, does not feel like she is lacking, lost, but instead feels whole, complete. Content. This man and his son have burrowed their way into her heart, taken residence there, made themselves comfortably at home.

'I'd like that very much,' she says.

William smiles and it is as if his whole body is celebrating. It is joy and it is love. He leans in, and over his sleeping boy's body, puts his arms around her, whispering, into her ear, 'I love you,

Rani. You make me so very happy. I have been afraid to love in case I am hurt again but you, you've broken through that reserve.'

She is happy, revelling in the music, the pure joy of his words, the truth of them soft in his eyes, his son whom she also loves nestled between them.

'I will never hurt you,' she whispers.

But she hurt Prasad. Her first love.

I love you, she opens her mouth to say...

The words evaporate as Prasad appears before her eyes. The young man she loved. Whom she inadvertently hurt. Her first love. 'You love *me*.'

William kisses her then, over his son's head, his son who has fallen asleep in their joined embrace. She tastes his love and is ambushed by an amalgam of feeling: love for this man even as memories of a lost love for a young man whose fate she doesn't know, whom she promised to run away with, created grandiose plans with, fight to take centre stage, so she is torn even as she kisses William back.

And that is when Andrew wakes.

He looks from his father to Rani. 'Did you ask Miss Raj, then, Daddy? Is she going to be my new mummy?'

'Yes.' William beams.

Andrew cheers. He throws his arms around Rani, kisses her cheek. 'I love you, my new mummy.'

And despite her mixed feelings, as she gathers the boy to her, his father's arms around her, William's soft gaze upon her, tender with love, her heart is full.

57

RANI

It is Andrew who breaks the news to Mrs Lewes.

After Andrew fell asleep again, snug in their joined embrace, William and Rani had kissed and talked and made plans, Rani promising herself in her head, *I will get it right this time. I will protect this beautiful, damaged father and son with my life. I will not hurt them.*

And all the while, the spectre of Prasad, whispering, *you promised to love me always and forever. You hurt me.*

As soon as he wakes from his nap, that eventful afternoon, Andrew looks up at Rani.

'Where's Daddy?'

'He's just gone to fetch us all a drink, my love.'

Andrew, looking worried, takes Rani's hand, his small palm warm, sleep-mussed hair standing to attention, 'Will you still be my new mummy?'

His vulnerability, the anxious hope in his eyes breaking Rani's heart, even as she gathers the child into her embrace, whispers, 'It will be my greatest privilege to be your new mummy.'

Andrew reaches up and kisses each of her cheeks. His innocent love, offered so seriously, this boy who has been so hurt by the mother he loves and misses, a benediction.

I will never take this for granted.

William comes in then, mugs in his hands, Mrs Lewes hot on his heels bearing a tray of her famous oat biscuits.

William's eyes soft and shining with love as he takes in the tableau of his son ensconced in Rani's arms.

'What's this new habit of spending all day in bed and being waited on, young man? And look at the state of my sheets!' Mrs Lewes grumbles, but before she can set down her tray, Andrew has jumped off Rani's lap and into Mrs Lewes' arms, upturning the tray and nearly creating an avalanche of biscuits.

William manages to catch it just in time, while saying, futilely, 'Watch out, son.'

But Andrew is not listening, for he is breathlessly addressing Mrs Lewes. 'Miss Raj is going to be my new mummy!'

Mrs Lewes pauses in the act of fondly setting Andrew's curls to order, looking from William to Rani and back again.

William's flushed gaze flusters away from Mrs Lewes' enquiring one. Even Rani finds it hard to meet her eyes.

'Is what this young man saying true?' Her hands going to her ample hips as she surveys each of them in turn like a stern mother bringing her erring children to book.

'I'm not lying, Mrs Lewes.' Andrew is indignant.

'Well, Mr Strong?'

'You're not lying, son,' William reassures Andrew. And to Mrs Lewes, briefly holding her gaze, 'Yes, it is.' He turns to beam at Rani, a smile which declares, *I can't quite believe my luck.*

Mrs Lewes catches it. She smiles at William and at Andrew. 'Well, well, that's good news. I'd better start saving coupons for the wedding feast. There's a cake to be made and the precious piece of chocolate I was saving for an eventuality such as this seems to have gone missing suddenly.' Her voice rising at the last.

Both William and Andrew look guiltily away.

Mrs Lewes' eyes meet Rani's and again, Rani has to fight the urge to look away. 'Congratulations, Miss Raj.' Her gaze gives a lie to the merry words for it is stark with warning, leaving Rani feeling chastised.

* * *

It doesn't take long for Mrs Lewes to corner her.

She is darning at the kitchen table when Rani, William and Andrew return from their daily walk, a jauntily celebratory one that evening.

Usually, by this time, she'd have retired upstairs to her room, the kitchen spick and span but grimly dark, blackout curtains drawn.

'Miss Raj, a word,' she says, when William takes Andrew up to prepare for bed and Rani starts making her excuses to escape to her own room.

Mrs Lewes' voice is just as strident with warning as before, when she had congratulated Rani.

Rani experiences a thrill of foreboding even as she scolds herself for it. *You're a grown woman making your own decisions. You're not answerable to her.*

And yet... she's grown to like Mrs Lewes. She values her opinion. Mrs Lewes is an integral part of this family Rani is soon to join properly. She is the only other person who also cares for William and Andrew deeply, and perhaps even more fiercely and protectively than Rani. She had been there for them before Rani. She'd held them together when they were deeply lost, abandoned by their wife and mother, tiding them through their worst. Rani wants, very much, for Mrs Lewes to approve of her decision to marry William.

Mrs Lewes looks at her and the dim light accentuates the lines on her face, adds shadows to her eyes. 'I've not seen them this happy since before...'

Mrs Lewes takes a breath, sighing deeply.

The ghost of William's absconding wife joins them at the table, which smells faintly of pickled cabbage despite Mrs Lewes' determined scrubbing.

'Thank you for making them happy,' Mrs Lewes says, but her voice is as grim as Rani has ever heard it, and there's no smile to alleviate the severity of her expression. And here comes the caution. 'Don't break their hearts. They've suffered enough. If you do, I won't forgive you.'

Rani holds Mrs Lewes' gaze, says with all the conviction of a heart that is suffused with love for a father and son who have welcomed her into their life and family, healed to a great extent her own broken heart, 'I won't.'

Mrs Lewes looks at Rani for several, unbending seconds – to Rani, it feels like a lifetime.

Then, her severe expression relaxing somewhat. 'I believe you.' And finally, she nods, and there... a smile! 'You are good for them.'

'I hope to be. I wish to be. I will be.'

Mrs Lewes pats her hand. 'Didn't you hear me just now, my dear? You already are.'

Rani is moved to embrace her, embarrassing both of them.

Mrs Lewes politely endures a moment or so of it before pulling away. 'Right then, goodnight, Miss Raj. I dare say you will have sweet dreams.'

And she winks.

58

RANI

William and Rani are married six weeks later (having decided not to dally due to the impatient excitement of a certain beloved little boy), in the church at Bletchley, all the codebreakers from the cottage, save Dilly, who is gravely ill, in attendance.

Rani wears the same dress she travelled to Bletchley in – no luxury of new clothes, even for a new bride, with the war on. The cream dress is now dull grey, sullied by age and wear, although Mrs Lewes has tried her very best to make it sparkle.

'You look very nice, although your dress is old,' Andrew says, scrunching up his nose as he says 'old' before possessively taking her hand. He will be leading her up the aisle.

'Andrew!' Mrs Lewes cries, but there's no heat to her admonishment. She's too happy to be annoyed, beaming widely at Rani in a way reserved until now only for Andrew and William.

'You don't look half bad yourself, young sir,' Rani beams down at her soon-to-be stepson.

He is looking very smart indeed, heart-warmingly precious. Mrs Lewes has starched his shirt, it is neatly tucked into his trousers and he's even wearing a tie. She has polished his shoes and wiped his face – always a little dirty in the way of small boys – shiny clean. She has pressed down his curls, combing them into submission. Rani can only infer at the emotional blackmail – most likely involving the lasting happiness of Rani and William and how much a well-turned-out little boy at their wedding would mean to them – that she must have employed to get the child to sit still and give in to her ministrations.

Rani can bet that before long, the curls will be flying all over the place instead of neatly wrestled into a side parting, the shirt will be awry and face and shoes dirty. She only hopes it lasts until Andrew walks her up the aisle.

Mrs Lewes had helped Rani get ready, tutting at her lack of passable stockings – all of Rani's had been darned over and over, the holes in them now irreparable. Mrs Lewes had tried to patch the holes with soot from the fireplace in the lounge. But it collected in patchy clumps, some of it dropping away in swirls of grey ash, so it appeared as if Rani was riddled by a strange affliction.

After they'd scrubbed the soot off, Mrs Lewes rocking on her haunches as she pondered the solution to the problem, there was a knock on the door, Andrew's sweet voice calling, 'May I come in?'

Mrs Lewes and Rani looked at each other, the soft smile lighting up Mrs Lewes' face mirroring her own expression, Rani imagined at the barely suppressed excitement in the boy's voice. 'In a little while, child. Give us a few minutes. She's not quite ready yet,' Mrs Lewes called.

They heard him skipping down the stairs, Mrs Lewes shaking her head and smiling as she mumbled, 'Dear, dear boy,' almost to herself.

Rani looked about the small room she would soon leave to move downstairs into William's bedroom, Mrs Lewes next to her, smiling fondly at Andrew's enthusiasm, this woman who'd taken her under her wing. And she was grateful even as she was swamped by a great big wave of longing, missing. She closed her eyes, imagining briefly, a different wedding day – her father and Opa looking on proudly, choking back emotion, Mama fussing with Rani's hair while Oma slipped the family heirlooms, pearls gleaming with a secret light, glittering emeralds, twinkling rubies around Rani's neck and hands, an over-excited Arjun dancing around them, getting in the way, Gertie waiting for a suitable moment to get Rani to herself, to ask her – again – if this was what she really wanted, saying seriously, 'Times are changing. Marriage is not the only avenue open to a woman, you know.'

As always when thinking of her friend, Rani is overcome with wistfulness, nostalgia, ache for happier times, even as she chants, over and over in her head, *Please let Gertie be safe.*

Rani heard from her friend just once after they parted ways, Rani to Bletchley Park and Gertie, an enthusiastic member of the SOE. Gertie's letter, as Rani expected, was cheery and upbeat, giving no clue as to how she was and what she was doing. Her friend had asked Rani to continue to direct all mail to the Foreign Office, promising she'd write again soon. But although Rani has sent several letters to Gertie since, inviting her to her wedding in her last, she has yet to receive a reply. It makes Rani terribly worried for her friend.

And her family. The one she is exiled from.

Her family...

She'd written to tell them she was getting married. No reply.

Surely if Mama had known, she'd have replied. She suspects her father didn't show her the letter. Was he always so vindictive and cold and unforgiving? Perhaps she never saw this side of him. No. No. Not her Baba. She chose to believe that his brother had intercepted the letter. That Baba never saw it at all.

And as for Prasad... She has decided he will stay firmly in the past as she creates a new future different to the one she had planned with him as they concocted plans among the branches of a peepal tree beside a drought-ravaged river, a weary buffalo bearing witness.

He will not intrude as she professes to love and honour another man, as she becomes mother to his son.

In the end, she attends her wedding bare-legged, bare-faced, biting her lips hard to inject colour into them. She wears the dress she'd worn when she arrived at Bletchley, the child she met and who won her heart that very day leading her proudly up the aisle to his father. William's eyes shine incandescent with love for both of them, the codebreakers from the cottage and Mrs Lewes bearing smiling witness.

This, then, her family now.

Both in the wider context of work and in her personal life – everyone important to her gathered here as she embarks upon the next stage of her life.

It is a stormy day, clouds glowering from an overcast sky, the steely, uncompromising grey of battleships.

It is as if the weather knows something Rani doesn't, flashing blustery warning with silvery scythes and ominous rumbles, the gusting wind sharp as it whistles caution, whipping her face with stinging force, causing the hair she spent so long tasking into submission that morning into whirling ringlets that obscure her eyes.

But when William beams at her, holding out his hand, his eyes moist with sentiment, vivid with love, all her doubts disappear, even as the storm breaks just as they exchange vows, his 'I do,' drowned by the thundering fury of tantruming heavens, the battering of rain on the church tiles so ferocious that everyone looks up, expecting the centuries-old bricks to give way, the eaves to bend with the force of the gale, devils dancing on the roof, making merry, growling in glee, celebrating with zigzags of electric mirth that split open the firmament, exploding more rain.

When it is her turn to take the vows, the bright-gold iridescence of lightning assuming the form of a jewel-tipped, steel-edged sword.

In the subsequent threat of thunder, the impression of a face at the corner of her eye. Insinuating upon her consciousness. Demanding attention she cannot spare, explanation she doesn't have.

It can't be...

Prasad.

Her childhood love.

But how?

She stumbles on her vows.

She shakes her head, determinedly clearing her mind of the past, concentrating on William, waiting patiently, looking at her with such love. His son beside him. Her future.

The storm holds the church ransom with a sabre-sharp, lightning-sheathed weapon, Rani's 'I do,' lost in its vehement outcry.

When she dares look again, heart pounding, towards where she thought she saw Prasad, she's newly Mrs Strong.

And the young man she once also promised to love forever, in front of his tired bullock, isn't there.

Of course he isn't. He's in a hot country across the ocean from here, pardoned by her father, long moved on from everything that happened, living a happy, fulfilled life, please God.

His likeness that she thought she saw just now is a figment of her imagination conjured by her guilty conscience as she finally sets her past to rest and moves forward with her life.

She shakes her head to clear it even as Andrew throws his arms around her. 'You're my new mummy now.'

Her heart fills with warmth, even more so as William draws them both into his embrace and kisses her.

Mrs Lewes kisses her cheeks while whispering in her ear, 'Remember what I said, Mrs Strong.'

Mrs Strong.

'I'll never forget,' she replies and Mrs Lewes smiles.

'Are you ready for the wedding feast, young man?' Mrs Lewes turns her attention to Andrew. And, tutting as she takes in the state of him, 'Now then what's all this? Look at you! Mucky hair, messy face. Scuffed shoes. Where has the smart boy who walked Mrs Strong, Miss Raj as she was, up the aisle, disappeared to?'

Andrew laughs. The sound so very precious. They can never get enough of it.

And in that moment, looking at her new family, laughing together, Rani herself joining in, she is happy. Grateful. Content. Replete. In love. Loved.

59

RANI

On their wedding night, when they are alone together, a very excited Andrew finally asleep and a very tired Mrs Lewes in her room upstairs opposite what used to be Rani's billet and is once again the spare room, and William reaches across to cup her face, she can't stop shivering.

'What's the matter?' he asks, very tender.

'I...' She cannot meet his eye, struggling to put into words what she wants to say.

'It's overwhelming, isn't it?' He is so gentle, tucking a strand of hair that is draping her eyes behind her ear.

She is overcome by an urge to cry. The words come out all in a rush, tasting of salt.

'I... I promised not to hurt you but I worry I will.'

'Why do you think so?' He asks softly.

'I'm scared. I don't know how to do this, be a wife.'

'Oh,' he says even more gently, his eyes liquid with an expression she now recognises as love. 'Have you never loved anyone before?'

The sceptre of Prasad takes centre stage, climbing into bed

with William and Rani on this, their wedding night.

'I... I loved someone once,' she whispers.

'*You still do,*' Prasad admonishes. '*You lied to your husband. You lied while taking your wedding vows. Your marriage is a sham. You love me. You promised to love me forever.*'

She can't take it any more. The hounding of her conscience in Prasad's voice.

And so, on their wedding night, she tells her husband the whole sorry story.

William listens patiently as is his wont.

He does not interrupt.

When she finishes, he holds her tighter, gently kissing her tears until he comes to her lips.

Then he kisses her lips.

And afterwards, the rest comes easily.

* * *

Much later, he says, 'It wasn't your fault.'

She sniffs. She does not want Prasad here any more. In her marriage bed, with her husband who has loved her so thoroughly.

He's already shouting at her in her head, *You betrayed me.*

'I can't help feeling guilty,' she says to William. 'I got what I wanted, an education. Here I am with you, Andrew and Mrs Lewes. Happy. And Prasad... I... I don't know his fate so I imagine the worst and feel terribly sad and guilty...'

'I do understand,' William says, kissing her gently, tenderly, with such love. 'It wasn't your fault, though. You did what you did out of love for him.'

He kisses her again. Loves her again.

And she manages to forget Prasad briefly, push him away and

live in the moment, in the glorious here and now with her wonderful husband.

* * *

Afterwards, William says, smiling at her ensconced in his embrace, 'Do you think we made a baby just now?'

It catches her by surprise. She is still lost in feeling, and so she can't quite school her face not to show the alarm that replaces the sated languor that had taken her over.

'Oh my darling, I'm sorry. I didn't mean to shock you,' William says. 'We can wait a little before we expand our family, but I would like nothing more than to be surrounded by several little versions of you and I can just imagine how excited Andrew would be to have siblings to love and boss over.'

She doesn't have to consider for very long. 'I'd like that very much too, as long as some of them are like you.'

He laughs. Then cheekily, 'Shall we try to make one now, if we haven't already?'

'Only if you promise he or she will be like you.'

'With your eyes,' he says, kissing them. And, 'Your smile,' kissing her lips.

Then there are no words, feeling taking over.

60

ESME

The letter is tucked in Mrs Lewes' battered Bible, just where she said it would be. Propping up the Ten Commandments.

And oh.

Oh.

There's also a photograph.

Esme is too wound up to sit inside the house even with the windows open and curtains flying in the breeze.

The garden is overgrown. Her little patch of paradise blooming colourful, joyful flowers arm in arm with riotous weeds singing in the heady glory of sun.

She sits on the bench among the lavender bushes from where she'd watch Robbie jumping on the trampoline, or digging industriously in his veg patch, again a weed haven.

Trepidation and excitement as she fingers the letter and the photograph. She's not looked closely at either. She's procrastinating. Nervous. What if it's nothing pertaining to her mother at all?

She strokes the velvet moss growing underneath the bench slats. Throws her head to the heavens so she won't see the weeds.

Closes her eyes, feels the sun-warmed breeze caress her cheeks.

Should she call her brother, wait for him so they can look at this together?

* * *

When she's next aware of her surroundings, coming to with a jolt, when her head, lolling in sleep, smacks against the hard back slats of the bench, darkness has fallen.

She can't believe she fell asleep! It's been this way since she started seeing the psychologist, Sally – her body, now she's sleeping again, catching up on all those lost hours it needs to make up.

She thinks of Philip – he is never far away, always hovering at the edge of her consciousness. The urge to see him, talk to him, hold him, kiss him, is overwhelming.

I must call him and apologise. But at the thought her body seizes up.

I'm not there yet, Philip. But I'm working on it. I worry though that by the time I'm ready it will be too late.

Please, no.

The sweet, smoky smell of settling evening and ripening fruit wafts at her.

An owl hoots somewhere among the trees beyond.

The rustle and scurry of animals among the overgrown vegetation.

She's cold now the sun has retired for the day.

She looks over at the house, windows open, curtains dancing a tango in the shadow-speckled breeze.

Her hands are numb.

She clasps them together to rub some warmth into them.

And then the events of the day rush into her groggy, sleep-numbed mind, as she realises she's still clutching the photograph and the letter.

She gathers them to her heart and goes indoors, as it's too dark to read on the bench. Night has arrived properly, stealthily, a seasoned spy.

The house is cold, but she does not notice anything except for the letter and photograph clasped against her frantically cavorting heart.

She does not close the windows, wafting in the outdoors on curtains billowing in the violet night air tasting of anticipation.

She collapses onto the sofa, ignoring the sighing balloon of dust it releases – time enough to give the house a good clean later.

Right now, she has something to do – she's procrastinated enough.

Taking a deep breath, telling herself if it turns out to be nothing, she will live with that, fingers trembling, she turns her attention to the photograph.

It is old, curling at the edges. Writing at the back in pencil. A woman's hand but not Mrs Lewes' handwriting, which Esme would recognise anywhere. The writing has bleached to a faded yellow but the beautiful cursive script is still perfectly legible: *Bletchley Park, 1942.*

1942. A year before Esme's birth.

Bletchley Park.

Dad had worked there during the war. He was a codebreaker but it was all hush-hush and they weren't allowed to talk about it. Esme only found out when visiting with Mrs Lewes and she said, while reminiscing about the war, 'We lived in that narrow house on the outskirts of Bletchley, while your father did that top-secret work at Bletchley Park, do you remember?'

This was before she moved to a nursing home, in the very early stages of what was later diagnosed as vascular dementia.

'Dad was a codebreaker at Bletchley Park?' Esme was amazed. Bletchley Park had been in the news recently – now that war time information was declassified, veterans were coming forward to share their stories. 'Like Alan Turing?' The man credited with shortening the war by at least two whole years.

'Oops,' Mrs Lewes said, clapping a hand across her mouth as with the other, she handed Esme her tea. 'I'm not supposed to talk about it. It's top secret.'

'Not any—' Esme began.

But Mrs Lewes had interrupted her with a sigh: 'But of course, you wouldn't remember anyway. We moved soon after you were born. My memory is not what it was. You won't tell anyone will you, my dear?' Winking at Esme. 'Now, is this strong enough for you, love? Shall I let the tea bag steep a bit more?'

Perhaps, Esme thinks now, grief at the memory of Mrs Lewes, accompanied by a vivid image of the woman she loved, ambushing, hurting, *this photograph is to do with her father after all.*

She turns it over.

A black-and-white shot – age tinting it sepia – of a group of people standing in front of a house. A rather ugly and rambling stately manor. They are a motley group, men and women of varying ages.

She squints closely at them. Hang on, one of them is very familiar. Is it... could it be Andy? Not possible. This photo is old.

She brings the photograph up to her nose. *Oh.* It's her *father*, younger than she remembers! She hadn't noticed how very similar her father and brother were, looks wise, but here, it's apparent.

A gift.

Thank you, Mrs Lewes.

She sniffs, blows her nose, studies the photograph again. Now her attention is drawn to the woman next to her father. Esme does not recall seeing her before, even in a photograph, and yet, she feels familiar. Not like her father did, when she thought it might be Andy. In a different, heart-tugging way she can't quite explain.

Her father has his arm around the woman, Esme notes. She's looking right at the camera, grave expression, watchful eyes. A captivating lady. Stunning in an exotic way. It is evident even in black and white that she's dusky complexioned.

Like Esme when she's caught the sun.

Is this the mysterious Rani? Esme's mother?

Esme has always wondered whether her father was so reticent to talk about the past because his children were from two different mums but she never raised it and pushed the question away when it popped in her head. It was hard to break the habit of a lifetime, learned from her father and brother – to let things be and not stir them up. And so she tried to squash the thought when it came. But it was always there, hovering...

And now, she gives it free rein.

Is Rani, like Mrs Lewes said, Esme's mother, but not Andy's?

PART IV

61

RANI

Bletchley, 1943

She's pretty sure she's being followed.

She slows down.

The sound of wheels behind her slows down too.

She starts pedalling faster. At her back, closer than before, is a reciprocal echo, loud in the chilly gloom of frosty dark. Open fields around her. Empty. Desolate. Shadow-coloured grass susurrating with secrets. The station is a way back. The village up ahead, a good five minutes of fast bicycling away.

What is she to do? Her mind is emptied of everything but terror.

She's returning home after the late shift. There is no one else around – her fault. She'd stayed back after her watch ended, caught up in the thrill of arriving at the solution for a particularly tricky code.

William is in London, cherry-picked for a top priority project – which is all he can say about it. He's been away for weeks now and has only been able to return home for a day during that time, quite exhausted and very happy to spend it as a tent day.

'I wish I had time for a tent night too, with my beautiful wife, whom I miss sorely, just the two of us in a white-sheeted world, bliss,' he'd whispered into Rani's ear, out of his son's hearing, making her blush, his apple-scented breath raising goosebumps.

When William found out she was on night watch, he'd made her vow not to stay back after her shift, knowing her only too well. 'No matter how close you are to cracking the code, promise me? I'm not there to accompany you home and I worry, my dear.' His eyes shining with love.

'I promise,' she'd said blithely, 'although I do think you worry too much.'

And now she's broken the vow she made to him. She hadn't even realised she was doing it, had vaguely heard the others leave, called goodbye, saying, to those who stopped by her desk, 'I'll just be a minute, you go on.'

Now, she's pedalling furiously in the pitch dark, and someone is following her. Stepping up and slowing down to match her pace. The whirring of bicycle wheels, rubber tyres smacking the cobbles – it is difficult to disguise the sound amplified by the pressing quiet of night, only broken by a mournful owl's persistent hoots, the distant hiss and chug of a train.

Her heart thuds too loud in the thick, all-enveloping cloak of silence.

Then it is broken by a word uttered softly. Intimately.

Her name.

A caress gently whispered into the velvet night by a voice that is familiar.

Known.

Completely disorientating as it is so very out of place.

He calls her name again in that same tender, conspiratorial whisper.

It can't be, surely...?

Goosebumps erupting upon her skin, wild thoughts rushing through her head as she turns.

He smiles, teeth gleaming in the dark. Eyes glinting.

Even as he says again, her name poetry in his mouth.

'Rani.'

And she is... transported across an ocean.

Back on the branches of a peepal tree arching over a parched riverbed, watched patiently by a wizened bullock, sharing mangoes doused in sea salt, making plans to change the world with her first love.

Prasad.

That sighting of him in the church as she was getting married.

That sighting that made her stumble over her vows.

That sighting she thought was a mirage.

Not a mirage. No.

Real. Flesh and blood.

She takes him in.

He is safe.

He is *here*.

She is happy. Happy happy happy. Her heart overwhelmed.

'I had to come to see you, Rani, my love,' he whispers.

He's travelled the ocean for her.

She flings her bike down beside Prasad's. The bike she usually takes such good care of because of her promise to a little boy she loves.

And Rani, who since India, has given thought to every decision, now recklessly, like the girl she used to be once, daring, unmindful of consequences, follows Prasad into the fields.

62

___

RANI

Prasad sets off down the path between the fields in purposeful strides, surefooted in the rustling dark, alive with secrets.

Prasad. In England. Here. At Bletchley. Her past colliding with her present.

She can't get her head around it.

And now, after the first, heady, disbelieving, fantastic joy of seeing him, this man who was the youth she loved, who she has worried about, agonised over, prayed for, wished and hoped was all right, she is ambushed by questions.

Is this really happening? Is it some sort of dream fantasy?

She pinches herself. Hard. Her skin scrunches up. And oh, how it hurts!

Not a dream then.

Rani looks around. Nothing. No one. Everything appears deserted. Pregnant with intrigue.

They are just a few metres from her home with her family, from the work she loves at Bletchley Park, and yet, with the moist grass gently tipping into her, enveloped by its green, earthy scent, night sky twinkling above, they might be anywhere.

He is just a silhouette ahead of her.

She is struck by a sudden qualm. Is it really him? 'Prasad...'

He raises a finger to his lips. *Shush.*

Beckons her with a nod of his head to follow.

Her curiosity aroused, accompanied by a thrill of fear.

She doesn't really *know* this man who was once the boy she loved.

The sighing of the breeze through foliage. The nostalgia-infused, sharply nippy scents of night pulsing with seductive promise, enveloping gently in a navy, velvet embrace.

Should she follow? Does she trust him?

'The girl I knew would never have hesitated,' Prasad tosses from ahead.

And then, of course she blindly follows him.

'The girl I knew also never could resist a challenge. She was feisty, inquisitive, always ready for adventure.'

She can hear him laughing. His laugh is still the same, cascading whorls of spun gold.

'She's still in there somewhere hidden under the boring, middle-class mother and wife front.'

That stings.

I'm still here, the person I used to be once, she tells herself, stumbling in Prasad's wake.

The grass, nearly as tall as her, swaying in dark swathes, shadow-sprinkled whisper and caress. The night taut with suspense. Is she mad to trust him?

He does not speak, just walks surefooted down the field, cutting through the vegetation.

Finally, in the middle of the field, nothing but blades of grass rippling with suspense, he stops. Turns to her.

She asks the first thing that comes to her head. 'How did you get here?'

'With difficulty,' he says shortly. His face grave.

And now, as her eyes adjust to the darkness, she sees the scars. They are gouged into his face and neck, hacked into the palms of his hands, all the skin that is visible – it is cold so he's wearing a long-sleeved cardigan and trousers – deep furrows of damaged flesh, as if someone has taken a knife repeatedly to it.

He is looking steadily at her, so she manages to stop herself from flinching.

'They are all over my body. But those are just the scars you see,' he says. 'There are many more here.' His hand upon his heart. 'And those are much more painful.'

As she properly meets his gaze… Something out of place.

And then she understands. And now she can't stop her gasp from escaping.

The glint in his eyes. One is alive, vivid, dancing. The other… the other not.

'I lost it recently. The war…' He shrugs, matter-of-fact.

'The war? You're in the army?'

'I had to get to you somehow. I'd found out from the palace guards that you were in England. And so I joined the British Indian Army.'

She closes her eyes, sways on her feet, ice-flecked, night-flavoured breeze chastising her with stinging strokes.

'The thought of you kept me alive,' he says softly. 'Through the beatings and torture at the palace, through the desperate times after, through the icy winds knifing stunned flesh unaccustomed to cold in foreign battlefields, fighting an alien war, through losing an eye and being invalided out. Our love, the promises we made to each other, kept me going until… until I found you.' His voice a keening lament. 'Then I discovered it was all a lie, that you are no different from your father, selling out on principles, promises, love, when it suits you.'

'I...' *didn't know your fate, thought you were dead, assumed you'd moved on, wished only the best for you...* Her words, excuses swallowed by the dark, dancing sea of nothingness, green grass tinted black with night, tightly holding on to its shadowy secrets, blue-grey awning of sky above, wide and benign, scribbles of stars.

'Why, Rani? Didn't you believe in us?'

What can she say? *There was no us. Not once my father retrieved the sword from you. I was sent here, to England. You were sent to jail.*

'I have kept my promise. I still love you. I always will. You're the only one for me. What about you?'

You are crazy to have followed this man here. Run, now, her conscience cries.

Above her, the star-pincered shroud of sky bears witness.

She should run.

And yet...

And yet.

He has suffered for her.

Prison. Abuse. Torture.

He has fought a war he doesn't believe in, lost an eye, come all this way for her.

'I loved you once. I don't know you now,' she stalls.

He says, 'I don't know you either, but I have steadfastly loved you anyway. The girl I knew promised to love me until the end of time and I believed her. When her father insulted her, I defended her honour by wielding the sword *she* had stolen, part of *her* grand plan, at his throat. She begged me not to hurt her father and in doing as she asked, I lost her and my freedom too. I would have been killed for treason, but she bravely stood up to her father, bargained for my life. She was willing to die for me, with me. She challenged her father when he accused me of committing treason. She said *she* had too, that if I must die, then she should too.'

'How do you know that?' Rani whispers.

'The palace walls have ears. There are servants everywhere and they gossip worse than fishwives.' A pause, then, 'The girl I knew was brave, devil-may-care. I cannot equate that girl with this staid woman who cycles to work and back and lives a quiet life with a second-hand husband and son.'

Fury. Biting hot. 'They're not—'

He cuts her off with, 'The point is, I don't know the woman you have become either, Rani.' He sighs, runs a hand through his hair. 'Look, I realise that this must be such a shock to you, me suddenly turning up out of nowhere... I do understand. We've both changed since we last saw each other. We have much to catch up on. Will you take the time to do so? Will you at least give me that?' he asks.

An image of Andrew and William rises before her eyes. Her family. Who were both so very serious and grave when she first met them. Who are happy now. With her in their lives.

'Don't hurt them,' Mrs Lewes had warned. 'They've suffered enough.'

But this man...

He is the youth she loved, whom she'd admired for finding happiness despite circumstances being stacked against him. Who knew by name every single person in his village, had charmed everyone.

Who is now broken. Scarred. Hurt. Because he dared to defend the honour of the girl he loved by holding the sword she had stolen against her father's throat. Who endured imprisonment and torture because she asked him to spare her father and he listened.

Who has come all this way for her.

He's suffered too. So very, very much.

And she is responsible. *She* came up with the plan to steal the sword, setting all the rest in motion.

He's paid very dearly for it.

'All I ask for is time to talk, for us to get to know each other again. I will not ask for anything you cannot or are not willing to give, Rani. I love you too much for that. You may not know me now, but know that you can trust me,' he says, in the middle of the fields, in the middle of the night, in the middle of nowhere, it seems.

A fitting setting for the past she thought was put to bed to come calling.

All he wants is to talk.

There's no harm in that, surely?

She's not hurting anyone.

And she owes Prasad this much.

'All right,' she says.

He smiles and it is a beautiful sight. He looks so much younger; he is the boy she loved.

63

ESME

Despite the lateness of the hour, Esme calls her brother.

'Did I wake you?'

'No, I couldn't sleep. I was reading.'

'You suffer from insomnia as well?' Why didn't she know this about her brother? Why didn't she notice that he looks so much like their father, that he too is a quiet, reserved man preferring books to people? Why hasn't she made more of an effort with him, one of her two living relatives now their father is gone?

'Sometimes. When I have a lot on my mind.' A pause. Then, 'You do too?'

'Yes.' She wants to ask what's on his mind, and she will, later, but first, 'Andy, Mrs Lewes did have a letter in her Bible, just like she said.'

'Ah.'

'I also found a photograph from 1942. Dad with his arm around a woman.'

'Rani.' Andy says. He sounds very sure.

'They're part of a group standing in front of Bletchley Park. Dad worked there, did you know?'

'I did. You were born there.' Again, he speaks with firm conviction.

'Andy? I thought you didn't recall much from early childhood.'

A pause that goes on.

And on.

Then, 'I... I've remembered who Rani is.'

'You *have*?' She's surprised. That it's happened so soon. Happened at all. How? And now it comes to her. 'Ah, that's what's been on your mind. It's why you couldn't sleep.'

His turn to sound surprised. 'Yes, how did you...?' Then, 'Never mind. Look, can I come round tomorrow after work? I'd like to look at the photograph and... I've so much to tell you. I'd rather do it in person.'

'I was going to suggest that, actually. I haven't read the letter yet. We can do that together.'

After Esme puts the phone down, she picks up the photograph, unease slithering up her spine. Her father and this mysterious Rani. What's the story here? How did Andy remember her so serendipitously? And why did her even-tempered brother sound so worried when he said he had things to share with Esme?

64

RANI

Bletchley, 1943

Prasad takes to meeting Rani every evening after her shift.

Mrs Lewes and Andrew are fast asleep when she gets home anyway, so they don't realise she's returning home later than usual.

If William was home, he would have noticed.

If William was home, it wouldn't have happened at all.

But he is not.

And so, she meets with Prasad and tells herself she's not doing anything wrong.

After all, they're only talking and if he takes her hand every so often, in the field in the dark, it is for old times' sake.

She allows it, pushing away the guilt, claiming her hand back when he holds it for a little longer than strictly necessary.

'Was it you at my wedding?' she asks Prasad the second time she meets him – he was waiting for her after her shift, hidden away in the shadows, making himself known once she'd bid goodbye to her colleagues, left Bletchley Park and was bicycling home on her own.

She had startled when he called her name in the whispering dark – while one part of her was expecting him, the other was wondering if it had all been a dream. He had laughed then – his beautiful, iridescent chuckles hadn't changed – and once again, she was transported to the past when she was young and daring and freshly in love.

She still can't quite get used to the idea of Prasad here – it's too fantastic. Her two worlds colliding so abruptly. During that first meeting, she was so disorientated that she hadn't said much, asked much, still digesting the fact that he was alive, that he, her past, was here, in her new life.

Right in the middle of it.

She couldn't sleep after her first encounter with him, although she knew she must. Andrew would come to wake her soon and then she had to go in for her watch. She needed to be alert to tackle the code. She was of no use tired.

Yet still she couldn't sleep.

The whole meeting had had a dreamlike quality. The clandestine nature of it. The dark. The field. A ghost from her past.

But...

The next day, he was there. Waiting when she finished her shift.

He had survived. He had joined the army. He had been invalided out. And then he had come in search of her...

'Yes, I was at your wedding,' he says, his voice steeped in pain. 'I finally found you again after years of missing, longing, suffering, and it was too late. You were getting married to someone else.' He's so bitter. 'I went away then. Tried to forget you.'

Ah. This explains why she didn't see him again for months.

'I couldn't,' he says softly. 'I've loved you, only you, all my adult life. You've got me through so much. I lived through torture, through war, through losing my eye for you.'

He is matter-of-fact. She is ambushed by guilt.

'I came back. I bided my time. It took a while but I didn't mind waiting. I'd waited so long without knowing where you were. Now, knowing you were close, I could wait a bit longer. Then he went away.'

Such anger in his voice when he talks of William.

'He's my husband.'

'*I'm* your first love. If we hadn't been separated, he wouldn't be.'

'But he is now.'

'Does he love you like I do? I've crossed oceans for you. I've suffered for you. Look at me.'

He lifts up his cardigan and she gasps, hot tears welling. Every inch of his skin scored with scars. Gouged flesh, mottled, clawed out. Wound upon wound upon wound.

Another midnight rendezvous, another question.

'What are you doing here?' she asks.

'What do you mean? I've come to find you. Ma and my buffalo both died when I was in prison. By the time I got out, my Baba was gone too – heartache took him. You've been my reason for living, for going on, Rani. I believed your promises of eternal love you see, fool that I was.'

When he speaks like this, she feels trapped.

He's an adult. She's not responsible for him.

But... she can't help feeling so.

He was imprisoned because she stole the sword. He was abused and tortured while she was getting an education at Cambridge.

He lost his parents, his buffalo, all who mattered to him, who cared for him, except her.

And so he came to find her. Only to find he'd lost her too.

'You are taken. You don't belong to me. Perhaps you never did.' His voice melancholy as storm-harangued wind soughing through denuded trees in the depths of winter.

Was he always this possessive? But can she blame him for it? Circumstances have made him this way, events that in part, she caused.

She feels guilty. She is trapped. She shouldn't be here.

Her place is with her family.

But Prasad...

For the longest time, he thought she was his family. He has no one else. She wishes she didn't feel so responsible. But she does. She does.

Which is why she keeps meeting him.

'You must go back, Prasad. Go home. Find a nice girl to marry,' she says. She can't quite keep the desperation from her voice.

Please, she thinks.

'I... I just want a few more days with you.' He's so close, she can smell his breath. Not mango flavoured any longer. He's so far from home.

Again, she experiences a renewed assault of guilt.

He reminds her of Andrew. At heart, still a lost little boy wanting love.

'How are you staying here? Where are you staying? Where is the money coming from?'

'I... I have some money.' He's cagey. Then, pulling at the grass around them in angry fistfuls, 'You are asking me to move on, look ahead, as if it's easy, Rani. I... when I imagined a future, it always included you. It got me through everything. *Everything*.'

65

RANI

Guilty.

She is guilty all the time.

When with Prasad.

With Mrs Lewes and Andrew.

With William when he managed to spare a few hours, come home for a rushed morning visit.

Before, she'd have thought the time with him was too brief.

But now the couple of hours with her husband couldn't go fast enough.

She was not comfortable in his embrace, guilt driving a wedge between them, colouring every action and conversation.

'You're different. What's the matter, love?' William asked.

'Nothing. I just... I wish we weren't apart. I worry about you in London.' Truth. Lies. Both.

'Not too long now,' William said. 'The project will be over soon and I'll be back for good.'

Before, she would have been uncomplicatedly happy and pleased.

Now, all she could think of was that she couldn't do this, maintain this deceit, with William home, portion herself in two no matter what she felt she owed to her childhood love.

Prasad simply *must* be gone by then.

* * *

'This has to stop,' Rani says to Prasad when she sees him next. 'We've talked, caught up. Now you must go home.'

Prasad does not say anything for a very long time, just plucks the dark blades of grass caressing their legs roughly and chucks them away.

When he looks at her, there are tears in his good eye. They pincer her heart. Gouge at her flesh, leaving invisible, indelible scars.

'They knifed me with the very sword that you stole from your father, repeatedly, to teach me a lesson I wouldn't forget,' Prasad had said.

Every time she looks at him, she imagines that lethal sword drawing blood, scoring his flesh.

She stole the sword. *He* paid the punishment. *He* bears the scars.

It breaks her heart.

'Don't you feel anything at all for me?' Prasad asks, a tear trembling on his lash briefly before settling on his cheek, glowing silver in the dark. 'I was hoping that when you talked with me, you'd remember what we had, realise that it was *me* you actually loved, that you'd come away with me.'

Guilty. She feels so guilty.

'You will always have a very special place in my heart,' she manages.

'Is that all?' he cries, and his voice is a raw howl of pain.

He pulls her to him in a rough embrace. It is so very sudden. She is too stunned to do anything but go along with it.

He has never touched her since he reappeared suddenly in her life here at Bletchley except to take her hand every so often – she's allowed that, but when his touch lingered too long she'd claimed her hand back.

He smells of fresh grass and festering past.

He kisses her. He tastes of earth. Raw, bitter.

And now, she pulls away.

'What are you *doing*? I'm married,' she cries.

'I wanted to remind you of what we had once. But I see now. You never loved me like I did you. Like I still do. When I heard from the palace servants that you'd stood up for me, were willing to die for me, I believed you did. It got me through. I thought what we had was true love. And that even though you'd been swayed by that *firangi* you've gone and married, you'd realise the truth when you met with me. But you've changed, Rani, just like you said. You were brave once, daring, principled, standing up for your love. But now you've become shallow, materialistic. This capitalist world you live in, with all its trappings, has changed you. You met with me out of pity,' he spits, pacing up and down the path between the fields.

Why is *he* angry when he's the one who's crossed a line?

She's *furious*. 'You told me I could trust you. You've broken that trust.'

'I don't want your pity. I want your love,' he tosses at her.

It is as if they are having two different conversations. It makes her even more enraged.

'Do you not see what you just did was wrong? I'm *married*. To someone else. I have a child.'

'And for me, for the longest time, you've been my life. My end goal. I've loved only you. I've endured for you. You think it's easy to leave now, go home, start again? When the purpose in my life is gone? Marry someone else, you say. It might be easy for you. Not so for me. I wish I'd never met you.'

Me too, she thinks, and she is so very, very sad. She loved this man once. She still cares for him.

'We can't go back, Prasad. We have to look forward.'

'Look forward?' He sneers. 'What do I have to look forward to? I can't get any jobs looking like this. A half-blind thug. Find someone else to marry, you say. Even if I wanted to, do you think they'd want me? What do I have to offer them? And when the woman who loved me once, who promised to love me forever, has chosen a comfortable, safe life over me, how can I expect anyone else to choose me?'

'Prasad.' She's despairing. 'We *can't* just turn back the clock.'

'If we could,' he says softly, 'would you choose me?'

'We can't, Prasad,' she sighs, the anger gone, just deep, deep pain in its place. 'It is what it is. We have to accept it.'

'It's because he has what I don't, isn't it? An elite education. A middle-class life.'

'It's no—'

'Look at you. You've sold out, Rani. You're no different from your father, well versed in betrayal, turning your back on promises when it suits you.'

'I'm nothing like...' She cannot finish. For, from his perspective, looked at his way, she *is* no different from her father.

It makes her realise something – that perhaps she should have given her father a chance, taken the time to look at things his way.

'It doesn't matter,' Prasad bites out. 'When we win – and we will, soon – we'll shape a world for the people, of the people. No more imperialism as practised by your father, or the capitalist society you've so easily embraced, you who used to spin dreams of a world where everyone was equal, nobody was marginalised, with me, once, remember?'

Like when he grabbed her just now, the change in him from despairing to passionate is too sudden, very disorientating. What's going on with this man she only really knew as a bright-eyed youth years ago?

Why is she still here, in the middle of the fields, in the middle of the night, alone with him, even after he grabbed her just now, listening to him spout the rhetoric she herself used once as an idealistic innocent?

Because she owes him.

She asks when she can trust herself to speak. 'Who's *we*?'

'We want change,' he continues, as if she hasn't spoken. 'A world where people are not discriminated against because of lack of wealth, "inferior" upbringing. No capitalist government can provide this. But if Britain's Russian allies win, well, we will make this world a reality, not just a dream.' His good eye gleams, radiating fiery light. 'The world is ready for change. A socialist world for the people. Where everyone is equal. With capitalism broken and fascism killing, maiming, destroying, socialism is the way to go.'

'Prasad?' she asks. 'Whose words are you...?'

'Don't you *dare*,' he barks. 'Just because I did not have the means to acquire a university education does not mean I can't think for myself.'

'I didn't...' She takes a breath. 'Look, what I meant was, where did you... You said "we"...'

'Why was I punished when you were at fault? Why did you get away scot-free? Because I was poor, with nobody to stand up for me, plead my case, like your father pleaded yours with his brother.'

'I pleaded your case.'

'Yes.' He softens. 'You did. But you were just a woman, with not much power. You managed to get my life spared, but I was tortured all the same. While you, with your father onside... Look at you, Rani, and look at me, and tell me this world we live in is fair, that it doesn't need to change.'

'But Britain is fighting for, bringing about that change. That is what we are doing at—'

'Britain is and always will be a capitalist society run by and for the rich. All of you working here, all privileged, with your degrees from highbrow institutions and your elite connections...'

'No, that isn't tr—'

'It doesn't matter.' Again, Prasad's manner changes, becoming impatient. 'Look, you want me to leave, don't you? Go far away, let you live your life, the one where I stay firmly in the past.'

She colours. It *is* exactly what she wants. He is her past. She wants him there, not here, intruding in her present. Perhaps he is right. She is more like her father than she thought, chopping and changing principles to suit her.

'I will.'

She lets out the breath she didn't realise she was holding.

'But you have to do one thing for me.'

Oh.

'What?' she whispers.

'Get information.'

'Information?' She's puzzled.

'From your husband.'

'From William?' she asks stupidly. Not understanding.

'For the cause. To create a fair world. For us to win, we need information. Which you can provide. Your husband is working on something right now that will be crucial to us.'

And then she gets it. 'You're asking me to *spy*?' She cannot believe it. 'On my *husband*?'

'For me,' Prasad says.

Is he mad?

'No.'

'You stole the ceremonial sword from your father for me.'

He *is* crazy.

'That was then. I was young, I didn't think things through. And look what happened with that – it didn't turn out well, did it?'

'But you did it. For me.'

'Prasad, you're asking me to steal secrets pertaining to international security, the *world's* wellbeing, from my husband.'

'*We* care for the world's wellbeing. All capitalist societies like Britain do is care for themselves only. Allowing the rich to get richer and the poor to suffer.'

She shakes her head. No.

'You used to agree with me, Rani, but you've been sucked into the capitalist machine, brainwashed…'

'It's you who are brainwashed, Prasad. Listen to you.' She's heard about them, these vultures who recruit spies. They prey on vulnerabilities, hone in on weaknesses. 'Who are these people who have you under their sway? Forget all this, Prasad.'

'You think it's easy? It's all I have, now I don't have you.'

They have given him something to believe in, this damaged man who had believed in the constancy and surety of the love he and Rani had once had, only to find she had moved on. He was disillusioned, flailing, until they recruited him.

'Please go home,' she tries.

'I don't have a home. I thought you were my home, my destiny, my future.'

'Prasad, please…'

'Rani, you owe me. *You* stole the sword. *I* was punished. I loved you. That was my only mistake. I still love you, more fool me. I should have killed your father when I had the chance. I was defending your honour when I held the blade to his neck. I stopped because you asked me to. I suffered. You are living your life at the cost of mine.'

True. All true.

'Do this for me, Rani.'

'Who are these people you're asking me to spy for?'

'They rescued me when I was at my lowest, having lost my eye, in pain, convalescing in a hospital here in the country that housed you and yet having no idea how to find you.'

Just as she thought. 'They helped you to find me,' she says.

'They did.'

They must have felt they'd struck gold when they realised she was at Bletchley Park, the hub of war intelligence. Or perhaps, an even more scary thought, they'd been watching her and found *him*, to get to her. Perhaps they did this with all the codebreakers at Bletchley: dug up the skeletons in their past and used those to get to them, get at them.

She asks, 'They set you up here in Bletchley?'

'Yes, and loaned me a bicycle. When I found out you were getting married and wanted to go away, they helped with that too.'

'But they urged you to come back. And, when William went to London, to take advantage of the fact my husband was not home, to approach me.'

'They might have done.' Now, he's cagey, defensive.

'In return, they want information. Oh Prasad, what have you done?'

'You will do it?'

He's hopeful. He's crazy. He's the boy she loved looking to her to come up with a plan.

In the intervening years, she's grown up. He hasn't. Can she blame him?

'No. But I can help you pay off...'

'I don't want your money,' he explodes. 'You can't buy me, buy them off. They told me you'd try. This is typical of capitalists, they said. But I never expected *you* to do it, Rani.'

'I'm only trying to help.'

'Then get me the information.'

Now it is her turn to explode. 'Do you have any idea what you're asking me to do?'

'You've stolen before. You stole from your father because you believed in us. Stealing information will be child's play for you after what you did.'

What we did then, Rani wanted to say, *was child's play. We were young. Infatuated. We made mistakes.*

Prasad has held on to that love. She understands why. He didn't get a chance to experience real love, honest and true, which is what she feels for William, she sees now. Prasad worshipped an ideal, clung on to it; he had nothing else.

'You're asking me to betray my husband, my country and my Jewish heritage.'

'You've betrayed your father. You've betrayed me.'

'I will not do it.'

'You are living the life you stole from me when you stole the sword. You are living the life you do at my expense. I took the fall for you. I have suffered at the hands of your family. Do this. It is the least you can do.' A pause. Then, again, 'You owe me.'

'I can't, Prasad.' Her voice a wail, a plea. She understands where he's coming from, even though she doesn't want to. He's desperate. She gets that. But now she's involved. And she can't be. She can't.

And now he changes once again. 'Please, Rani. These men are dangerous. My life depends on it. Please. You don't love me? You can't be with me? Then at least do this for me. I'm now in this bind because I came to find you.'

'I didn't ask you to.'

'They will kill me. It will be on you. I don't deserve to die, just as I didn't deserve to be imprisoned, tortured, punished through no fault of mine. I deserve a future after all I've endured. Do this for me. Then I will be out of your life.'

And with this, Prasad leaves her there in the middle of the fields.

When she stole the sword, she didn't pay, not really. Yes, she was exiled from her family, but she was getting an education, the education she'd always wanted. She's always felt guilty, wanted to give back. Known there was a reckoning coming.

But this?

Her legs give way as all that happened this evening catches up with her. On her knees, among the shadow-dusted fields, susurrating night settling on her slumped shoulders, she sobs, grass blades depositing moist velvet caresses upon her cheeks, silver-sweet dew mingling with her tears.

66

RANI

Every evening, Prasad accosts her. 'They are getting desperate, Rani.'

Every evening, she says no.

No.

No.

No.

She wants, more than anything, to tell William. Write to him. Ask him to come home. Put this on him. He will sort it out. Everything will be resolved.

But the guilt...

How will she live with the guilt?

If she were to confide in William, she would be selling Prasad out again. He would be punished. Again. She can't do it.

And Prasad knows it. He knows it.

He is what she and her father have made him.

Once before, he paid dearly for her wrong judgement.

Now he is collecting his dues. Now she must pay.

67

RANI

And then...

As she is getting ready to go to work, dreading the usual nightly encounter with Prasad, his pleading, scarred, blinded face demanding justice, recompense, she experiences what feels like an actual kick aimed at the lining of her stomach as if by a minuscule but very determined foot. She dismisses it as a flight of fancy.

It happens again.

And again.

Oh.

She has always had an irregular cycle, so when she stopped bleeding these past few months, she thought nothing of it. She had attributed the bouts of nausea and more recently, the fluttering in her stomach, to indigestion.

Awe as she gently strokes her stomach, the burgeoning bump there.

She had attributed her increasing girth to happiness and contentment in her marriage and family life and despite the often pressured nature of it, work. This was before Prasad came on the scene of course, disrupting everything.

She strips then and stands in front of the mirror she barely glances at, preferring to see herself as reflected in William's eyes.

But now she looks at her rounded stomach and as she stands there, she sees clearly the impression of a little fist pushing against her belly. She blinks, and there it is again, a foot this time.

A miracle growing within her all this time and she, an observant codebreaker who takes pride in that she misses very little, if anything, clueless to the mysterious, wondrous machinations of her own body...

* * *

That evening, when Prasad waylays her, again: 'Please, Rani. Just do this and I'll be out of your life.'

'No,' she says. For William.

'They will not leave me alone, Rani.'

And again, 'No.' For Andrew.

'I will not leave you alone, until you do this. Nobody need find out. You get to live the life you have chosen and I'll begin one without you in mine.'

'No,' Rani says. Surreptitiously stroking her bump under her coat, the new life she and William have created.

'Rani, how can you be like this? Don't you have any compassion? Any care? You used to be so daring. All you have to do is find out information, give it to me. That's it. That's all. No one will know. Your husband will be none the wiser.'

'I will know.'

'Well, you have to either live with it, or with me in your life.'

And with this parting shot, Prasad leaves.

And Rani stands there, her hand on her stomach which houses her growing child, knowing – a part of her has always known since Prasad walked into her life – that unless she sets the past to rest, she will not be able to enjoy the present, move into the future.

Something must be done.

68

RANI

With each day that passes, Rani is more desperate.

Mrs Lewes and she have barely seen each other since Rani was assigned the late watch – 4 p.m. to midnight – Rani sleeps late into the morning and then she has to get ready for work. So Mrs Lewes has not cottoned on to her pregnancy yet. But she will and soon, Rani is sure. Nothing misses Mrs Lewes' eagle-eyed scrutiny.

'They should vet the kind of people they take on over at your workplace,' she grumbles, when a groggy Rani comes downstairs midmorning to find Mrs Lewes washing up with loud and lemon-scented gusto. Andrew is in his room, busily concocting something or other from some cardboard Mrs Lewes has found for him – Rani has just been in to see him. He'd told her what he was doing but it's gone out of her head in the time it took to descend the stairs. Absent-mindedness – another symptom she puts down to pregnancy – along with nausea and occasional light-headedness.

'Why?' she asks Mrs Lewes as she pours herself a glass of water. She can't stomach the chicory tea any more; it exacerbates her nausea.

'Well there's a funny-looking man hanging about during the day – he must be on the night watch like you. Don't know if you've seen him; his skin is all puckered and bruised. Poor dear must have been wounded in the war. He must be billeted nearby. I think, to be honest, my dear, that he's not quite right in the head – walks about aimlessly, looking lost, mostly up and down our street. He should be sleeping, if he's on nights. And those people you work for should have checked before they took him on. I don't think he's up for working, if you ask me.' Mrs Lewes has been rabbiting on, looking out the window, as she washes the dishes. But as she reaches for the tea towel, she sees Rani's face.

'What's the matter, love? You look quite peaky, as if you've seen a ghost...'

That afternoon, during their walk – Andrew and Rani have still persisted with the walks, even without William and with Rani on late watch; they go after lunch while Mrs Lewes is having what she calls 'a little lie down' – Andrew, who was running about letting off steam in the meadow behind the pub, comes up to her, quite breathless.

'There's a scary man following us,' he says, tugging at her hand. 'He said to me when I was laying in the meadow and looking up at the racing clouds, "I used to know your mother in India." Did you? Is he from India?'

'I don't know him, son,' she says, one hand going to her heart, which is throbbing so hard, she thinks it might explode, the other to her stomach to stroke her bump. 'You must have misheard.'

'But he said your name. Rani.' Andrew's trusting gaze upon hers. This boy she loves so much, whom she will do anything to protect, keep safe.

'It's to do with work. Top secret.'

'All right,' Andrew says, trustingly tucking his hand in hers. 'I saw ten clouds and a pigeon.'

'A pigeon on a cloud?'

He smiles, strange man forgotten, for the moment at least.

69

RANI

That evening, she pounces on Prasad, 'You are not to approach Andrew again. Keep away from my family.'

'You don't trust me, Rani? I would never hurt—'

'Keep away from him,' she growls.

'Ah,' Prasad smiles, 'there's the brave tigress who once stole a sword, stood up to a king, bargained for my life. I thought she was gone forever.'

'Enough whimsy, Prasad. I'm not joking.'

'I'm not either.' His smile quite gone. His gaze boring into hers, frost-flavoured night sharp and stabbing with icy vigour. 'Will you do it then? Get me the information from your husband and I'll be gone from your life. I've heard he's back soon. Perfect timing.'

'How do you...?'

'We have our sources.'

'Can't they get you the information then?'

'Ah, only your husband is privy to it, sadly. And those at the very top, whom we do not have access to, though not for want of trying.'

He speaks like a seasoned spy, like he's one of them, parroting their words so confidently.

He used to be happy once, content despite caring for an ailing mother, not being able to find work and thus eking out a hand-to-mouth existence in a mud hut, beside a temperamental river that flooded during the monsoon and vanished over long, overheated summers.

Since then, he has suffered abuse, torture. He has changed.

And it is all because she crossed paths with him, irrevocably changing the direction of his life.

He was poor but he was happy. He was the darling of the villagers. He was a charmer. His future wouldn't be much different from his father's, he had the expectation of a hard life but he knew what he had to face, was accepting of it.

Until she entered his life, showed him a different way, spun dreams of a happy ever after together.

If he is who he is now, it is because she caused it.

And that is why she agreed to meet with him, talk to him when he turned up in her life out of the blue.

That is why she is *still* meeting with him, putting up with his stalking, his pressuring, his blackmail.

That is why she hasn't shopped him to William.

That is why she will do this.

No one need find out, especially not William. But... it will create a scar in their marriage, skewering it with the lies she will keep from him, sullying it with the betrayal she will always know she has wrought even if he doesn't.

In her stomach, her child moves.

This is also, mainly why she will do it: so her beautiful children's lives will not be tainted by the sins of her past. So she can guide them into a future hopefully free of, unshackled from her past.

She strokes her bump. 'Just this one thing.'

He beams. 'Rani, you are a gem.'

'And once it's done, you will go?'

He nods, smile disappearing. 'I will go.' Then, 'And unlike you, I keep my promises.'

70

ESME

'Yes,' Andy says, taking one look at the photograph. 'That's her. Rani.'

A multitude of expressions cross her brother's usually sedate face. Pain. Hurt. Tenderness. Love?

He looks up at her, an assessing gaze. 'You look like her, actually. That same lilt to the eyes...'

She recalls Mrs Lewes' gaze boring into hers as she said, firmly, in response to Esme's question as to who Rani was: 'Your mum.' It is still a bit of a shock, all the same, for her brother to confirm this.

Her brother notices. He gently takes her hand, leads her to a chair, sits her down. It is, curiously, their closest interaction since childhood.

They'd drifted apart as teens, each withdrawing into their own sullen world, and had never quite managed to bridge the distance, which kept getting wider with the passing of years, a chasm of things unsaid, lives unshared, until they were only bound by their father and Mrs Lewes, both also lost in their own worlds, one willingly, the other not.

So is it strange, or strangely fitting, that Esme and her brother have come together now they've lost the two people who'd brought them up?

She's procrastinating. Digressing. Her mind pondering everything except dealing with her brother's confirmation of Mrs Lewes' declaration as regards to her mother.

Some part of her had instinctively recognised the woman. She'd seemed familiar even though Esme was pretty sure she'd never seen her before. She'd felt drawn to her, even before she noticed her father's arm around hers.

She notes the exact moment Andy reads the knowledge in her eyes. His whole body relaxes, even as he pulls out a chair and sits down opposite her.

How is it that they've not been close and yet they can communicate seemingly without words? Is this how it is with siblings?

Siblings...

Or...

Half-siblings? She has pondered if that was the great mystery surrounding their past, why their father never spoke of it. She's wondered if she was a child from a secret affair. She never allowed the thoughts room but they spawned anyway, especially when every so often, the differences between herself and her brother glared at her. Robbie, ever perceptive, even as a child, had observed, when only five, 'You and I look alike, Ma, but you and Uncle Andy do not. At all. Not even a teeny bit.'

And her brother called Rani by her first name just now, rather than 'Mum'...

'Is Rani your mum too?' Her voice is husky. Barely louder than a whisper.

But her brother hears her. He shakes his head. 'No.'

Ah. Just as she thought.

Andy is saying, a wistful smile on his face, 'I remember their wedding.' His voice soft with reminiscence. 'Dad looked so smart. And Rani even lovelier than usual, although she was wearing an old dress. I remember asking her why and she'd laughed, said it was war time and we all had to make do. Mrs Lewes was sighing and complaining about rationing although there was quite a spread as I recall. I think Mrs Lewes bullied and blackmailed everyone into sharing their coupons. The cake looked so magnificent that I remember sneaking a bite and being awfully disappointed as it tasted like cardboard! That's because it was! The real, depressingly small and not very sweet cake was inside the cardboard outer!'

'How,' her voice is harsh now, too loud, causing Andy to baulk, wiping the nostalgic smile from his face. She seems to have lost her ability to modulate it. 'How do you remember everything in such detail, suddenly?'

'I...'

She blinks. Is her staid brother *blushing*? This is a day of firsts.

'When I... when you said Mrs Lewes had mentioned Rani... The name, it wouldn't go away. I knew it was important. That she meant something to me...'

'And what, it just all came back suddenly?' Still too loud. Argumentative.

But this time, Andy doesn't flinch. He's busy blushing, even more so now.

'My...' He clears his throat.

Is he *nervous*?

Oh my. What's happened to her dry, sedate brother? She's always secretly thought that when they created a stereotype for scientists, they must have had Andy in mind.

'My friend suggested hypnotherapy,' he says all in a rush.

'*Hypnotherapy?*' Her voice is a squeak of amazement. 'But

Andy, you don't believe in it. You think it's all mumbo jumbo. I recall you saying so when Robbie mentioned it once at Dad's.'

'Well, I... I changed my mind.'

'I see.' She absolutely doesn't. 'And it worked?'

'Like a treat.' He's enthusiastic in a way she hasn't seen before. 'In fact, I'm planning to write a paper on it.'

'Wait. Back up.' She's still processing everything he's said. 'Dad and Rani – my mum – were married? Do you know, I always had this idea at the back of my head that I was a product of a secret affair.'

'He loved her.' And again, that wistful expression on her brother's face, that softness to his eyes. *Love.* 'I did too,' he says simply.

I love Philip. And yet, I pushed him away. Is this what happened with Dad and Rani?

'Tell me about her. Everything you remember.'

And so he does, right there, as they sit side by side on the moss-carpeted bench in her overgrown garden. Ambushed by the scent of lavender and heartache, her brother tells Esme about an intelligent, loving, kind, fun woman who healed the broken hearts of a man and a boy, taught them to love again. Esme's mother brought to vivid life through her brother's words.

'So what happened? What went wrong?'

'I don't know. This bit I can't remember, or perhaps I was too young to understand. I'm hoping the letter you found will tell us.'

'How old were you when all this happened?'

'Four when Rani came into our lives.'

'Old enough to retain memories. So why did you forget until now? Why did you need hypnotherapy to remember?'

'Jay says it's because it was just too traumatic for me to process. First, my mum disappeared.'

'She disappeared?' Esme is shocked.

'She ran off to America with her lover.'

He's very matter-of-fact, but Esme can guess at the pain behind the bald words.

'I'm so sorry.'

'Anyway.' Andy is keen to move on. 'First Mum disappeared and then Rani. And nothing was ever talked about or discussed. The topic was so taboo that Jay thinks I mentally blocked it.'

'Jay is the hypnotherapist?'

And now, once more, her brother goes bright red. 'No er... he's um...'

'He's...?'

'The friend who suggested I see a hypnotherapist.' He's fiddling with a button on his shirt, avoiding meeting her gaze.

But now she sees. 'He's more than a friend, isn't he?' She can't keep the smile from her face, her voice.

Her brother blushes even brighter red if possible. And even as she watches him, she's thinking, *Rani – my mum! – is why I go bronze, not red in the sun.*

'He... Robbie introduced us.'

'*My* Robbie?' she asks.

'He was his GCSE drama teacher.'

Oh. The flamboyant man, in dress and manner, with his penchant for bright scarves and exotic headgear. His exuberance, his enthusiasm.

That wildly outgoing man with her introvert brother?

'I remember him. He's not someone you forget. He made Dad blush once...' Esme says.

Andy, having shared a rare confidence, is nervously kneading his hands together, his gaze fixed on them, but the way he sits, ears cocked, alert, she knows he's waiting, listening, so she gathers her thoughts.

'It was when we went to watch Robbie as Ariel in the school's production of *The Tempest*. Jay told Dad he was too handsome for words, then before Dad could protest, he'd kissed him on both cheeks.'

Andy chuckles. A light-hearted, infectious sound, like wine fizzing in celebration. Esme realises she hasn't heard it since childhood.

'He's wonderful,' she says.

And now Andy meets her eye. 'I certainly think so.'

Before reserve intervenes, she acts on impulse and throws her arms around her brother, hugging him for the first time since they were children. 'I'm so happy for you.'

And she is, even as her heart aches for her own love, Philip, who proposed marriage and even though every cell in Esme wanted to accept, she did the opposite.

Her brother wraps his arms around her, as easily as if he has done it always.

He smells so familiar, of bergamot and childhood and comfort and love.

And then she's sobbing, for her father, for Mrs Lewes, their broken family, all the lost years and the distance, for herself and what she has done to Philip, breaking up with him even though she loves him, for what she has learned, a woman in a photograph connecting with her across time and worlds, the mother she didn't know, not even that she *was* her mother.

Her brother holds her and he lets her cry.

71

RANI

Bletchley, 1943

She uses their baby to get the information out of William.

He arrives home just a couple of days after she agrees to Prasad's request, just like Prasad said he would.

After the joyful reunion with Andrew, after he's finally asleep, much later than usual, wanting story after story from his father, when they are alone together, after they've loved each other, once, twice, sated their missing, when they are lying spent in each other's arms, she says, 'I'm pregnant.'

He beams at her and it is as if his whole body is smiling, aglow, alight with joy.

He kisses her, and in that kiss that goes on forever, he tells her what he cannot in words, how happy he is, how delighted, how blessed.

Oh William, if only you knew what I'm about to do. But it is for us, for our family. And you need never know.

Surreptitiously, she crosses her fingers behind her back.

He can't stop smiling, and her black heart rejoices in his joy even as she prepares to use him. Betray him. Steal from him. Betray her country and her Jewish heritage. Opa and Oma had been so proud of her and now... Now what she is setting out to do will betray their memory.

Baba's long-ago words reverberating loud and potent in her head: '...the choices you made to get what you wanted, to betray your family for a lonely prize...'

'I did hope so,' William says, still glowing. 'Just now, when we... I did think, hope, pray that...'

She swats playfully at him. 'You noticed I was plump and just didn't fancy a fat wife.'

He is immediately serious. 'I love *you*. I don't care if you put on weight or lose it, Rani.'

Will you still love me if you find out what I'm going to do? I hope you never do.

But I will know, and I must live with that knowledge of having betrayed you, tainted our love.

My punishment.

'I know, my love,' she says, managing to smile. 'Same goes for you too, you know.'

'I know.' He's beaming again, his hand stroking her stomach where their baby grows.

'Keep your hand there. Baby kicks around this time.'

His face lights up even more. 'He does?'

'How do you know it's not a she?'

'Ah, I would love a daughter the image of you.'

The baby moves then. Awe upon his face, as he whispers, 'It *is* a girl.' A kick. 'Look, she's agreeing with me, talking to me, telling me I'm right.'

And with his hand upon her stomach, as he coos to their babe, Rani asks, 'What was it you had to do?'

'You know I can't tell you,' he says, softly, his face still incandescent with wonder, happiness. 'If Dilly was still here, they wouldn't have asked for me – a shame about Dilly.' His eyes clouding over as he remembered the great man who had recently succumbed to his prolonged illness.

'Was it dangerous?' she pushes.

What *she's* doing is dangerous.

'I worry, William. Even more so now we are bringing a new life into a world still at war. I worry about your safety. Our children need you. I need you.'

She's the one compromising their safety. She is wilfully taking a sword to their love, lethally slashing its cream purity, staining it the scarlet of lies, the bloody carmine of betrayal.

'I was never in any danger, love. Far from it. I was decoding very classified, high-level intercepted information about a planned German offensive on the Eastern front against the Soviet Union.'

She holds her breath, even as she wills him to talk without realising what he's giving away. Now she understands why Prasad and his 'friends' are so interested in this information. It concerns an attack on the Soviet Union, on whose behalf they are spying.

William goes on revealing what he has been doing as he gently strokes her bump and the baby dances within, responding to its father's touch, as if recognising its parent on a primaeval level. She commits it all to memory.

It is only when he has finished talking that William, his face losing that luminescent glow of happiness, turns red, realising what he's done, how much he's given away.

She kisses him then, even as her double-crossing heart sighs with relief. It's done. Finally, after what feels like years of being afraid, torn, worried, guilty, she will be free of Prasad.

But not of guilt. You will always carry that. Not only for Prasad but for what you have done, are doing, now.

She lies, gently. 'You know it won't go further than our marriage bed, or should I say tent.' She pulls the sheets around their heads, enclosing them in a swaying, white cocoon.

He laughs, pulls her to him, kisses her.

She kisses him back, backstabbing viper that she is.

72

RANI

'There,' she says, after she's finished relaying the information she stole from her husband, her heart heavy, torn, broken, weighed down by guilt. 'That's everything.'

Prasad smiles. 'It's a goldmine. You've come through, Rani. For me.'

She'd almost turned back several times, not wanting to go through with it.

She had stayed on in England, working for the war effort at Bletchley instead of returning to the family she missed sorely when Baba, after years of silence, invited her back, because she felt guilty about Prasad paying for what she had done. It was her way of making amends.

But now she was being a traitor to the country she loved, the job she loved, the husband she loved, for Prasad. Oh, the irony. If she wasn't so sad, so divided, so broken, so torn, so *guilty*, she would have laughed.

William, who'd wanted to accompany her so she wouldn't have to bicycle alone at midnight now he was home, had said he'd come by when her shift was finished.

'No, you rest. You have the day watch to do and you told me you'd been working all hours up in London.'

His face colouring at the knowledge of everything he'd shared with her, confidential information given away in the marriage bed, in a few moments of weakness. 'But—'

'I've been coming home on my own all this time. Once more will not make any difference.' *It will make* all *the difference. I haven't been alone all this while, but after tonight, I will be. You stay put, William.*

'Just this once. But you really should not be doing late watches when—'

'Don't fuss, please. I'm fine. If it gets too much, I'll ask for a change of shift, I promise.' She leant in to kiss William and that was that.

And now, it's done. She has betrayed her husband, her country, the Jewish half of her. She has sold her soul.

Prasad's scars are visible, but 'There are many more here,' he had said, his hand upon his heart.

Now she has wrought a new indelible scar upon her own heart, blemishing her marriage with the brutal claret of deceit. All her life, she will be lying to her husband, the knowledge of what she has done infecting their every kiss, hug, conversation, interaction guilty purple, remorseful blue.

'It goes against everything I believe in.' She sniffs, not quite able to keep the wobble from her voice as she thinks of William, so happily innocent, so innocently happy as he stroked her stomach where his child grew and walked right into her manipulative trap, feeding her the information she wanted. 'But I've done it. Kept my side of the bargain. This is goodbye, Prasad; we are done.'

She flinches from the pain in his eyes.

'If that's what you want,' he says tightly but it can't quite hide the tears braiding his voice.

And despite everything, she's sorry. She loved him once. With her all. So much so that she came up with a foolish plan that's led them here, across the world from India, in a field in the middle of the night, in the midst of war, open space, pressing darkness. Sorrow. Goodbyes. The end of what was once.

And for her, the beginning of new guilt, fresh remorse.

A solitary tear gleams dreamy silver on his eyelash, glinting like jewels on a ceremonial sword.

In her stomach, her baby moves. The future. Reminding her to forge ahead. The past is what brought her here. It ends now.

She takes a breath. 'Yes, I do,' she says. 'Now, we're even. Goodb—'

But she can't finish, for he's changed, become a snarling tiger pouncing on her.

'No.' So close she can smell his breath. Acrid spiced with the outdoors. 'We will *never* be even,' he growls.

She agrees. It was the wrong choice of words.

'Look at you. Your life. You have an education. A husband. A family. A future. While I...' He swallows and in that bobbing Adam's apple, in those sorrow-burnished eyes, she sees the boy with whom she used to spin grand dreams. 'I thought I had the love of the most beautiful, the bravest girl in the world, a girl who was not above stealing ceremonial artefacts, challenging kings and besting fathers for her love. Turned out it was just a fantasy.'

'You have your cause,' she whispers. 'You have a future.'

He continues as if she hasn't spoken. 'We will never be even.' He is so weary, bringing to mind his buffalo, which used to swish its tail in a half-hearted attempt to swat at the flies that collected upon its person, the action mired in exhaustion built up over a lifetime, its liquid eyes brimming with pathos. 'But I will get out of your life. You won't see me again.'

The relief is immense, mingling with shame at its extent, the release she feels, and sadness.

She looks at him standing there, defeated.

She could squeeze his hand, close the gap between them, embrace him, perhaps, a hug for old times' sake.

She nods. Keeping her distance. Stroking her bump. 'I wish true love for you in the future, Prasad. I wish you well. You will always have a special place in my heart.'

'We could have had everything, Rani.'

'You have what you want, Prasad. Goodbye.'

And with that, she walks away from her past, carrying into the future, a new child and a turncoat heart breaking under the burden of her guilt.

73

RANI

When William climbs into bed beside her a few nights later – he asked for their watches to be switched around; she's on days now and he's on lates – she knows something's awry. He's not his usual self.

She never quite falls asleep as deeply as when he's beside her, spooning her, one hand on her now really very big and quite unwieldy bump.

'Hello you,' he says, kissing her and, 'hello little one,' kissing her stomach.

Their baby obligingly kicks hello back.

'What's the matter?' she asks. 'You're mulling over something.'

'There's something going on. The head of MI5 drove up from London late this evening and is holed up in the commander's office.' He rubs his chin, his voice speculative. 'I wonder if it's to do with the work I was called up for in London – the impression I got was that our victory hinged upon it. I do hope nothing has gone wrong.'

He's been much more open since he confided in Rani the details of what he was actually doing in London. She wishes he wouldn't be. Her black defector of a heart doesn't deserve his trust.

And this...

This she certainly didn't need to hear for it ignites fear, bright hot, danger red.

Has the information she passed on to Prasad caused the Allies' defeat? Is that why the head of MI5 is at Bletchley Park?

She knew what she was doing was wrong, that it would have repercussions, but she'd not really given much, if any, thought to how what she'd done would play out on the world stage, more worried about her perfidy on a personal level, agonising over her betrayal of William's trust.

Please no.

She buries her face in William's chest.

He smells of outdoors, frosty night, tobacco from the cigar smoke pervading the cottage at Bletchley Park that clings to clothes, and that lemony, honest, trustworthy scent that is uniquely him.

She makes the decision in that moment. She will come clean, tell him what she did. There is a strong chance that she might lose him, this wonderful, kind man she's had the privilege of loving, and creating a family with, and she will most certainly hurt him, thus breaking her promise to Mrs Lewes and to herself.

It breaks her heart to even consider what the knowledge of her perfidy will do to him, to them, to the family they have made together.

But if there is a chance her mistake can be rectified, whatever harm her spilling of state secrets to Soviet spies has caused to be contained, then she will take it.

She only hopes it's not too late. Why did she not think of this, of the consequences of what she had done for the world and the war, she who prides herself on her ability to solve even the hardest of codes? Because she did not want to think too much about what she had done; she'd tried to put it away, hoping that with Prasad gone, that was the end of it...

She caresses her stomach, takes a deep breath. 'William, there's something I want to—'

She is cut off by staccato rapping on the front door, downstairs.

Her heart pounds fearfully in time with the knocking as William sits up hurriedly in bed, reaching for his glasses.

It can only be bad news at this time of night.

They exchange looks, Rani hugging her stomach, her body jellied with panic, William's face furrowed, befuddlement crowding his eyes.

Andrew comes into the room, blearily rubbing sleep from his eyes. 'Daddy, who's at the door?'

'Let's see, shall we, son?'

William goes to answer the door and Rani gathers Andrew to her, needing the comfort of his warm little body to ease the terror that has taken her over at this unexpected, late-night intrusion.

'Nobody maintains any standards any more. Just because we are at war doesn't mean the rules of basic politeness can't be observed,' Mrs Lewes grumbles as she comes down the stairs, knotting her dressing gown, looking almost unrecognisable with her hair down.

74

RANI

A consignment of William and Rani's colleagues lurk in the doorway, unsmiling.

Rani, having reassured and settled a sleepy Andrew in her and William's bed, is perched on the stairs, in the same position that Andrew was peering from when Rani had first arrived here with William. Oh, how excited she was then, full of enthusiasm to do her bit for the country while also missing and aching for her family. Now here she is, traitor to the beautiful family she has gained, that she loves more than life itself. How did it come to this?

'Ah, Ben, Tom, Harry, Geoff, what can I do for you at this late hour?' William's hearty tone belying the incomprehension and bewilderment Rani can read in his gaze. This spot on the stairs offers a bird's eye view of the goings on at the front door and she sees now why Andrew – the solemn child he was then – preferred it.

Her heart strains against the confines of her ribcage, her mouth filling with bile.

She knows then with absolute conviction that her sins have come to roost, that these iron-faced men know what she has done.

And that they will tell William before she has had the chance to.

She cradles her bump with one hand, and Andrew (who, unable to sleep with all the commotion in the middle of the night, has come down the stairs and is sitting beside her), with the other, the family she so desperately loves, even as she breathes in the man she loves, who, once he finds out what she has done – not from her but in this callous way – will loathe her, will never look at her with that special regard, his eyes glowing with love, again.

If she had known that their hug just now would be their last, she would have held on, not let go. She would have finished confessing before this intrusion – it would have been kinder for him to hear from her about her betrayal of his trust and, especially, why she had done so.

'Let them knock,' she would have said. 'They will leave eventually. There's something I have to tell you.'

A salty, roiling sea in her mouth, thick and bitter with everything she wants to confess to her husband, her love.

Wait, she wants to cry to the grave men, the colleagues who usually laugh and banter with William and Rani, now hard-faced strangers. *Give me a minute, please.*

How did they find out?

She hasn't seen Prasad since she passed on the information she stole from William. She thought it was because he was honouring the promise he made to her. But what if it was for an altogether more sinister reason?

They are speaking now, tight-lipped, crisp, incriminatory words falling like sharp, stinging bullets of hail from their grim mouths. Through her stunned fear, self-recrimination loud in her head, she only makes out a few words here and there: '...security leak... believe we've located the source... all points to the same person.'

She waits, one hand cradling her stomach, her child cavorting beneath her protective clasp, the other around Andrew, for her name to be called, for her to be damned. If only they'd come when William was still at work.

'The information you worked on in London was leaked.'

'I was told only I had access to it.' William's voice wavering.

'Yes.'

Rani can't help it; she gasps, sitting there in the dark on the stairs, giving herself away.

And now, William looks at Rani. It is as if he is seeing her for the first time, as the memory of their conversation, Rani in his arms, night heavy and soft around them, the scent of love and happiness and celebration, honey sweet, is reflected in his shocked, red eyes. The knowledge that she'd used the news of the child they'd created together to manipulate him hollowing his face.

He'd held her against him, so close, she couldn't tell if it was his heartbeat or hers that she heard, stroking her bump, their child dancing to his touch. His minty breath warm as love on her cheek, the hair on her ear standing to attention, Rani shivering with goosebumps of guilt and remorse.

And then he told her.

Now, his gaze: perplexed befuddlement replaced by intense, agonised hurt. Pain so raw, it hurts to meet his eyes.

And she knows then that she has lost him, this man she loves. In that look, she hears his heart breaking and hers breaks too.

How could you? William is asking with that tortured gaze. *I trusted you.*

She flinches from the anguish in his eyes, the pain there that she has caused. But the least she can do is meet his gaze, reply through her own, *I'm sorry. So very, very sorry.*

And before her eyes, his own eyes shutter, become opaque screens. His mouth, his whole face hardening as her beloved morphs into a stranger to her, transformed by her betrayal.

She strokes her bump with one hand, a puzzled Andrew with the other, imparting reassurance she doesn't have, with hands that tremble even though she tries to stop them doing so. She appears to have not only lost her love, but also control over her own body. Nevertheless, she takes a deep breath, pushes back her shoulders and waits for the men to take her away.

But...

'William Strong, come with us, please.'

And she stands there, numb, as her husband, her love, the father of her children is led away.

William's back straight, shoulders rigid, not turning to look at her, only pausing to reply to Andrew, who is asking, anxiously, 'Daddy, where are you going?'

'Something came up at work, son, I'll be home soon. Go back to bed.' She can only guess at how much effort it must take to make his voice sound so very steady, reassuring, for his son.

And as the door closes behind them, what she feels amidst the upset, the fear, the angst, the sorrow that William had to find out in this way, that he had to find out at all, what she is ashamed of and her conscience outraged by is the relief mingling with the other emotions, that, for now, she is spared.

75

RANI

She puts Andrew to bed.

The child acquiesces quietly, chewing his bunny. But the look he gives her, solemn, silent, wide eyed, brings to mind the boy she first met when she came here as a lodger, not the bright-eyed, inquisitive, happy soul he is now.

He's a very sensitive boy and must have picked up on the atmosphere, must instinctively know something's wrong and must be worrying about it.

She does not know what to say, how to fix this.

I've caused this, she agonises, as she holds him. It is the only thing she can think to do, as, silently, he closes his eyes, clutching Bunny for dear life, not asking for a story as he usually does when he wakes in the night.

When, finally, his breathing evens out and she comes out of his room, Mrs Lewes is there, hands on hips, a large, looming shadow. 'What's going on?'

Nothing misses her eagle-eyed gaze and she has a nose for picking up on undercurrents.

She too resembles more the woman who blocked Rani's way

into the house on her very first day here than the woman Rani has grown to love and respect.

She is regarding Rani with undisguised suspicion.

'In all the years Mr Strong has worked at Bletchley Park, this has never happened.' She looks sternly at Rani, her gaze appearing to reach right into her guilty heart and to access the truth lurking there.

'A misunderstanding.' With difficulty, Rani keeps her voice steady. 'It will be sorted by morning.'

Because by morning, William would have told them the truth. That it wasn't him but Rani who leaked the information. That his only fault was to confide in his wife whom he trusted implicitly.

'It had better be,' Mrs Lewes says. It is a threat, a grim warning.

She knows. How? Is Rani's guilt written all over her face for the world to see or is it Mrs Lewes' particular skill to hone in on the truth?

And Mrs Lewes' parting shot: 'The boy's mother has left him. He needs his father in his life. He can't lose him too.'

It hurts, like Rani is sure Mrs Lewes meant it to. Rani thinks of *herself* as Andrew's mother. But what Mrs Lewes is implying, rightly, is that Rani loses the right to claim ownership of the son if she is responsible for the trouble his father is in...

* * *

Rani can't sleep of course. She can't even bear to look at the bed where she and William have spent so many, many happy hours together, where they have created the child she is carrying, where she used that same child to manipulate him into giving away information that *she* has leaked and for which *he* is now implicated.

She paces up and down, up and down, worrying about what is happening, what they might be doing to him.

In the end, *no time to spare*, she decides, and, getting dressed, walks out into the night, only to be completely swallowed by the darkness of blackout. Lost in worry, she has lost track of time. It is that all-consuming, all-enveloping, stifling, suffocating velvet dark hour of deepest night that precedes dawn.

Even if she made it to Bletchley Park, she wouldn't get past the gates. There is a system of passwords for the staff working the night watch and it changes daily. She does not have access.

She will have to wait.

* * *

She returns home and waits, shivering – she can't get warm. She waits for the knock that will determine her fate.

Surely William would have informed them by now that they've got it wrong, that it's not him but Rani who is the spy.

Andrew wakes and comes to the bedroom where she is pacing. The boy is silent, his huge, anxious eyes asking the question he cannot voice as he chews Bunny's ear.

'Daddy's not home yet,' she says.

He nods. In just a few hours, the child has regressed to the boy he was after his mother left, having somehow, in the way of children, picked up on the adults' unvoiced anxieties. He appears to understand that this time, his father's leaving is different to when he stayed away in London for work. Andrew was happy then, a normal, chatty child.

Now he isn't.

She opens her arms but he shakes his head and she hears him make his solemn way downstairs, hears Mrs Lewes' determined chatter, one sided, too hearty.

She knows he will sit at the kitchen window and keep an eye out for his father, a silent, sombre vigil.

Her heart breaks for him even as her conscience chides, *Your fault*.

She waits and waits, ignoring the growling in her stomach that reminds her that despite everything, she needs sustenance, not only for her, but for the child she is carrying. Hers. William's.

William.

That look.

She can't bear to think about it, about him, how he must be feeling, her husband, who had been broken by the unfaithfulness and subsequent abandonment of himself and his son by his first wife, only to fall in love with a woman whose betrayal is even worse.

'It is the absolute worst thing I can imagine, to be accused of betraying my country,' he'd confided to her once when, for some reason, they were talking about spies.

Why hasn't he told them yet that it is *she*, not he, who is the traitor? Why are they not pounding on the door, ready to take her away?

* * *

She bicycles to Bletchley Park when it is time for her watch, bidding a falsely cheery goodbye to Andrew and Mrs Lewes.

'Will Daddy come home with you?' Andrew asks.

'I'm sure he will, sweetheart,' Rani reassures, keeping her fingers crossed.

Mrs Lewes snorts, then sighs in the next breath, her gaze resting on Andrew, worry and love.

'Mrs Strong, I'm sorry, but you don't have clearance to enter.' The sentry at the gates to Bletchley Park bars her way.

'But I...' She can't continue.

It is, after all, what she expected.

'Where's Daddy? Why are you back home again so quickly?' Andrew is even more concerned.

She gathers the little boy to her, kisses each cheek, his button nose.

How she loves him! And yet, she has done this to him, caused him this anxiety, this upset.

I thought I was doing it to save us, our future, from the blot of my past. Instead, I seem to have destroyed our future, undone everything, caused heartache, wounded you all, Andrew, William, Baby, Mrs Lewes. I'm so very sorry.

'He will be home soon,' she says.

Before Mrs Lewes can snort, a knock on the door, backing Rani's assertion.

But it is not William.

A different set of officers to those who took William in. And yet wearing identical grim expressions.

'Mrs Strong, if you'll accompany us, please.'

76

ESME

Esme and Andy open the letter, found in Mrs Lewes' Bible, together.

Such a simple word: *together*. And yet so nuanced.

Esme hasn't experienced the closeness the word implies with Andy since childhood.

She does now.

The letter is penned in the same handwriting as at the back of the photograph. Her mother's handwriting. Slanting to the right. Beautiful. Like glittering pearls on the page.

Esme takes a moment, strokes her mother's words, her other hand upon her overwhelmed heart. She is touching the same page her mother touched once; it is the closest she has ever been to her.

She reads it out loud, to Andy, her mother's words in her voice, a young woman faced with a terrible dilemma, making the wrong choice with devastating consequences resulting in the breakup and destruction of the family and life she had created with a broken man and his vulnerable son.

So many revelations, like dominoes dropping one by one.

Once she finishes reading, Esme sits for a while, eyes closed, taking it all in, her brother beside her doing the same. His presence a great comfort.

A gamut of emotions ambushing her.

Shock. Anger at Rani for her betrayal.

I don't understand you. I have nothing in common with you. I would never do something like this.

It is only when Andy asks, 'Wouldn't you? If faced with the same circumstances?' that she realises she's spoken out loud.

She had taught her son not to judge people, condemn the choices they made, for you could never fully understand why they were doing so, what they'd been through that had coloured and informed their decisions, unless you'd lived their life. And now here she was sitting judgement upon her mother.

'People do all sorts of things for love. And with the war, it was a difficult time. Loyalties were stretched.' Andy sighs. 'And she paid dearly for what she did.' A pause, then, 'In any case, it did not cause harm, have repercussions on the world stage. I've read up on Bletchley Park and its singular role in the war extensively since wartime information was declassified in the 1970s as I knew Dad worked there.'

'How did you know?' Esme asks. 'We moved away just after I was born and you didn't remember anything from before then until recently. And Dad certainly never spoke about it.'

'Mrs Lewes and I were reminiscing and she let slip that Dad was a codebreaker at Bletchley when I mentioned that I vaguely recalled living in a tall house.'

'Ah,' Esme smiles. 'That's how I know too.'

They share a moment, eyes shimmering as together, they mourn the woman who brought them up: fiercely loyal, dependable, protective and loving, their indomitable Mrs Lewes.

'Coming back to what Rani did, Esme, I've been learning even more about Bletchley recently, since my memory of that time returned. The Russians, I've discovered in the course of my reading, for the most part chose not to believe the information they received from Bletchley Park and subsequently did not act on it. It did not affect the war, one way or another.' Another pause. 'Rani was a remarkable woman who made a bad choice. We all make mistakes.' He sighs, rubbing a hand across his eyes, the gesture weary. 'There are as many truths as there are people. Each person's war, whether actual or metaphorical, is different, defined, shaped by their imperfect lives, their individual experiences.'

Esme looks at her brother. 'I didn't know you were so wise.'

He emits that lovely chuckle, albeit a little wet – they've both been crying, her staid brother for the woman he loved, whose memories he'd repressed because they were too painful, Esme for the mother she's only just coming to know. She hasn't heard her brother's chuckle since childhood and is only realising how much she missed it now that she's hearing it again.

'There's a lot I don't know about you,' she says, taking Andy's hand. 'But I'm going to rectify that.'

It's too late to mend bridges with her father. But not with her brother.

And please, let it not be too late with Philip, her love, whom she rebuffed when he proposed marriage because she was afraid of commitment.

77

RANI

Bletchley, 1943

A roomful of men, sombre expressions on tight-lipped faces.

Her stomach cramps with a savage wave of pain.

It takes her a searing moment to understand that this pain has nothing to do with facing judgement and everything to do with her child.

The baby is coming. Too soon. The stress of all that's happening must have brought on labour.

As she prepares to face the consequences of her actions, fisting her palms to ride out the pain that is swamping her, trying her best to keep a straight face, keep from crying out – the pain is excruciating, like nothing she has ever experienced – her main concern is how to protect this child, this innocent created from an unexpected, glorious love, bring it safely into the world while her own is in jeopardy.

The wave of pain thankfully eases just as her interrogators begin their questioning.

'Mrs Strong, were you aware of your husband's activities?'

She's shocked, more blindsided than when the pain struck, unable to process what they are asking for a few stunned minutes.

Not, *Why did you do it and allow your husband to be blamed?*

But this...

William *hasn't* told them. Her husband, a stickler for rules, a patriot, who never puts a foot wrong if he can help it, hasn't betrayed her, despite her own treachery, even though he's enduring being branded a traitor when he isn't, when all he has done wrong is to love her.

His love as pure and selfless as hers is deceitful and selfish.

'Has it caused a lot of damage?' she asks, keeping her fingers crossed. *Please, let my actions not have had too many adverse repercussions on the world stage.* It's too late to hope for the same in her personal life.

The men look at each other as if deciding what to tell her, if anything. Then, shortly, 'No. We managed to contain it just in time.'

The relief is immense.

'But, nevertheless, it shouldn't have happened. Do you have any knowledge of any other information your husband might have shared? Have you an idea of how long this has been going on?'

She opens her mouth to tell them the truth. Clear William's name. She has brought this upon him. She must get him out of it by owning up to her mistake.

Pain. Overwhelming. Overpowering. Stealing her breath. Taking her prisoner.

It is all she can do to not cry out, to school her face not to reveal her agony. She clenches her hands into fists, nails drawing blood from the soft flesh of her palms.

The baby wants out.

'I... I must go. My child... is coming now.'

The men's grim expressions replaced varyingly by confusion, distaste, embarrassment on Rani's behalf. They do not want to talk about or think of such personal and indelicate matters as imminent births of children of traitors when national secrets have been spilled by one of their own.

'I must go *now*,' she says, appealing to each of them in turn.

'Please Mrs Strong, answer our question and we will take you urgently to wherever you need to go.'

Another contraction takes hold. Through the blinding pain, which she tries to school her face not to betray, she agonises on what she will tell them, these uncompromising men whom she once worked beside.

The pain tears at her, reminding her that she's not at liberty to make decisions based on herself alone any longer. William, by not giving her away, by taking the fall, is protecting her and the child they have created together. She must too. She will bring this babe safely into the world, *please*, and then, she will confess.

'I was not aware of what William was doing,' she says, once the pain has blessedly eased, in this way betraying the husband she's betrayed once already yet again. 'The first I knew of it was when you arrived to take my husband away.'

78

RANI

She is being assaulted, torn apart by agony the likes of which she has never experienced before.

'Mama!' she calls. 'Baba!'

'Oma, Opa!'

'Arjun!'

And lastly, only, the one she wants, needs, craves, whose arms and assurances will make everything better, in whose eyes she finds a better version of herself.

'William!'

Silence.

Only pain keeping her company, breaking her.

Undoing her.

Then, 'Push, Mrs Strong.'

Mrs Lewes.

The prickly, judgemental woman Rani has come to love, fiercely safeguarding those she loves and takes under her wing, to whom Rani has said, a thousand times, 'Please call me by my given name.'

Who has replied just as many times, 'It doesn't feel right, Mrs Strong.'

'Andrew?' she manages.

'Asleep,' Mrs Lewes says tersely. 'Exhausted from his broken night.' Her mouth a thin line.

Rani had been dropped off by one of the men who had interviewed her after she betrayed William again – although she doesn't recall much of the journey home on account of the pain.

Now, it occurs to Rani that she is clutching Mrs Lewes' hand as if her life depends on it.

'I'm not going anywhere,' Mrs Lewes says dryly. 'But the babe wants out and you must push.'

And in the room, on the bed where she made love to her love, created this child, where she also manipulated him, stole from him, using this child, she pushes with all her might as her baby prepares to arrive into a world torn asunder by war, into a home rent by Rani's betrayal.

Gushing release followed by a plaintive wail.

'There, there, little one. My goodness, aren't you beautiful?' Mrs Lewes coos, her voice infused with awe, soft with wonder.

Ignoring the aches and complaints of her exhausted body, Rani sits up, arching aching arms to reach for the slippery bundle, gathering it in her arms.

'She wasn't early, Mrs Strong. Well, perhaps by a couple of weeks. But she is well. A strong un, living up to the Strong name, aren't you, my love? Look at those lusty pair of lungs on you!' Mrs Lewes is exulting.

It was entirely possible that Rani had miscalculated given the irregularity of her periods. For she gently wipes the blood and gore away and there she is, the most exquisitely perfect cherub ever.

Her baby girl.

Her pain, ache, torment easing as she drinks in her child's angelic features, as she kisses every one, each baby snail finger and each curlicue toe.

'Esme,' she whispers, the name, meaning beloved in French, arriving in her head as if the magic of this moment has enchanted it there. 'Hello there, my beloved.'

79

ESME

'I wish you'd had the opportunity to get to know Rani, Esme,' Andy says. 'You're very like her. Smart, loving, kind, caring. You single-handedly brought Robbie up and he's a real credit to you.'

Esme sniffs, overwhelmed, the tears she's thought she's exhausted erupting again. She'd not known her brother thought so highly of her. It means the world. 'Thank you,' she manages. And then, 'I think you're wonderful too.'

He chuckles, bashful. Then, 'I've been meaning to tell you what a great job you've done with Robbie, but I...'

She squeezes her brother's hand. 'I know. We're not a family who talks to each other, are we? We've been more like islands.'

'With the exception of Robbie, who's at ease with everyone.' A smile gilding Andy's voice. 'Which is where you've bucked the family tradition, and thank goodness for that and for Robbie.'

'Well *we've* bucked the family tradition too, today. We've been talking, shock horror, about deeply personal things, mentioning mothers and digging up never to be disturbed pasts.'

'We have.' Her brother smiles.

'I think now, finally, I understand why Dad was so reserved.

Why he never held on to things. Why he kept himself at a distance, a remove. It was because he had been hurt so badly. He had loved completely, and been betrayed and had his heart broken, once and then again by the two people who'd vowed to love and honour him and whom he must have trusted absolutely. So he did not allow himself to love completely again. He held a bit of himself back. He did not get attached to possessions, to people; he even held himself back from his children. He was scarred, scalded, branded by love.'

'Yes,' her brother agrees softly.

Such sadness, Esme thinks, *such hurt we inflict on those we love, bound by our whims, our choices, our mistakes. Harsh words flung thoughtlessly, barbed wounds that last a lifetime or several, that bleed and chafe, seeping their poison down generations.*

I need to make things right with Philip. There's no love without risk. I'd rather love and risk rejection than not love at all. Tomorrow is not certain. I need to grab life with both hands, savour it. Enjoy it.

My father and mother lived in prisons of their own making, cages they constructed through the choices they made. I cannot perpetuate this and spend the rest of my life wallowing in regret.

I will live life to the full, taking risks, no matter if I'm hurt, wounded in the process.

No longer afraid to love.

No longer afraid.

80

RANI

Bletchley, 1943

She holds her baby in her arms, learning her every feature by heart.

She is perfection itself, innocence personified. And she appears bouncy and hale – Mrs Lewes checking her thoroughly and declaring her in 'smashing good health'.

Andrew comes in, dragging his bunny, his hair even more mussed than usual. The solemn gravity leaves his face, replaced by curiosity, his eyes coming alive, as they land on the diminutive bundle in Rani's hands.

He approaches carefully, looking from the baby to Rani, questions burning in his eyes. They are expressive, the anxiety replaced by inquisitive, barely suppressed excitement and for that, Rani is grateful.

A few days ago, Rani and William had sat Andrew down and explained to him that he was going to have a new brother or sister. He has been impatiently waiting for the new arrival ever since, asking every morning if his new brother or sister is here yet, stroking Rani's stomach and grinning with joy when the baby has responded to his touch, promising to be the best big brother ever.

'Would you like to hold your sister?' Rani asks.

'My sister?' His face alight, eyes shining. In this moment, he is all little boy, animated and adoring and awed, not a sombre child too old for his years.

'Esme,' she says.

'Esme,' he repeats carefully, rolling the syllables in his mouth as if getting a feel for them.

Mrs Lewes looks on, smiling.

'Here.' Rani pats the bed beside her.

Andrew climbs up next to her and for the first time that she can remember, drops Bunny carelessly, without thought to where the stuffed rabbit lands. He holds his arms out and gently, Rani places his sister in them.

He looks down at her sleeping face, the wisps of flyaway hair, delicate as angel wings, the barely-there dot of a nose. 'My sister,' he whispers, tenderly. 'She's beautiful.'

Mrs Lewes sniffs loudly and Rani is too choked up to do anything but nod.

And then the little bud of a mouth puckers, the eyes flutter open, shut, open, shut and she lets out a small mewl of a wail, revealing very pink gums, a teeny, tiny tongue.

'Shh... Esme, it's all right; your brother's here,' Andrew coos. 'I'll look after you.'

Mrs Lewes blows her nose.

Esme opens her eyes and looks up at her brother for a brief moment, trying to find the source of the voice. Her cherubic lips lift upwards in a quick little, barely-there twitch.

It's enough for Andrew.

'Did you see that? She smiled at me! She did!' He beams. He glows. He laughs.

Startled by the noise, Esme lets out a wail.

'She's loud for a baby,' Andrew exclaims, his admiring gaze affixed upon his sister, and they all laugh. 'Daddy will be so happy to meet her,' Andrew says, and they all stop laughing. 'Is he gone away too, like my first mummy? Is he never coming back?' Andrew asks, now, finally dragging his gaze away from his sister to look up at Rani, eyes wide with worry.

'Of course your daddy is coming back,' Rani says at the same time as Mrs Lewes cries, 'What's this nonsense, child? He's just gone to work; it's top secret so he can't send word, that's all.'

Andrew is sombre, his shoulders slumped, his joy dissipated in the face of anxiety with regards to his father. It is apparent that for perhaps the first time in his young life, he doesn't believe either Rani or Mrs Lewes.

'He will come back, I promise,' Rani says to the boy she loves, who holds his sister in his arms gently, carefully, like she is the most fragile, precious treasure in the world.

It is this little boy's heart that is the most fragile and precious. And right now, Rani's own heart breaks as she senses the crack that had splintered Andrew's heart when his mother left, which had healed somewhat when Rani came into his life, rupture, creating several more in the process.

Esme mewls and as Andrew shushes her tenderly, Mrs Lewes raises an eyebrow at Rani, as if to say, *Don't make promises you can't keep. You blithely promised not to hurt them when you married William. Well?*

Rani cannot meet Mrs Lewes' gaze. Instead, she concentrates once again on the tableau of her two beautiful children, her glorious, innocent angels, Andrew's tousled head bent over Esme's scrunched up little face.

Her children, whose father she has betrayed twice over, who hasn't had a chance to meet his daughter yet.

She has done this. She will right this. She will keep her promise to Andrew.

She will.

And if she has to lose the family she loves with her all, where she's happy, accepted, trusted, loved, it is just punishment.

Esme starts wailing harder.

Rani gently gathers her from her son and settles her against her breast, while Mrs Lewes holds her hand out to Andrew. 'Come, child, Esme is having her dinner. Let's get yours.'

And watching him go, his slumped shoulders, the potent anxiety that his meeting with his baby sister briefly displaced, Mrs Lewes sighing in his wake, her daughter suckling from her, she feels William's absence keenly. William, who has shown her true love, taught her that it involves making sacrifices.

If you love, you win even when you lose.

Once before, she had let another man suffer the punishment for her mistake. She never got over the guilt.

Now, once again, a man she loves with all her heart, the father of her children, has taken the fall for what she did.

She can't allow it.

It is up to her now to do what is best for her family, right the wrong she has wrought upon them. If she gives herself up to the authorities, there might be a trial, worse. She cannot allow her children, her pure, perfect stars, to be tainted by the ignominy of her actions.

She does not want them to have to carry the burden of her mistakes, like she has done for all of her adult life. She does not want them to be manipulated into doing something they don't want to because of the past hanging like a deadly sword, casting an ominous, sabre-toothed shadow over their lives, arched to spring, maim, cut, destroy their pure, unsullied present with the bloody crimson stain of *her* past, *her* sins, *her* transgressions, like it has done William.

She knows what she must do. It is the only way.

It will be the hardest thing she will ever have done, the most difficult choice she will ever make.

But it is the right one.

81

ESME

When her brother leaves with a promise to meet up at the weekend, introduce her to Jay, she dials Robbie's number.

The phone rings at the other end.

And rings.

He must be out.

Of course. The social butterfly.

She's just about to put the phone down when...

'Hello?'

Her son.

She revels in the cherished music of his voice.

Voices in the background. Laughter. Chatter. The clink of glasses.

He has people round.

'Shush, you noisy lot,' he says in his party voice. He sounds jolly drunk. 'I'm on the phone here.'

'Robbie love,' she breathes.

'Ma! How's life treating you?'

'I'm fine, darling. And you?'

'All good. You have news, I can tell.'

'How?' She laughs.

'I can interpret every note of your voice, even down the phone with my loud friends in the background. I'm not even joking. So are you going to spill or what?'

She takes a breath. 'You know how I told you Mrs Lewes had mentioned a letter from my mother?'

'Was it from her? You weren't sure.'

'It was. She... It's a long story. I'll tell you at the weekend. And you can read the letter then too. You *are* coming down?'

'I am. Can't wait to get to know my ma's ma.'

She can hear the smile in his voice. Her lovely boy.

'It's helped you. I think,' he continues, 'finding out about her. You sound lighter.'

'Do I?'

'Definitely.'

'You are perceptive even when drunk.'

He laughs, celebratory drums. How she loves this boy!

'Now at the weekend,' she says, 'we're meeting Uncle Andy and—'

'Jay,' he says at the same time as her. 'He's told you then, has he? About time.'

'Can you believe it?' she asks.

'Absolutely. They complement each other perfectly. Which is why I introduced them.'

She laughs, amazed and proud. 'Quite the matchmaker, you are.'

'Talking of matchmaking, have you grovelled to Philip, told him that you panicked, that you love him and accept his proposal?'

'How did you...?'

'I'm not stupid, Ma. He makes you happy. Go on, tell him you love him.' Then, gently, 'He won't wait forever.'

The very thing she's afraid of. 'What if he's already...?' Her voice an apprehensive whisper.

'He hasn't. I know that for a fact.'

'How...?'

'He calls me. We have a bond. Just because you're too afraid of commitment doesn't mean we're the same.'

'Oh.' She's touched. *Oh Philip.* He's kept in touch with her boy. They have a bond.

'He's waiting. But like I said...'

'He won't wait forever,' she whispers.

'That's what I said. He, however, maintains you're worth waiting forever for.'

82

RANI

Bletchley, 1943

Holding her child, whose every limb she's kissed, every feature she's learned by heart, she writes two letters.

One to William.

The other to the commander at Bletchley Park.

Then hugging her baby close, her Esme, she kisses every inch of her once again as she rocks her to sleep.

She lays her sleeping child in the basket she has prepared for her, bolstered by bedding made from her softest dresses – all quite tatty and mended over and over given clothes rationing – recalling, as she does so, the time when she was falling in love with William, when she'd dearly wished for a new dress, tired of her 'make do and mend' clothes. How frivolous that feels now!

She places the letters in the basket beside her babe and, as an afterthought, also tucks in the photograph of herself and William with Dilly, Harriet and the other codebreakers, taken at Bletchley Park the year before – a record of happier, more innocent times, albeit in the midst of war.

Then, hugging and kissing her sleeping daughter one more time, she carries her downstairs in the basket.

Mrs Lewes and Andrew are in the kitchen. She positions herself just behind the door, Esme at her feet. Mrs Lewes is chatting away. Andrew sits at the table, listlessly twirling his mash with his fork. She breathes them in, commits them to memory, the stout, matronly woman and the little boy she loves with her all.

She swoops down and inhales the newborn scent of her child. She kisses her one last time. Then, making sure Esme's basket is in Mrs Lewes' line of sight, the letters and photograph on top of her sheets, she lets herself very quietly out of the house where she found so much love and happiness, where she became a wife, a mother twice over, where she loved and betrayed her husband.

* * *

She walks, every step heavy and weighted with heartbreak, past the meadow where she raced with Andrew during their daily walks, and he laughed for the first time after his mother left, past the field where she had her rendezvous with Prasad, and where she sold William out, where she said goodbye to her past while taking a sword to her future.

She walks past the railway station where she'd arrived as a recruit from Cambridge, fired up with the zeal to make a difference and right the mistakes she had wrought in her past, and up to the gate of Bletchley Park, retracing the steps she took on her first day and the thousand days after.

Again, like on that first day, she's stopped by the guard, barred from going further.

'I'm just saying goodbye,' she says and he allows her to stand at the gate.

Bletchley Park, these grounds, verdant green, the lake twinkling and glimmering, radiating exquisite, painful memories. The place where she found love, and a purpose: codebreaker.

This place that has shaped her destiny.

A lone swan glides serenely on the water of the lake, regal, dignified, pure as her children's hearts.

83

ESME

Her son's laughter ringing in her ears, Esme drives to Philip's cottage.

The hydrangea they'd planted together is in resplendent bloom.

He's in the arbour, pruning, framed by a cascading cornucopia of roses. Sweet-smelling blossoms the delicate cream of a sparkling new dawn.

He straightens as she approaches, sets the secateurs down.

She hungrily breathes in every detail of his beloved face.

'I'm sorry. I've been a fool,' she says.

His sunset-amber eyes glow and shimmer as he stands there, the man she loves, framed by his roses.

She gets down on one knee, looks up at him, her love.

'I did not know who I was. I worried I was like my father. There was this emptiness within me. I was terrified that I'd infect you with it too. What I didn't realise, what I understand now, is that you complete me. You fill the emptiness; you *are* my life.' She takes a breath, her eyes not wavering from his burnished-gold gaze. 'Philip, I love you. Will you marry me? I will understand if you say no, turn tail and run—'

'Esme.' He's reaching for her, gathering her to him, his eyes, his face awash with love, and then he's kissing her, the taste of his tears and hers mingling. The salty sweet flavour of love, in the arbour, surrounded by his carefully cultivated prize roses aptly named Wedding Day.

84

RANI

She goes to the lock at Fenny Stratford.

They had spent the most glorious day there – William, Rani, Andrew, Mrs Lewes – a few months before William was called to London and Prasad re-entered her life. And now, counting back from Esme's birth, Rani is sure that Esme was conceived that night, when they returned home, exhausted but very happy.

Both William and Rani had the day off and since it was a bright, sunny day, they decided, on the spur of the moment, to pack a picnic and get away.

'I know just the place,' William had said.

They'd splashed in the river, even Mrs Lewes getting her ankles wet!

They'd spent hours choosing the choicest sun-warmed pebbles, at Andrew's instigation, for his 'collection', he'd said.

'You haven't got one,' Mrs Lewes had pointed out.

'That's why I'm collecting them,' Andrew had said with perfect logic and they'd all laughed.

The sun had shone all day and they'd drowsed beneath the weeping willows on a bed of dandelion and daisy strewn grass, the water whispering and gurgling and tumbling, the swans ignoring them, the ducks coming up to them, snooping and quacking and gossiping, angling for crumbs and waddling away in fright when Mrs Lewes emitted one of her trumpet snores.

The fish-paste sandwiches were soggy, Mrs Lewes' famous oat biscuits hard as the stones in Andrew's 'collection', the chicory tea undrinkable, and yet it was the best picnic they'd ever had, flavoured with laughter, seasoned with happy chatter, sweet with contentment.

William had shown Andrew how to skim stones and they'd even tried to fish with rods fashioned from the willow-tree branches and worms dug from the wet earth upon the bank.

When the sun had finally set, a peach orb in a rose-gold sky chased by violet shadows, they'd made their way home, pink with exertion and wellbeing.

And that night, when William gathered her to him, and loved her, they had created Esme.

She gathers stones, like they had done that day. Perfect treasures for her own collection. She fills her pockets with them.

The ducks waddle up to her, curious.

Even more so when she follows them into the water.

They quack in alarm and warning when she keeps on walking, past them and towards the pair of swans gliding serenely in the middle of the river, their long necks bent towards each other to form a heart, the sky, the bright white of purity, framed inside. She closes her eyes as the water reaches her neck, her chin, her mouth, her nose, her eyes, her forehead, as it envelops her in its liquid embrace. She fancies she hears Opa and Oma beckoning for her, their voices doting warmth: '*Bubbale*', beloved, their caresses benediction, and as she joins them, she pictures Baba's face alight with pride as Rani made an impassioned argument for socialism, Mama's gentle smile, her fond affection, the taste of her *schnecken*, sticky sweet, an edible kiss, Arjun throwing his arms around her neck, crying, 'Didi! How I missed you!', Mrs Lewes' gaze tender as she looks at Andrew, Andrew's starburst laughter, Esme's perfect features, William's smile, glowing with love as he leans in to kiss her...

EPILOGUE
ESME

It is a small wedding, just as Esme wanted.

Andy, Jay, Robbie and a couple of his friends are present, as is Philip's close friend Rob and his wife, and Philip's cousin Martin and his family. Philip's parents died a few years ago and he has no siblings.

Esme and Philip's beloved people are gathered in Philip's rose arbour where Esme proposed to him. They are exchanging vows with the Wedding Day roses framing them in abundant glory. The creamy velvet petals confetti-ing their union, their sweet perfume sanctioning it, the magpies, robins and thrushes twittering amongst its branches, and the wasps and bees attracted to the blossoms, providing witness alongside family and close friends as Esme and Philip promise to navigate a future – together.

There will be lunch at the pub (Philip's local) after, fish and chips and a glass or two of red.

Robbie has baked a wedding cake, a multi-tiered concoction of chocolate, topped with raspberries.

'What do you think, Ma?' He'd grinned when he'd removed the lid of the box to reveal his delectable creation.

She'd gasped in awe. 'You baked it yourself?' Her voice was choked with emotion.

He'd thrown an arm around her, planted a kiss on her cheek. 'For you, Ma. You don't get married every day.'

'It is absolutely divine,' Esme had managed, overwhelmed by her son's thoughtful kindness.

'Looks too good to eat,' Philip had agreed, while whispering in Esme's ear, '*You* look absolutely divine, my love.'

She was wearing a simple white shift dress she'd picked up in the sales at Marks. But she had to admit, it suited her, flattering her body, accentuating her curves. Her hair was up in a bun and she'd applied mascara and lipstick.

'Definitely better than Rani and Dad's wedding cake, which was mostly cardboard. I was fooled and sorely disappointed,' Andy had said and they'd all laughed.

Philip and Esme have written their vows themselves.

Esme's simply says, *Philip, I vow to love and cherish you. I promise I will never take you for granted for I have waited long enough to know what I want and what I want, my darling, is to spend the rest of my life with you, each night and day with you by my side.*

Jay, dressed flamboyantly in a purple and orange silk kaftan and matching turban – 'A nod to your Indian heritage, Esme' – is officiating.

'Are you ready for your wedding present, Ma?' Robbie asks.

'I thought the cake was your present.'

'Well, this one is a joint present. Uncle Andy and Jay helped and even though it is his wedding, Philip helped too. His research skills came in useful.'

'Well, I'm intrigued,' Esme says. She cannot think how this day could get any better. Her husband-to-be smiling at her, eyes soft with love. Her husband-to-be! In a matter of minutes. And the thought, instead of scaring her, fills her with joy.

Her family and friends gathered around her as she steps into a new phase of her life at long last. She fancies the shimmering radiance at the edge of her eyes, summer sun slanting through the rose bushes splintering into kaleidoscopic rainbows, are the ghosts of her beloved lost watching and cheering: Dad and Mrs Lewes and Rani, her mum, whom she's recently found out about but feels like she's coming to know.

'Your insistence on a fast-forward wedding made life difficult,' Robbie is saying.

Once Esme and Philip decided to get married, they moved quickly. 'Before the roses stop blooming,' was Esme's only consideration.

'But thanks to Philip and Uncle Andy and Jay, we managed, just about, to get your present here on time,' Robbie adds.

'I'm really curious now, Robbie, although I can't think of anything that can top that stupendous sculpture of a cake.'

'I promise this will.' Robbie grins.

Esme smiles. 'I'll take your word for it.'

'Tada...' Robbie sings.

Her family, grouped among the rose bushes, steps aside and she notices a man walking towards her, smiling gently.

An older man. She's never seen him before and yet... he's strangely familiar. Greying dark hair. And, she realises with a jolt, features that she sees when she looks in the mirror.

'Esme,' he says. She loves the sound of her name in his deep voice, his Indian accent lending a musical cadence to the syllables. 'You are the image of my sister.'

His voice catches when he says, *my sister*. 'I am Rani's brother. Arjun.'

'Arjun,' Esme breathes, overwhelmed. 'Rani's brother.'

Her mind processing his words, which render her eyes moist with emotion. *You are the image of my sister.*

'How I loved her. She was my sun, my star. My *didi*, big sister, who could do no wrong. She led and I followed.' His voice a lament, a chant, an incantation. 'I miss her terribly. I always will. But now, I have found you.'

He smiles at Esme, his eyes, so like Esme's own, iridescent with jewels of tears.

I have found you. She reaches out, takes his hand.

And the part of her that has been flailing since she lost her father and Mrs Lewes settles.

'Tell me about Rani,' she says. 'My mum.' Her *mum*.

'She was brilliant. Fiercely intelligent. Feisty. Very loyal. Good to have on your side.' His eyes soft as he reminisces. 'She cared intensely, perhaps too much.'

'Yes,' Esme says, thinking of the choices Rani made, because of just that.

'She was so upset to be abandoning Mama to the zenana, the women's section of the palace, when she was sent to Cambridge. If she was here, I would tell her that it wasn't for long. After the dissolution of the princely states post Indian independence in 1947, Mama and Baba travelled the world together, like we had done when we were growing up, and I joined them during my holidays. Rani would have liked that.' His eyes sparkle bright gold with wistful longing. 'Baba tried to get in touch with her after the war but by then, it was too late...' His lashes sequinned with sorrow, cheeks dusted with it.

Esme squeezes his hand.

'Ma, do you like our gift?' Robbie asks.

She cannot speak, only nod, mouth, 'Thank you', as she clutches her uncle's hand. Her *uncle*!

She pictures Rani and William and Mrs Lewes smiling from above, and a sudden breeze scented with roses gently strokes her cheek and it is benediction and confirmation: *we are here with you.*

Esme beams at her family, her husband-to-be, her son, her brother, his dashing boyfriend, her uncle beside her, all gathered under and framed by Wedding Day roses, a festive cascade, the extravagant cake on the table in front of them, an image she will remember and cherish all her life, a wedding day she will never forget.

ACKNOWLEDGEMENTS

I would like to thank my wonderful editor, Francesca Best – SO very lucky in you.

Thank you to all the amazing team at Boldwood for helping make this book the very best it can possibly be, and for making it travel far and wide.

Thank you, Hayley Russell, for overseeing the process of shaping the manuscript into a book.

Thank you, Emily Reader, for your eagle eye and wonderful suggestions during copy edits for this book. Thank you, Rachel Sargeant, for proofreading this book.

Thank you, Ben Wilson, for overseeing the production of the audio version of the book.

Thank you to my lovely author friends, Angie Marsons, Sharon Maas, Debbie Rix, June Considine (aka Laura Elliot), whose friendship I am grateful for and lucky to have.

An especial thanks to my nephew, Jaisal Simon D'Silva, for explaining why chess skills are useful for codebreaking, and to him and his sister, my niece, Eila Maria D'Silva for being all round wonderful – I will always fondly remember editing this novel to their delightful background chatter and laughter.

A huge thank you to my mother, Perdita Hilda D'Silva, who reads every word I write; who is encouraging and supportive and fun; who answers any questions I might have on any topic – finding out the answer, if she doesn't know it, in record time – who listens patiently to my doubts and who reminds me, gently, when

I cry that I will never finish the book: 'I've heard this same refrain several times before.'

I am immensely grateful to my long-suffering family for willingly sharing me with characters who live only in my head. Love always.

And last, but not least, thank you, reader, for choosing this book.

AUTHOR'S NOTE

This is a work of fiction set around and incorporating real events.

I have taken liberties with regards to the Indian setting, picking characteristics, such as food, vegetation and customs, from different parts of India to fashion my fictional villages and cities; the areas I have set them in may not necessarily have places, cuisine, flora and fauna and rituals like the ones I have described.

I apologise for any oversights or mistakes and hope they do not detract from your enjoyment of this book.

ABOUT THE AUTHOR

Renita D'Silva is an award-winning author of historical fiction novels. She grew up in the south of India and now lives in the UK.

Sign up to Renita D'Silva's mailing list for news, competitions and updates on future books.

Follow Renita on social media here:

 facebook.com/RenitaDSilvaBooks

x.com/RenitaDSilva

instagram.com/renita_dsilva

bookbub.com/profile/renita-d-silva

Letters from
the past

Discover page-turning
historical novels from
your favourite authors
and be transported
back in time

*Join our book club
Facebook group*

https://bit.ly/SixpenceGroup

*Sign up to our
newsletter*

https://bit.ly/LettersFrom
PastNews

Boldwⲟⲟd

Boldwood Books is an award-winning fiction publishing company seeking out the best stories from around the world.

Find out more at www.boldwoodbooks.com

Join our reader community for brilliant books, competitions and offers!

Follow us
@BoldwoodBooks
@TheBoldBookClub

Sign up to our weekly deals newsletter

https://bit.ly/BoldwoodBNewsletter

Printed in Great Britain
by Amazon